DEADLY SPIRITS

Also by Mary Miley

Roaring Twenties mysteries

THE IMPERSONATOR
SILENT MURDERS
RENTING SILENCE *
MURDER IN DISGUISE *

The Mystic's Accomplice mysteries

THE MYSTIC'S ACCOMPLICE *
SPIRITS AND SMOKE *

* *available from Severn House*

DEADLY SPIRITS

Mary Miley

SEVERN
HOUSE

First world edition published in Great Britain and the USA in 2022
by Severn House, an imprint of Canongate Books Ltd,
14 High Street, Edinburgh EH1 1TE.

Trade paperback edition first published in Great Britain and the USA in 2023
by Severn House, an imprint of Canongate Books Ltd.

severnhouse.com

British Library Cataloguing-in-Publication Data
A CIP catalogue record for this title is available from the British Library.

ISBN-13: 978-1-4483-0684-8 (cased)
ISBN-13: 978-1-4483-0686-2 (trade paper)
ISBN-13: 978-1-4483-0685-5 (e-book)

This is a work of fiction. Names, characters, places and incidents
are either the product of the author's imagination or are used fictitiously.
Except where actual historical events and characters are being described
for the storyline of this novel, all situations in this publication are
fictitious and any resemblance to actual persons, living or dead,
business establishments, events or locales is purely coincidental.

All Severn House titles are printed on acid-free paper.

Typeset by Palimpsest Book Production Ltd.,
Falkirk, Stirlingshire, Scotland.
Printed and bound in Great Britain by
TJ Books, Padstow, Cornwall.

ONE

During the final days of 1924, our neighborhood greengrocer fell down his basement stairs and broke his neck, a tragedy that left his family without a breadwinner. He was a nasty man, violent when drunk, and because he drank most of the time, his wife and children mourned only the loss of his earnings. Some neighbors wondered if he had been pushed; none wondered aloud. After the funeral, the widow was surprised to discover an enormous cache of liquor squirreled away in the basement, enough to last a lifetime and beyond, and all of it perfectly legal because federal law had provided for a one-year grace period starting in 1919 where folks could lay in as much alcohol as they wanted before Prohibition took effect.

The greengrocer's widow, a far-thinking woman named Mrs Ward, decided against selling the liquor case by case or even bottle by bottle. She realized that more money could be made by selling it glass by glass, so she turned her basement into a cozy speakeasy. Everyone knew her liquor was honest – none of that bathtub gin made with embalming fluid or poisonous wood alcohol. Her oldest, fourteen-year-old Dan, left school to run the place while she took over the grocery upstairs. Customers came and went discreetly through the store, usually picking up a head of lettuce or sack of potatoes as they left. Both businesses prospered.

The speakeasy, predictably called the Greengrocer's by locals, was located at the corner of my street, half a block from our house in Chicago's Near West Side. I went there three or four times a week, sometimes after a séance if it wasn't too late, sometimes during the afternoon while Baby Tommy napped and I wanted a little company. Baby Tommy and I had lived at Madame Carlotta Romany's house only a few months, but I had come to know some of our neighbors and made a few friends. It was a nice neighborhood with honest, hard-working people doing their darndest to keep heads above water. There was always someone I knew at the Greengrocer's.

One windy Saturday afternoon in August, I came to the grocer's for cherries. Carlotta had heard Mrs Ward say she was expecting a crate of fresh cherries and had got it in her head to make a pie. Tommy was napping, so I popped across the street to get them.

The shop bell tinkled. 'Leave the door open, Maddie, dear,' called Mrs Ward from behind the counter. 'The breeze is welcome.'

'I hope the cherries came in,' I said, pushing a brick against the door with my foot so it wouldn't slam shut. 'Carlotta's already made pie crust.'

Her hands full, Mrs Ward gestured with her elbow to the corner where two crates of bright red cherries sat one atop the other. I filled my basket with what looked like a pie's worth and handed it to her to weigh. Sounds coming from below my feet reminded me of the basement speakeasy. Someone had turned the radio up quite loud. 'Who's downstairs?'

'Josephine and Dizzy. Mary Lou and her mom. Sandra Baker brought a gentleman friend, Marcus What's-His-Name from around the corner. Unless one of them slipped out while I was in the back room. Go on down. My boy Dan's made a batch of lemonade that goes nice with gin.'

The basement steps were steep and the treads narrow. Thoughts of the late Mr Ward and his accidental tumble made me place my feet cautiously. Basements can be dreary, damp places, but Mrs Ward had rigged out the area with easy chairs and checkered tablecloths so it felt more like a comfortable home than a cellar. A few well-placed lamps augmented what little natural light filtered through the high windows, and scented candles cut the cigarette smoke. Mrs Ward didn't permit cigars.

Mary Lou waved me over. I'd met her mother last March when she moved in with her daughter's family after her home was destroyed in that monster tornado that swept through southern Illinois, flattening whole towns and killing near a thousand people. Young Dan Ward nodded at me from behind the bar. 'Can I get you something, Mrs Pastore?'

'Your lemonade, please, Dan.'

'Gin or no?'

'Gin, yes. Please.'

'Is Freddy busy tonight? I haven't seen him in a few days.'

Carlotta had more or less adopted Freddy, a streetwise orphan boy, when she moved into her house two years ago. He turned out to be very useful, handling the spooky effects for Carlotta's séances – mysterious noises, thumps, flames extinguished – her 'spiritual enhancements' as she called them. If she didn't need me to act as a shill at a particular séance, I usually helped him.

'He's been spending lots of time at that chess bar lately,' I told Dan. The fancy chess set I'd given him for Christmas had captivated Freddy, as I had hoped, and he spent hours every week at Carl's, an unusual sort of speakeasy where chess outranked booze. 'You should take up the game, Dan. There are fellas at Carl's who'd like nothing more than to teach you.'

The radio man was going on about the recent Scopes monkey trial down in Tennessee, and we sipped our drinks while we listened to the report and speculated as to whether we were descended from apes or not. The radio had been an inspired addition to the speakeasy. It was a real draw – no one in our neighborhood could afford to splash out a hundred bucks for such a contraption. When the news ended and the music resumed, we began gossiping about a local woman who had been summoned for jury duty.

'She's the first I've heard of,' said Mary Lou. 'I'm glad it wasn't me.'

'Why?' I wondered. 'Wouldn't you want to serve on a jury? You wouldn't be afraid, would you?'

'Heck no!' said Mary Lou. 'I'm glad the law was changed so that women can be called up. I just don't want it to be me. Not until I see how it goes. You know what I heard? That there's a woman who's just been elected governor out west.'

'No fooling?' said her mother.

'Wyoming, I believe it was. Can't remember her name.'

'I think jury duty sounds fascinating,' I said. 'Imagine

listening to the testimonies and hearing all the details about the crime. I'd be proud to serve.'

'I think it would be exciting, too,' said Mary Lou's mother. 'I'd go in a flash if I was called up, I would. Why should men have the only say in who's guilty or who's not? Besides, when it comes to judging character, women do it better than men.'

We could all agree with that.

When it turned out that the women's vote didn't destroy American democracy, as so many men had predicted, opportunities for women continued to grow. Cook County, the largest county in Illinois because it included America's second largest city, had recently passed a law allowing women to serve on juries. Our neighbor had been the first we knew of to be summoned. Summoned, and actually seated.

'Juries are corrupt,' said Mary Lou. 'They're paid off by thugs from the Outfit or the North Side Gang or the Gennas. The lawyers are bribed. Or the judges. Or the cops. Or all of 'em. Everything's a racket nowadays since Prohibition started. I don't want anything to do with it. A plague on all their houses, that's what I say.'

Footsteps on the stair turned heads. Boris Jankowski, a longshoreman who lived one street over, came into view.

'Anybody want tickets to tonight's show at Early's? It's the early show at ten. Get it? The early show at Early's? Ha ha! I got two tickets but the missus is taken with one of her headaches. We can't use 'em. Free, did I say?'

That was the key word, for me anyway. After several seconds of silence, I spoke up. 'If no one else wants them, I do.'

There being no other takers, Boris handed over the pair. 'Enjoy the show, Mrs Pastore.'

'Thank you kindly. I hope Mrs Jankowski is feeling better soon.'

'Aw, she will by tomorrow. Poor girl. These headaches come over her now and then, no rhyme or reason to 'em.'

'I have a friend who gets fierce headaches. Migraines. Has your wife tried Bayer aspirin?' asked Mary Lou's mother.

'Aspirin, cold compresses, and a dark room does her best. Good day, ladies.'

I followed him out a few minutes later, carrying my basket

of cherries and a bunch of fat carrots. When I got home, Carlotta wasn't in the kitchen. I called her name.

'In the parlor, Maddie, with Officer O'Rourke. I mean, *Detective* O'Rourke,' she corrected herself with a giggle.

Officer Kevin O'Rourke had been promoted to detective the month before, owing to his success in solving two or three murders, success due in large part to me. He got all the credit for bringing the guilty to justice, and I was happy for it to be like that. No way did I want anyone knowing what part my investigations had played, not even O'Rourke. O'Rourke believed that it was Carlotta's mystical connections to the Great Beyond that brought most of the information we were able to share with him, but really, it was all my doing. He'd come to Carlotta last autumn after she and I had solved the Weidemann murders, asking for her psychic help with future cases.

'Maddie, dear,' began Carlotta. She patted the space beside her on the sofa and I sat. 'Detective O'Rourke has some disturbing news.'

He cleared he throat. 'Yes, Mrs Pastore. There has been a vicious attack. An elderly woman who lived on the South Side was stabbed and her jewelry and money stolen.'

'Was she killed?' I asked.

'Thankfully no. She's in the hospital now, but I hear she'll survive.'

'And you want our help solving this attack?'

He shook his head. 'It's outside our district. Far outside. What concerned me was the fact that she was a spiritualist. A medium, like Madame Carlotta here. Her attacker was a male client. Have you ever . . .? I mean, I know you've had a couple of violent incidents at your séances and I wanted to warn you about this, in case, well, in case one of your clients became dissatisfied. You could be in danger too.'

It was Carlotta's turn to shake her head. 'That woman may have called herself a medium, but I don't imagine she was anything like me. I can't think I'm in any danger, detective. All my bangles are tin and paste, and anyone is welcome to the few dollars I have in the sugar bowl. As you know, I don't charge my clients like other mediums do, and I don't cheat them out of their money. Everyone knows there's nothing here to steal.'

It was true. Carlotta didn't charge clients. There was no law against holding séances or telling fortunes; there were, however, laws about bilking people out of their dough, so she made sure she never charged for her services. She accepted donations. One of my duties as her shill was to encourage donations by putting a ten-dollar bill in the basket as people left. It worked pretty well.

O'Rourke stood to take his leave. 'Well, consider this visit a warning. Have a care when choosing your clients. You've no man in the house to protect you.'

'There's Freddy,' I protested.

Carlotta had happened upon Freddy when she was moving into her house. He was hanging around and she needed help carrying boxes, so she offered him a ham sandwich and a quarter for a few hours of his time. He proved a good worker, so she asked him to return the next day. When she found the boy later that night shivering behind a pile of bricks in the alley beside her house, she fashioned a pallet on the floor in an upstairs room. He was still there.

O'Rourke smiled. 'That kid? What is he? Fifteen, sixteen? He can't weigh more than ninety pounds. A good lad, I'm sure, but it pays to be cautious. Prohibition laws have made Chicago more dangerous than ever.' And with that warning, he took his leave.

By this time, I'd been working for Madame Carlotta for nearly a year, if 'work' you could call it. I'd run across her in the Maxwell Street Market last summer when I was down to my last dollar, a just widowed brand-new mother with no family except my two-week-old baby. Though I hadn't seen her for a decade, I recognized her right away: Myrtle Burkholtzer, mother of my schoolfriend Alice who had long ago married and moved to southern California. Marriage had changed my name, and Mrs Burkholtzer had changed hers too, but not through marriage.

'I go by a name from one of my earlier lives,' she'd explained to me that day. 'I'm Carlotta Romany now. That was my name a hundred and twenty years ago when I was a gypsy queen in Austria-Hungary. Isn't that amazing? Knowing about that past life explained so much! It freed me from the iron bonds holding me back from my true vocation. I've always had the gift of spiritual connection, you know – or maybe you didn't know, but ever since I was a child, I've had strong feelings about the Far Beyond. And when I met my spiritual guide, the archangel Michael, bless him, I was able to unlock the door to my true essence and begin using my unique gifts to help others. When I was poor Mrs Burkholtzer, I was a lonely, unhappy woman, not much use to anybody, but Madame Carlotta Romany welcomes clients who are despondent, confused, or grieving, and helps them move on with lives. It is so fulfilling!'

She paid me a dollar that night just for showing up at her séance, posing as a grieving widow (which I certainly was), and pretending to reach my late husband's spirit (which I certainly didn't), thus encouraging the others at the table to believe her powers were genuine. I was a shill, something common in olden days. Traveling snake-oil salesmen always planted one or two in their crowds to drink some of the elixir and boast of their miraculous cure. Magicians relied on shills in the audience to help certain tricks. Auctioneers used them to bid up the price of the item on the block. It may not have been an honorable occupation, but it was an ancient one.

In no time I'd expanded my duties. With facts gathered from investigating the wills, obituaries, graveyards, neighbors, and homes of the deceased, I could feed Carlotta the sort of details 'no one could have known', details that made her séances eerily accurate, convincing clients that she was indeed the Real McCoy. I wasn't exactly proud of what I did, but I was proud of how well I did it. And it beat selling myself on the street or to Al Capone and his Outfit.

I'd first met Capone at my husband's funeral. He gave me a wad of bills and promised to avenge Tommy's death. Of course I'd known that Tommy drove a delivery truck for the Outfit. Heck, half of Chicago was involved in the illegal liquor business in some way, so his job was nothing to raise eyebrows. What Tommy hadn't told me was that he'd been promoted to handling more than simple runs. When thugs from the rival

North Side Gang swiped one of the Outfit's trucks, Tommy and some Outfit boys went to get it back. During the fight, a bullet found Tommy's forehead and there I was, a widow with a baby on the way. Within a week, I went from my comfortable house and a bulging bank account to begging for a temporary bed at Hull House, the Jane Addams settlement home for immigrants, thanks to the conniving trollop who claimed to be Tommy's legal wife and who took every dime we had. Mrs Burkholtzer – ahem, Madame Carlotta – saved me and Baby Tommy. She was more a mother to me than my own mother had ever been. I owed her everything.

The Early tickets slipped my mind until just as Carlotta, Freddy and I were sitting down to dinner. Little Tommy was safe in his kiddie coop and I was looking forward to boiled ham and potatoes and a slice of warm cherry pie.

'Oh, Carlotta, I have a nice surprise for you tonight. Somebody at the Greengrocer's had extra tickets to Early's floor show this evening – free! I thought you and Freddy would like to go. It's for the first show at ten.' Freddy frowned. He'd never heard of the place. 'It's a nightclub on our side of town. I've never been there, but I've heard of it. It should be a quick trip on the L.'

'Don't you want to go, Maddie?' Carlotta asked.

'Not really. I'll stay home with Tommy and finish my library book. You and Freddy deserve a night out.'

'*I'll* stay home with the baby, Maddie. You and Freddy go.'

After a bit of back-and-forth, she convinced me she was serious, so I changed into my gray, knee-length dress with all the bugle beads, a leftover from the days when I was married and could afford nice clothes from Marshall Field's. Hemlines had risen a bit since then, hovering now just above the knee, but this dress had been a favorite of my late husband's. He said the silvery bugle beads made him think of glittering icicles. A wintery image for this summer night.

And so we went to the early show at Early's, Freddy and me, him wearing his one dark suit and me in my glad rags and coral lipstick, for what I expected would be an uneventful night of musical entertainment.

TWO

Whoever owned Early's didn't worry about police raids. The sign on the three-story former warehouse was large and well-lit. No peephole, secret knock, or Joe-sent-me password, just big double doors to welcome the stream of ritzy customers. The owners might be paying the local beat cops to look the other way, but for an operation of this size, I figured it was higher-up palms getting the grease.

Inside, lights were low. Small round tables hugged by chairs and topped with candles were packed together in a semi-circle around the stage, giving everyone a clear view of the show. No bad seats at Early's. That said, our tickets put us in the busy back corner near the bar where there was a lot of coming and going from waitresses and cigarette girls working the crowd.

Freddy and I ordered gin rickeys.

'Geez. Fifty cents each!' griped Freddy.

'They can charge more at a place like this because of the show. You can switch to beer if you want. Those are just a quarter.'

'Naw, it's a class joint. Too classy for beer drinking. Check out this swell audience. No one my age and everyone's all dolled up.' He was right. I was glad I'd worn my silvery frock.

At a few minutes past ten, the lights dimmed and a man with a goatee stepped slowly up to the piano at the back of the stage. The crowd settled down. He played a flourish that acted as a signal for another man's entry, this one an energetic gent who bounded onto the stage and took his place in the spotlight. Handsome, thirtyish, with a thin Douglas Fairbanks mustache and thick hair parted at the side, he stood with his back ramrod straight and his chin lifted, surveying the crowd with a confident smile as he waited for silence.

'Ladies and gentlemen, good evening, one and all,' he began. 'I'm your host, Sebastian Dale, bidding you welcome to

Early's. And do we have a show for you tonight!' The pianist's fingers danced from bass to treble in another musical flourish. Sebastian Dale's smile stretched to his ears as he acknowledged the musician with a slight bow. 'First and foremost, allow me to introduce our musical maestro, the esteemed Ray Donovan of the Chicago Symphony, who will be accompanying our talented vocalists this evening and also entertaining you with his own renditions of some of today's most beloved tunes.' Applause brought the pianist to his feet for a curt bow. The emcee continued. 'For your listening pleasure tonight, we have three outstanding musical acts, the crème de la crème of the music world, brought here by popular acclaim and held over by popular demand. We will begin with a duet, an extraordinarily gifted pair that has recently returned from London where they performed at the Royal Palladium, the enchanting Mabel and Bruce Wisterley. Ladies and gentlemen, let's hear a warm welcome for the Wisterleys!'

The couple climbed on stage, hand in hand, sporting toothy grins and matching sequined vests. Their first number, 'When My Baby Smiles at Me', was followed by another romantic favorite, 'I'll Be With You in Apple Blossom Time', after which they switched to an amusing little ditty I'd never heard called 'After You Get What You Want You Don't Want It'. A few more numbers and they left the stage to generous applause.

A piano number by Ray Donovan brought up the lights and gave the audience the chance to order refills and visit with one another. Some minutes later, the emcee returned to introduce Walter Fulbright, a colored tenor who performed songs that ranged from the lighthearted 'The Moon Shines on the Moonshine' to a sentimental ballad about a railroad man.

'I thought this would be like vaudeville, but it isn't, is it?' said Freddy during the next interval.

'How do you mean?'

'Well, I've been to a few vaudeville shows, and they have more acts, maybe nine or ten, and more variety but shorter acts.'

'Like one animal act, one kiddie act, a singer, a dancer, and so forth?'

'Right. Here we got all singers.'

'The marquee out front advertised three acts tonight. The third one's the headliner. A woman.'

The pianist gave a lively rendition of some marching music that sounded like John Philip Sousa while everyone chatted and ordered more booze and smokes. A thick haze had developed, drifting up to the rafters and swirling lazily about the lights like Lake Michigan fog on a cool morning. When the lights dimmed once again, the emcee returned to give a fulsome introduction to the third act, Sophie Dale.

'She must be his wife,' I whispered to Freddy. 'Same last name.'

'Or sister. Or mother.'

'Point taken.'

'Ladies and gentlemen, I am honored to present to you tonight a star of the very highest magnitude, a chanteuse whose voice critics have likened to the nightingale, a woman who has been compared to the legendary Jenny Lind, a woman whose success on the Orpheum Circuit, the Broadway stage, and the theaters of Europe has brought her accolades from foreign princes and movie stars alike, my own favorite vocalist in the whole wide world, the beautiful, the talented Miss Sophie Dale!'

'Criminey!' said Freddy when she walked on stage. 'She ain't his mother, that's for sure.'

Sophie Dale slinked onto the stage like a runway mannequin who knows every eye is on her pretty face and trim flapper figure. Her backless silk gown stopped at the knee with a handkerchief hem, baring shapely gams and arms. Most of her dark hair was covered by a violet turban sporting white ostrich feathers that wafted through the air with every blink of her eyes. Taking her time, she surveyed the room, giving the impression that she had personally acknowledged everyone there. I wondered if she was searching for someone.

Sebastian Dale had not exaggerated. Her voice, a warm contralto, soared effortlessly across the room, bringing a complete hush to the audience that had continued to murmur throughout the previous two performances. She began with a sentimental favorite, 'Alice Blue Gown', but switched to lighter fare with the amusing 'Prohibition Blues' and an old Gilbert and Sullivan song with the words cleverly changed to bring them up-to-date.

As I watched, fascinated by her skill and stage presence, a strange feeling crept over me, pricking my thoughts, teasing my memories, and bringing ridiculous ideas to my head, ideas I kept pushing firmly aside. The thing was unthinkable and I'd better stop thinking about it. It had been a long time . . . It was a preposterous notion . . . It was too far-fetched to bear contemplating . . . There was no possibility, no earthly chance . . . but if you thought about the unthinkable long enough, it became quite possible.

Finally, as she finished her last song and folded her slender body into a gracious bow, I turned to Freddy and spoke over the applause.

'I think she's my sister.'

The surprise showed plain on his face. 'How can that be? How can you not know for sure?'

The crowd continued to applaud and whistle in an attempt to bring her back to the stage. No luck. The lights came up and the last-call bell sounded.

'When I left home, my sister was nine or ten. I haven't seen her, or any of my brothers or sisters for that matter, since then.'

'I didn't know you had brothers and sisters.'

I shrugged. My former family wasn't something I talked about. 'I'm third of nine.'

'Jeez Louise, I thought you were an orphan like me. All alone.'

'I may have grown up in a big family, but I was always alone.'

People were leaving. The second show audience would begin coming in soon. Waitresses bustled to clear the tables of glasses and wiped them clean for the next customer surge. I looked at the door behind the stage where Sophie Dale had slipped out. 'I've got to know. You can wait here if you like.'

'Hell, no. I'm coming.'

We threaded our way through the tables and chairs toward the back door. 'Where is Miss Dale's dressing room?' I asked a waitress who came through, balancing a tray of clean glasses in one hand. 'She's expecting me.'

She pointed with her free hand. 'Up the stairs, on the right.'

Freddy and I passed a tiny kitchen that was large enough only to wash bar glasses, climbed a grimy wooden staircase that reeked of spilled beer, and followed the voices to an open door on the right.

'. . . too old-fashioned. I think another—'

'But you do it so beautifully, darling, and it's perfect for your range.'

'I thought applause was weak. What about the moonbeams song?'

'It's up to you. As always.'

I knocked on the open door. Sebastian and Sophie Dale turned as one and regarded my intrusion with some displeasure. I gathered few fans had nerve enough to get this far.

'Excuse me, but are you . . . I know this is a really bizarre question, but are you by any chance Sophia Duval?'

The chanteuse's eyes grew round as recognition dawned. 'Oh my god! Maddie? Maddie!' And she shot out of her seat and threw her arms around my neck in a ferocious squeeze. 'I can't believe it's you! You look the same! Well, different. Older, but the same.'

'And you look very different from the little girl I remember.'

'But even so, you recognized me!' She hugged me again, then remembered her husband. 'Do you believe this, Seb? This is my big sister, Madeleine. I haven't seen her in – what? – ten years?'

'Pleased to meet you, Madeleine,' he said, holding his hand out for a friendly welcome. 'I'm Sebastian Dale, Sophie's husband. And manager.'

'And owner of Early's,' she added. 'Did you catch my act or have you just arrived?'

'I saw you. You are marvelous! I thought there was some-thing familiar about you but I couldn't believe it was possible. Your voice – I had no idea you could sing.'

'Neither did I, until Seb discovered me.'

He grabbed her hand and gave it a kiss.

'And your career! You've been to Europe and performed for royalty!'

'Oh, well, that . . . no. Not really,' she confessed with a giggle. 'Seb's always exaggerating.'

'Nonsense. I just stretch the truth a little,' he said. 'There was that German count in the audience last year, remember?'

'We really did play the Orpheum circuit, Maddie. For two years, all over the country. Seb and I had the cutest act – he sings too, by the way—'

'—only not so good as Sophie.'

'But we got tired of jumping to a new town every week and boarding house life ain't exactly the Ritz. So Seb got this place and here we are!'

A distant bell rang.

'That's my cue, ladies,' said Sebastian, glancing in Sophie's mirror to check that his slicked-back hair was still in place. 'Excuse me, Madeleine.'

'Maddie, please,' I corrected him. My brother-in-law. Imagine that! I had a brother-in-law.

'Maddie then. I'm delighted you've found your sister, but you'll understand that a real reunion must be postponed. Sophie's working and, as you can tell, she's the key to our success.'

'Oh, Seb, that's not so. You're the one who's made Early's the best nightclub in the city.'

'Well, OK, let's agree that we're a good team.' He lifted her pert chin with one finger and touched her lips in a make-believe kiss. 'Take a few minutes off, sweetheart. But get Maddie's telephone number and address so we can all get together on a Sunday. That's our one day off,' he explained to me. 'But not this coming Sunday – we have that birthday party we're working, remember. Delighted to make your acquaintance, sister-in-law.' And he slipped through the door, giving Freddy, who was hovering in the hall, a curious glance as he passed. Embarrassed that I'd forgotten the boy was out there, I quickly introduced him to Sophie.

'Come and sit a moment,' she said. 'You too, Freddy. I have so much to tell you! Have you seen Mama and Papa lately? Or any of the others?'

I decided to leave out my last visit to our parents' home, when my pleas for a place to stay a few weeks until my baby could be born were met with insults – they called me a whore and my unborn child a bastard. Not that Sophie would be surprised at any of that, but I had vowed never to let the word 'bastard' come within ten miles of my son, ever. It was too close to the truth. Instead I merely said, 'I was home a few years ago when I told them I was getting married.'

'I remember that! I wasn't there when you came, but I heard about it. An Italian boy. They were disgusted. Did you marry him? How is he? I'll bet he's real nice.'

'He was. Real, real nice. He was killed last year in a gang fight.' Her hand flew to her mouth as she gasped, but I forged ahead. Too much sympathy dragged me down. Much better to focus on the good parts of my life. 'But I have a lovely son named Tommy and we live with someone you might remember. Do you recall my friend Alice Burkholtzer's mother? Their family lived a block over from us.'

Sophie frowned in thought. 'Wide as she was tall?'

Freddy snorted.

'That's her. Now she's a mystic named Madame Carlotta and she conducts séances to connect people with the spirits of their dead loved ones. Baby Tommy and I live with her in a house on the Near West Side. Freddy lives there too.' She gave Freddy a curious look, so I gave as plausible an explanation as I could. 'He's a cousin.'

That was enough about me. I didn't need to dance around the touchy parts of what I did in my investigations for Madame Carlotta or what Freddy and I did together for séance enhancements. No one could know about that, not even a sister. It wasn't hard to change the conversation. Sophie was eager to talk about herself.

'I did what all of us kids did and ran out as soon as I could. I took off when I was fifteen and never looked back. Worked a while waitressing in a bar. Seb found me there and took care of me, and he discovered I could sing real good. We played the Orpheum Circuit for two years, like I said, and we were headliners most of that time. Made a pile of dough, sure, but the gypsy life wasn't for us. It's exhausting like you wouldn't believe, jumping from town to town every week, living in crap boarding houses. I thought I was gonna have a baby so we got married, then I lost the baby. We came back to Chicago and settled down here last year. Seb's swell. He can do anything. Do you ever see any of the other kids?'

I told her what little I knew of our brothers and sisters – which was virtually nothing since each of us had escaped the violence of our wretched home at the first opportunity. Without a parent or another relative to serve as the hub of a wheel, there was no way for the spokes to keep in touch. We had all gone our separate ways. America was a big country. I hadn't left Chicago, but one brother had gone to St Louis, or said he was going to. I never expected to encounter any of my siblings again. It was pure luck that I'd stumbled onto this one little sister.

A waiter wearing an eyepatch came to the dressing room door. 'Miss Sophie, Mr Dale said to tell you five minutes.'

I stood. 'Come on, Freddy. We've gotta get out of here so Sophie can do her job.' I snatched up a piece of paper from her desk and took a pencil out of my handbag. 'Here's my telephone number. Call me and we'll arrange to meet on a Sunday or whenever you're free. I'd love you to meet my little boy, Tommy, and we can talk all we want. About the good times,' I added. She frowned, as if trying to remember any good times, then gave me a smile that deepened her dimples.

'And you know where to find me now, too.' With another hug and promises to get together soon, we parted.

'A sister!' I gushed to Freddy as I practically danced my way home. 'Imagine that. I have a sister! Someone who knew me back when. It's a miracle.'

It was three days later when I heard her name spoken again. Sebastian telephoned the house to let me know that his wife Sophie Dale was in the Cook County jail, charged with first-degree murder.

THREE

Behind the Hubbard Street Courthouse sits Cook County's jail, a plain two-story stone building that housed men and women waiting for their trials and others who were serving sentences too short to warrant moving them to the state prison down in Joliet. The courthouse itself was an attractive structure with an exterior that looked more like a nice museum or Gold Coast mansion than a place of government business. I'd never been inside, but I knew from Detective O'Rourke to go around behind it to the jail entrance on Illinois Street. I was going to visit my sister, something I gather wasn't very common since it took O'Rourke some fancy footwork to get permission for me to get inside to see a prisoner.

'Don't bring anything with you,' he'd warned me.

'But she'll be wanting some fresh clothing, maybe some soap and a comb and such.' It had been four days since Sophie had been arrested. Four days is a long time to go without a toothbrush.

He shook his head sadly. 'It's not allowed.'

'Surely I could bring her a book or—'

'Nothing. Not for now, anyway. I'll try to get approval for that sort of thing later, but for now, just you. She'll be housed in a separate area for women. It's a little better than the men's side, not that you'll think that when you see it. Trouble is, they cram twice as many people in there as it's supposed to hold, but what else can they do? The city won't vote the money for a new facility.'

The worst thing about the jail was the smell. Worse than the filthy floors, worse than the grimy windowpanes in the front office, the smell of vomit and sweat hit me like a gale-force wind as I stepped through the public entrance into the lobby. I wondered how the guards and deputies and office workers stood it; no doubt they grew used to it after a while. I fought back the impulse to put my handkerchief to my nose as I approached the reception desk and gave them my name and Sophie's.

'Wait here,' said the bulldog behind the desk. He motioned with his head to a bench against the wall where a few other forlorn-looking Chicagoans sat. No one moved to make room for me – no one even glanced in my direction – so I remained on my feet.

While I waited, I went over in my mind what Sebastian had told me when he'd called with the dreadful news.

'It's terrible, Maddie. Terrible. I'm completely . . . I don't know what to do! I mean, I know enough to hire a lawyer. I did that. Asked around and hired John Farnsworth. Heard he was one of the best criminal lawyers in the city. Never mind the cost; dollars don't matter. Nothing matters but that Sophie needs the best.'

'Calm down, Sebastian. Take a deep breath and tell me what happened that night. Sunday, wasn't it? Where were you?'

'It was that party. A birthday party. For Nick Bardo. Nick and his wife come to Early's pretty regular. They're big fans. Me and Sophie know them. So they asked would we come to Nick's birthday party, not like guests, but Sophie would entertain and I'd tend bar. It was a fancy party, a real big deal, and they're very rich. Of course we said yes. I don't know why we said yes. We really didn't need the money. We were doing swell. Why did we say yes? If we'd said no, none of this would ever have happened and we'd be home now, happy as kings.' His sobs came through the telephone wire like he was right there beside me.

I tried to calm him as best I could. 'That's OK, Sebastian. It's OK. You couldn't have known. Just go on, tell me what happened at the party.'

'Yeah, sure. Yeah, so . . . at the party, I'm tending bar. There are maybe two hundred people, so we brought another bartender, Doc, from Early's and a boy, Stanley, to help. Doc's working one room; I'm working another; Stanley's back and forth with a tray full. Sophie's in the living room where there's a grand piano. She sings a bunch of tunes. I can hear her but not see her. Anyway, she sings great, as usual. After a while, she comes to me at the bar and says she's not feeling too good. What's the matter, I say, you sick? You wanna go home? I dunno why I said that; we can't go home. But she's looking pretty woozy, so I find Ellie – that's Nick's wife, Ellie Bardo – and I tell her Sophie's looking like she might keel over any minute. Is there a quiet room where she could rest? And Ellie, she says sure, and she leads the way upstairs to a guest bedroom at the end of a hallway where it's cool and quiet. Sophie lies down on the bed and is out like a broken light. Ellie and me, we close the door and go back downstairs, she to her guests, me to the bar. Next thing I know, there's cops coming through the front door.'

'What time was that?'

'No idea.'

'About.'

'Oh, maybe two.'

'What time did you take Sophie upstairs?'

'About midnight. No, about one. I dunno. I don't wear a watch.'

'So who called the cops?'

'I dunno. The way I heard it, some lovebirds were looking for a place to nest, checking the upstairs for an empty bedroom, you know, and they walk into the guest room and find Nick on the floor, dead as the dodo. Head bashed in. And lying on the bed is Sophie, with a big candlestick in her hand. Bloody. So the woman screams and people come running and they call the cops. And they get Ellie who goes crazy.'

'But you didn't see any of that?'

'No. None of us was allowed upstairs. I kept asking, where's Sophie? Where's Sophie? But I figured she's all right, like still passed out somewhere far away from all the ruckus. All I saw was the cops coming in and then they come down the stairs minutes later with Nick on a stretcher. We didn't know then that he was dead. Only later do I see other cops coming down with Sophie. She could hardly walk, so they're almost carrying her, one on each side. They don't let me come in the paddy wagon with her, so I follow them to the police station. They don't let me see her, no matter what I say. I been at the police station twice, but they won't tell me anything. They still won't let me see her. I hired the lawyer, that Farnsworth fella, and they're letting him in to see her today. He says he'll make sure I see her soon.' He broke down again, sobbing.

'Try not to worry, Sebastian,' I said, thinking how stupid that sounded. Of course he was worrying! Anyone would be frantic with worry. But what else could I say? What could I do? I felt so helpless. 'You've done the right thing, hiring that lawyer. He'll make everything right.'

'The thing is, she couldn't have done it. I know Sophie and she's not a killer, no matter what. I know she didn't do it. I'm sure of it. But I thought you should know, Maddie. You're the only family she has. The only family that cares about her. I don't have anyone else. She's all I have. She's everything to me, Sophie is.'

That was two days ago. Tuesday's newspaper carried the story – anytime a gruesome murder happened, the reporters were on it like buzzards on a corpse. I didn't learn anything more from the article than Sebastian had told me.

Right away, I did the only thing I could think of, and that was to call on Detective O'Rourke for help getting into the jail. What else could I do? Maybe something would come to me after I spoke with Sophie. My sister. The stranger I barely knew. Was Sebastian right that she couldn't have done it? Or could she have? I had no way of knowing, not really.

After an hour of waiting in that stinking lobby, a stocky woman with muscular arms and a head of thick iron-gray hair, pulled back in a tight bun, burst through the door and called my name. The nametag on her bag-like black garment identified her as D. BAKER.

'Come with me,' she ordered curtly, leading the way through a thick wooden door reinforced on both sides with sheets of metal. Impossibly, the stink grew worse. 'I'm Matron Baker,' she began, without turning her head. 'You'll be searched first, then you have thirty minutes with the prisoner.' We passed through another door, this one she had to unlock with a large key, then we turned into a small room with a stool, a wooden chair, a small table and a curtain to divide the space in half.

'Leave your handbag here.'

I set my bag down on the table.

'Take your hat and shoes off and raise your arms over your head.'

Wincing at the prospect of standing on that floor in my clean stockings, I complied. The matron patted me down quite thoroughly, not neglecting to feel my hair to make sure I wasn't hiding a file in my chignon. She examined my shoes and hat for the same reason, I presume, then allowed me to put them back on. Detective O'Rourke had warned me about this, so I'd worn my simplest dress, a no-waist cotton frock with a pilgrim collar and short sleeves as if to imply that I'd nothing to hide. No jewelry. I'd left off corsets before my marriage so my soft underclothing posed no threat to jail security. Eventually the matron gave a grunt, which I interpreted to mean she was satisfied, and we left the room.

August in Chicago can be hot as Hades, but today was *not* one of those miserable oven-like days that leave you gasping for air, even in the shade. Nonetheless, it was stifling in the cell block. What little air there was wafted in through slits in the exterior walls, reminding me of arrow slits in castle walls that medieval archers used when shooting at enemy attackers. The heat made it hard to breathe. I couldn't imagine what this place would feel like on a more typical blistering summer day. I could only pray that Sophie wouldn't be here long enough to find out.

I expected to be taken to Sophie's cell. Instead Matron Baker led me past several large cells, all of which were crowded with inmates leaning against the walls, reclining on metal beds, or sitting on the cement floor, and into a room with several tables. Each table had two chairs. Some were occupied by haggard-looking women sitting across from a man, probably a husband or lawyer. A few inmates had female visitors. None had children. I spotted Sophie at once, alone at a table in the corner, waiting for me. No one else looked up.

'Thirty minutes,' barked the matron.

Sophie gave a cry and fell into my arms.

'Sit!' called the matron. 'Rules say you sit the entire time.'

I released my sister and followed orders.

Sophie looked dreadful. Her long dark tresses, wavy where mine were stick straight, had been braided into a messy queue with a halo of escaped tendrils circling her head. Her eyes, blue like mine, were red from crying. Her hands shook. Someone had replaced her pretty clothes with a shirt and long skirt made of a coarse, stripey, gray fabric, and she wore thick stockings and heavy black shoes without laces that looked like they were meant for men. Every prisoner in the room was dressed the same.

'Sophie, Sophie,' I crooned. 'Sebastian told me. I have a friend who pulled some strings to get me in. Try not to worry, honey. Everything is going to come out all right, you'll see.'

Those wet, red eyes just stared at me, wanting to believe my words but losing hope fast. She looked so young, so fragile. I could see the little ten-year-old I remembered from all those years ago and it like to broke my heart.

'Has Sebastian come to visit you?'

She sniffed and nodded.

'And the lawyer? Farnsworth?'

Another shaky nod.

'What did they say?'

'They said the cops think I killed Nick,' she said, chewing her fingernails as her words spilled out in a jerky fashion. She glanced about the room nervously, avoiding my gaze. 'They found him in the room with me. Where I was lying, upstairs. Dead. On the floor. His head bashed by a candlestick. A brass candlestick. It was beside me on the bed. My fingerprints . . .'

'What do you remember?'

'That's what everyone keeps asking me! And I keep answering – nothing! *Nothing!* Stop it!' Her voice rose hysterically. 'I remember nothing at all!'

Others turned to look at us. The guard frowned and headed our way. I signaled with one hand that we would keep quiet, and the guard resumed her watchful stance from the corner. I spoke to Sophie soothingly. 'Let me try an easier question. Do you remember singing in the living room?'

She nodded grudgingly.

'And that was about what time? Ten o'clock? Eleven?'

'Eleven.'

'What did you sing?'

'Silly songs. "Yes We Have No Bananas", "Toot Toot Tootsie". That sort.'

'Did the guests applaud?'

'Of course. Nick – Nick requested those. And some others.'

'Did you sing the Happy Birthday song?'

'Not then. That was for later.'

'But later never came, right?'

She nodded miserably.

'What were you drinking?'

'Soda water with lemon.'

'Nothing alcoholic?'

'I don't drink alcohol.'

'You're a teetotaler?'

'I mean I don't drink when I'm performing. Alcohol hurts my voice.'

'How's that?'

'Makes me sound raspy. Can't hit the high notes. I never drink before a performance.'

'So you weren't tipsy. Or drunk. Or hitting the opium pipe?'

'No!'

'How did you feel after your performance?'

'Normal, I guess.'

'You didn't feel sick? Light-headed? Stomach pains?'

'I don't think so. Nothing like that.'

'I'm just wondering what made you collapse so suddenly.' *Could she have been drugged?*

'I collapsed?'

'Sebastian says you seemed ill and he asked for a place where you could lie down.'

She rubbed her temples with both hands. 'I don't remember.'

'OK, let's think about after your performance. Who did you talk to afterwards?'

'I tried to mingle with the crowd. That's part of my job. I talk to people. Make 'em feel good.'

'Anyone in particular?'

She squinched up her face, trying to recall. 'Nick's daughters. He has two. Older than me. Older than you. Like, more than thirty. They were there. He's told us about them before. They hate each other. All their lives, they've hated each other, and now they hate their father for marrying Ellie and they hate Ellie. I was curious about them, whether they were as bad as all that. They were there that night, so I made sure to see what they were like.'

'And what were they like?'

Her lips tightened into a thin smile as she remembered. 'One's smart and ugly as a troll. The other's a Dumb Dora but a looker. Nick used to say that between the two of them, they woulda made one decent person. His words, not mine.'

'What did you think of them?'

'They were just the way he described them.'

'Sophie, has Nick ever, well, you know, come on to you? Has he ever tried anything fresh or suggested that you and he should, you know, get it on?'

'No! Seb and me have been with him and Ellie half a dozen times and honest, Nick's always behaved like a gentleman. He's crazy about Ellie. He wouldn't step out on her.'

'OK, so after you mingled with the guests, what did you do?'

'I don't know. That's the last thing I remember. Seb said the cops came and took me away in the paddy wagon, but I don't remember any of that. The next thing I remember is waking up in a jail cell all alone and being scared, not knowing where I was. Or why. There was no one to tell me what had happened. I thought I'd been kidnapped. It was a whole day before Seb and that lawyer fella came and told me about Nick being killed. They think I killed him.'

'And you don't remember anything about it?'

'Maybe I did kill him. It's my fingerprints clear as day on the candlestick. And Nick's blood. Do you think I did it?'

'I don't know what to think, but I know one thing. You're innocent until proven guilty. They'll have to prove you guilty and we'll – Sebastian and the lawyer and me – we'll prove you innocent. In the meantime, listen, Sophie, I'm trying to get permission to bring some things to you, like a comb and a toothbrush. Is there anything you particularly want me to try to bring?'

Dull eyes met mine. She shook her head. 'I just want to go home.'

'And we're going to get you home, soon. Real soon. I promise.'

FOUR

'I just don't think she did it,' I insisted for the third time. Detective O'Rourke had come by the house to see how my jail visit had gone, and Carlotta was holding court in the parlor. Freddy was nowhere to be found. He always high-tailed it out the back door the moment O'Rourke knocked at the front – that boy would never feel easy around cops, even decent ones like Kevin O'Rourke. Carlotta kept insisting that O'Rourke was sweet on me. I thought he was angling to get our help solving murders. No matter if he *was* romantically inclined, I was not and never will be again in this lifetime. Tommy Pastore was the love of my life. No man could ever live up to him.

Every window in the house was wide open to catch the morning breeze, so we could hear kids arguing on the sidewalk over a game of marbles and another gang in the distance playing kick-the-can. Although the calendar still said summer, early September brought soothing fall temperatures to Chicago and the leaves turned gold and orange overnight. Carlotta was pressing O'Rourke to take a second piece of cinnamon cake, still warm from her oven.

'I don't think she did it.'

'You're pretty much alone in that opinion, I'm afraid,' he replied.

'Surely the investigation will turn up some other suspect, someone who wanted Nick Bardo dead and is happy to have his murder pinned on my little sister.'

'That's the thing, Maddie. The investigation is finished. It's a cut-and-dried case. Victim on the floor, head bashed in, suspect holding murder weapon. No one else around. What's to investigate?'

'But she was unconscious! And she wasn't drunk – she doesn't drink before performances.'

'So she says.'

'She wasn't using opium or cocaine or any of that.'

'Again, so she says.'

'She was ill and had fallen deep asleep. So deep she didn't hear when someone came into the room, whacked Nick Bardo, and stuck the candlestick in her hand.'

'Maddie, I didn't work the case. My information is second-hand, but here's what the boys at headquarters are thinking: Sophie goes upstairs to lie down. Nick follows her, comes on to her, maybe tries to have his way with her. She grabs the nearest thing – the brass candlestick on the table – and whacks him on the head.'

'But Nick never pushed himself on her before.'

'So Sunday night was his first try. Maybe he was drunk. A little too much birthday celebration and he was ready to open a shiny new present. Whatever the story, after she brains Nick, she collapses back onto the bed, passed out cold. Try not to worry too much. Your sister has a good lawyer who can probably prevent her hanging. He can probably get charges reduced by saying she was defending herself. Maybe as low as third-degree murder or even manslaughter. Although, to be frank, that won't be easy since she had no bruises or scrapes on her anywhere that could testify to a struggle. Still, she might get off with ten or twenty years.'

My stomach gave a sickening lurch. Ten or twenty years? She'd be an old woman by then, if she lived through it. And that was the optimistic scenario! 'So you think Sophie's lying? When she says she doesn't remember anything?'

He shrugged. 'Let's just say the investigating detective didn't believe her. I'm willing to believe it's possible that she honestly doesn't remember, but it doesn't change the outcome.'

'I just don't think she did it,' I said, unwilling to give an inch. Stubborn as a mule, my brothers used to say.

O'Rourke stood to take his leave. 'Are you still set on attending the funeral this afternoon?'

'Yeah. Funerals are good places to pick up information. I'll wear mourning clothes and a veil so no one will recognize me, and I'll not speak to the family. It doesn't really matter if I do, I suppose, since no one knows I'm her sister.'

'Just take care.'

'I always do.'

'I'll watch the baby, Maddie,' offered Carlotta. 'And won't you take another piece of cake home with you, detective?'

I was certainly no police detective, but I'd been investigating suspicious deaths for over a year now as part of my job helping Madame Carlotta with her séances. Although I hadn't met Sophie's lawyer, I was sure I could help him by sharing whatever information I uncovered. Like I did with O'Rourke. And I could go places he couldn't go, tease out information he couldn't find. People often talked more freely to a woman, especially when she was carrying a baby with her. I'd start with Nick Bardo's funeral.

I'd already been to the library to read his obituary in yesterday's *Chicago Tribune*. An obituary is usually full of helpful information, some of which can lead down other avenues. Obituaries give me facts to feed Madame Carlotta as she communes with her spirits, details that impress her clients because it seems to them that no one could possibly know those things. Nick's obituary was no exception. Nicholas A. Bardo was fifty-six years old, the father of two grown daughters, Vivian Wilcox and Gladys Selinko. Vivian, the elder, was a divorcée. Gladys was married to Warren Selinko. No grandchildren. Nick's first wife, Flora, predeceased him by ten years. He and his second wife, Ellie, had been married for two years. Evidently Nick's money came from his hotels, for his obituary listed several, including the Adler, one of Chicago's finest grand old hotels. I knew the place. Tommy and I had dined there on our anniversary, the last one we would ever have. Obituaries always make the deceased sound like they had lived blameless lives and were universally admired and loved, so pardon my cynicism if I snorted when I read about all of Nick's charitable goings-on. Supposedly he'd been a leader in the Chamber of Commerce, the YMCA, the Union League Men's Club, his local Catholic church, and half a dozen organizations I'd never heard of, and a long-time member of the Chicago Yacht Club. He kept a boat at Monroe Harbor and enjoyed competing in the Mackinac Race every July – that part rang true. Typically, the last sentence of the obituary revealed the time and location of the funeral.

After I'd noted all pertinent facts, I traipsed down to the Cook County courthouse to see if his will had been probated yet. No dice. I'd have to return later. Back home, I fed Baby Tommy rice pudding and mashed carrots, dressed him in the clean cotton gown I'd ironed last night, and put him in his baby buggy for the ride to the morgue.

Not the dead-people morgue, the newspaper morgue. Sometime last year, a librarian had told me that the big newspaper publishers kept all their back issues, something that wouldn't be much use to anyone except that they had a filing system that worked like the library's card catalogue. You could look up a name or subject and find out the dates of any newspapers with stories about that person, place, or event. And also the page and column so you could find it fast. A real help for a spiritualist's investigator like me. The downside was simple: these archives weren't usually open to the public. They were meant for employees, mostly reporters, and police investigators. I'd lucked into access to the *Chicago Tribune* morgue by accident, thanks to Baby Tommy.

The *Chicago Tribune* morgue was managed by Mrs Waterman, a fierce old woman who guarded the storeroom of back issues like it was a museum full of Old Masters. She would let you look at a newspaper but even think about removing it from the premises and you were likely to get stabbed with one of the sharpened pencils she kept stuck in the bun on top of her head. A reporter friend told me that she seldom allowed anyone but *Tribune* employees into her lair, but she let me come again and again because she loved seeing Baby Tommy. She liked to fuss over him while I read through the newspapers I'd requested. I never went to the morgue without him.

'No, he's not walking yet, Mrs Waterman. And at fourteen months, I'm getting a trifle concerned. What do you think?'

'I think you should count your lucky stars, girl. I had one who walked at nine months. Ran me ragged. After they take their first step, it's Katie-bar-the-door. Here, give me the little tyke,' she said as she swapped him for a stack of newspapers. I sat at the big library table to read.

There had been a number of articles mentioning Nick Bardo

in the recent past. I thought it most efficient to start with the present and work my way backwards. Many were about the Adler Hotel, which he acquired in 1920 from the family that built it decades earlier. One article told about his marriage to Ellie, a gaudy 'society' wedding that had been ignored by Chicago's proper society. It was held at his own hotel, the Adler, complete with doves released from cages and enough hothouse flowers to shame Versailles. The catty society reporter noted that Nick's daughters were not among the guests. I guess I could understand their pique – Ellie was probably ten years younger than they were – but after all was said and done, Nick was their father and could it have hurt too much to sit quietly at a corner table during the reception and pretend to smile? The other articles were interesting but contained little other than general business information. Evidently Nick Bardo didn't speak to reporters, for he was never quoted. I hoped I would learn more at his funeral.

There's nothing drearier than a funeral on a rainy day. Chicago skies opened up just as the mourners were gathering at the church, and the downpour continued for the length of the service. I arrived early so I could plant myself in the back where I could watch people coming in and going out without craning my neck and calling attention to myself. Half the pews were empty, but considering the size of the church, it was still a respectable showing. Nick's body was on display in an open casket up front, before the altar. I followed the example of others and walked down the aisle to view the deceased before finding my seat. It would be my only chance to see the victim and I wasn't going to miss it.

For a fella whose skull had been crushed, he looked pretty good. Like he was asleep. A hat on the top of his head covered up the wounds. He was tall, over six feet, big chested but not fat. His hands, folded across his stomach, were enormous and there was a large diamond ring on one finger. Would they leave that on for the burial? Or maybe the stone wasn't real. I wondered, too, how a little thing like Sophie could whack a big guy like Nick. She had to be a foot shorter and couldn't amount to half his weight. Could she even reach the top of his head with the brass candlestick? How was it he didn't see or hear her coming? How was it he didn't defend himself? Did that worthless police detective think of that?

From my perch in the back pew, I watched mourners shuffle down the aisle to pay their respects. Some sniffed into handkerchiefs; others stared stoically ahead, seemingly lost in contemplation. All at once I was aware of a man in a dark raincoat flanked by two thugs with hands deep in their bulging pockets, strutting down the aisle like he owned the church. And maybe he did. Al Capone, head of the Outfit and, God help me, godfather to my precious son, had come to the funeral to . . . to what? Pay his respects? Was Nick Bardo one of Capone's men? Nothing I'd read in the papers had suggested that. What in heaven's name was Scarface Al doing here? Was Nick an enemy? A rival? An employee? Was he making sure Nick was really dead?

Capone stopped at the side of the casket and stood there, hat in hand, for maybe a minute. I couldn't see his face but I knew it all too well: piggy eyes, fat lips, disgusting smirk. The scars on his cheek came, some said, from his younger years when he insulted a woman and her brother slashed his face. I knew how much Capone loathed his Scarface nickname, and he hated those scars so much he wore make-up sometimes. I'd seen that with my own eyes. Heck, whenever he had his photograph taken, he made sure the cameraman took his right side so the scars wouldn't show.

Capone and his bodyguards turned around, but instead of sliding into a pew for the service like you would think, they retraced their steps all the way down the aisle, their heads bobbing from side to side as they scanned the congregation for threats, and left the church. I thanked my lucky stars I'd worn my hat with the mourning veil. Even if he'd looked directly at me, he wouldn't have recognized me swathed in all this black netting.

It was only last winter that Al Capone had inherited the top spot at the Outfit from its previous boss, Johnny Torrio. What happened was this: the North Side Gang tried to murder Torrio and very nearly succeeded, but the docs patched him up. After he was released from the hospital, he wisely decided it was time to turn over the Outfit to Capone, his second-in-command,

and retire to his home back in Italy. Smart guy, I thought. Get out while the getting was good. My late husband had worked for Torrio, at first just delivering beer and booze, but eventually he was promoted and that's what got him killed. The Outfit likes to boast 'we take care of our own', so Capone made a big deal about honoring my husband by becoming our son's godfather. I nearly threw up when he showed up at the baptism uninvited, but there was no way I could prevent it. Enough said. I try to keep myself and my boy as far from Capone as I can.

The priest droned on for over an hour. Finally the service ended. And so did the rain, almost. Pallbearers closed the casket and carried it outside to a hearse. The burial was to be private, so the two daughters and the widow greeted mourners outside under the dripping trees.

It almost made me laugh to see the three women, huddled under their umbrellas, carefully distancing themselves from one another. One daughter stood far to the right on the sidewalk, the other stood with her husband far to the left. And Ellie, the widow, held court on the steps, shaking hands as mourners came out of the narthex. Each woman was surrounded by a small clutch of people who murmured their condolences before moving on to the next. I put up my umbrella and found a place under a tree, avoiding all three of them. How could I explain myself? 'Hello, I'm the sister of the woman the cops say killed Nick and I'm looking for clues to help me prove her innocence. So sorry for your loss.' Not a chance.

But I watched. Intently. So intently, I hardly noticed the woman standing behind me, swaying slightly from side to side like a mother soothing a fussy baby. When she started talking, I could ignore her no longer.

'They're a pair, aren't they?' she began.

'Excuse me?'

'Those girls. The daughters. Vivian and Gladys. Snakes, the both of 'em.' Then she seemed to catch herself, for she dabbed her crimson lipstick with a handkerchief and paused briefly, until she could think up a neutral remark. 'You a friend of the deceased?'

She was standing close enough that I could smell the liquor on her breath. 'No, not a friend. An employee. I worked with him at the hotel.' Best not to mention which hotel, in case she worked there too. 'And you?'

'Hmph. Hardly knew him. It's my husband . . .' And she looked across the sidewalk to a group talking with the widow. 'My husband's his lawyer. But everyone knows about those girls.'

'I suppose they're nice enough, but I don't know them.'

She needed no further encouragement. 'Nice? I'd sooner, what do you call it, send my laundry to the Chinese.' Yes, she was drunk all right, but a drunk is often an excellent source of information.

'Tell me about them.'

'Well, my dear, that one . . .' She pointed to the one nearest us, standing on the sidewalk beside a man holding a large black umbrella over them both. 'That one is Gladys, married to Warren, beside her.' Gladys was pretty in an overripe way, the sort of woman who peaks at eighteen and fades gradually thereafter. She should have known better than to use so much kohl on her eyes – her tears and her swipes with her handkerchief had smeared it dreadfully and now she reminded me of a raccoon. But then again, perhaps that was the impression she was trying to give: a bereft daughter mourning her beloved father.

Her husband Warren looked to be about forty, a solid body topped by a large head with a receding hairline. His ruddy complexion suggested gin in the morning, whiskey at night, and brandy after meals. He looked bored, like he couldn't wait to get back to the bar.

'Warren's a real dolt if there ever was one. Works for Nick but doesn't work, if you get my meaning. And Gladys is the looker in the family but she's got the brains of a . . . of a . . . fruit fly.'

'And the other?' My gaze traveled to her sister holding court on the opposite side of the pavement in front of the church. Where Gladys was plump, her sister was stocky. Where Gladys painted her face, her sister disdained all forms of make-up. Her bobbed hair looked as if she'd cut it herself with a dull knife. She was standing with a group of friends and all were laughing rather coarsely. A bit more decorum would have been nice. It was, after all, her father's funeral.

'That's Vivian. She got the brains. Used to be married to a builder until he ran off with his secretary.'

'How sad.'

'Nah. She drove him away. A real bitch. At least, that's what my husband says.'

'What about the widow?'

'Oh, her? Ellie's her name. She was a showgirl, you know.'

'I didn't know.'

The lawyer's wife was delighted to find someone who knew so little about the family, someone she could impress with her behind-the-scenes knowledge. With my most flattering tone of voice, I encouraged her.

'Yep. Burlesque. Hoochie-cooch, you know? Well, just look at her, it's obvious, isn't it? That figure! Nick knew what he was getting when he married her, although my husband tried to talk him out of it. Just keep on with her, he said. Just let her think there's an altar at the end of the road, you know? To keep him safe from her gold-digging grasp. But no, Nick wanted her all to himself so he married the little tart. His girls nearly shit bricks, you know?'

'She does look rather young for him.' Young and pretty. Under that dark kohl and rouge was a very attractive woman. Bottle blonde, sure, but with an hourglass figure few men could resist. I gave Ellie credit for some smarts. Getting a rich older man like Nick to propose must be every burlesque dancer's dream.

'Young? I'd say! She's not twenty-five if she's a day. My husband tried to warn Nick off, saying she was a gold digger, but he thought she loved him. Imagine that. Men are such fools!'

Or maybe she really did love him.

'The girls hate each other,' she continued.

'Really? Because of their father marrying Ellie?'

She shook her head so hard she lost her balance. Clutching my arm to steady herself, she burped in my face. 'They've hated each other since they were born. One pretty and stupid;

the other ugly and smart. A bomb waiting to explode. No, a bomb that exploded every day! Ha ha! You'd think, since they both hate their stepmother, they'd come together over that, but no. They're both lazy, grasping sluts. Look at them, thinking now he's gone and they can push out Ellie and get his money. Ha ha! They'll get their comeuppance soon enough. I can't wait!'

'Wait for what?'

She gave a cagey look around as if checking that no one was listening. 'The will. They've been cut out. Ha ha! They get nothing.'

'Surely that's not true.'

Her back straightened with offense. 'You think? I'll tell you what's what, missy. I know because I overheard my husband when he was in his office at our house with Nick just a coupla months back, trying to persuade him to leave something to the girls but no. No! Nick was so angry over the way they'd treated Ellie, he couldn't forgive. Wait 'til they find out!'

'They don't know?'

'Not until the will is read. That's later tonight.'

'I'll bet he changed his mind.'

'Nope. He might have, eventually, but being murdered killed any chance of that. The will says everything goes to his wife. Oh, not everything, you know, some to charities and so forth, sure, but most to that showgirl. Imagine! What will a little tramp like her do with all that fortune?'

'The daughters don't know yet?'

'No one knows. Wait 'til the press gets a hold of this, huh? That'll be soon enough. The law says you have thirty days to file a will, but my husband will file it as soon as he reads it to the family. Wish I could be a fly on the wall tonight. Ha ha!' She lost her balance, then cursed the wet leaves for making the pavement slick.

A tall, graying man limped toward us on a stiff leg. War wound? Had to be her husband; he looked like a lawyer. 'Elizabeth?' he said, shooting an uneasy glance in my direction. With my face obscured by the veil, he had to act polite in case he knew me. But I could tell he was worried about what his blabbermouth wife had been saying. 'Excuse me, miss,' he said as he peeled her away. 'Come, Elizabeth dear, the chauffeur is waiting.'

With the lawyer's wife gone, I moved closer to Nick's widow, close enough to hear the conversation she was having with an older couple. Friends of Nick's from one of his businesses saying the trivial words one says at a funeral. The same words people blathered ad nauseum when my Tommy died, words that meant nothing, but the bald truth was, nothing would have sounded better.

I studied the widow. If you didn't know she'd been a showgirl, her professional, artful make-up, dyed hair, and melodramatic poses might have given it away. But who was she? The conniving gold digger who pulled the wool over Nick's eyes or the adoring wife who happened to fall in love with an older man? The evil stepmother faking grief or the innocent victim of her stepdaughters' machinations? Did she persuade Nick to alter his will and then have him killed? (She couldn't have done the deed herself; she was even smaller than my sister.) I shifted my gaze to the daughters. How I wished I could be there this afternoon when the lawyer read his will! Never mind, it would be public soon enough.

As Madame Carlotta's investigator, I'd become adept at mining information from wills. Not only did they reveal a lot about the deceased and his family relationships, they often provided small details about his possessions, property, and personal interests that spiced up our séances and gave the bereaved client reason to believe Carlotta's connection to the spirit world was genuine. Yes, I put my hopes in learning something significant from Nick Bardo's will as soon as it became public.

The crowd had thinned enough that my lingering presence on the fringe would look odd, so I made my way toward the nearest L station. In less than half an hour, I'd reached Early's.

Early's nightclub occupied the main floor of what used to be a large warehouse. After the devastating Chicago Fire of 1871, city fathers sensibly forbade any more wooden buildings. All subsequent structures, whether commercial, residential, or civic, had to be built of stone, marble, brick, tile, terracotta, or concrete. The cheapest of these was brick, especially the rough local bricks called 'Chicago Pinks' due to the pinkish cast they took on during the firing. The warehouse that was home to Early's had been built of these pink bricks, large and coarse ones, but sturdy and fire-resistant.

Late afternoon is slow at any speakeasy, and Early's was no exception. But the bar was open and a Victrola played jazz from the corner. I knew the way without asking, so I threaded my way through the tables and chairs and climbed the back stairs to Sebastian Dale's office, next to Sophie's dressing room.

'I thought I would find you here,' I said when he answered the knock on his door.

'Maddie! What a surprise! Come in, come in. I've just been . . .' He gestured to the mess of papers on his desk. 'I've let things slide, I'm afraid. I just can't seem to keep my mind on my work.'

I understood. I'd been having trouble sleeping myself.

Sebastian's office was large, with a partner's desk at one end and a seating area at the other. A bentwood hat rack held his hat and a flashy jacket I presumed he wore when introducing the acts. On each of three walls was an interior door – one connecting to Sophie's dressing room, the one opposite to another room – and on the fourth outer wall was a large window hung with ugly brown draperies. The room was stuffy, but the window was closed. I considered suggesting that he open it and a few of the doors to create a cross-breeze, but didn't.

'Have a seat,' he said, gesturing to the small sofa. 'It's so good to see you. Have you seen Sophie today?'

I shook my head. 'Not today but yes, I've seen her and will go again if they let me. A friend of mine . . . a cop . . . is trying to get me permission to bring her some things. I thought I'd get her brush and comb and some items from her dressing room, if that's all right with you.'

'Of course! She would appreciate that so much.'

'What have you heard? From the lawyer, I mean.'

'Well, they won't let her out on bail because the charge is

murder. And there's no date set yet for the trial, although he says it should be soon.'

'What does "soon" mean?'

He shrugged. Sebastian Dale had had as little experience with the Illinois court system as I had. 'The police investigation has concluded. It shouldn't be long now.'

'Well, *my* investigation hasn't concluded. It's just starting.'

'Bless you, Maddie. You're our only hope. You and the lawyer, of course.'

'Does he think Sophie is guilty?'

'He says it doesn't matter what he thinks. He'll try his best. I have to hope it's good enough.'

'Sophie didn't do this, Sebastian. She couldn't have done it.'

'What do you mean?'

'For one thing, she's so much smaller than Nick Bardo. How could a slip of a girl like Sophie attack a big fella like him? Even with the candlestick, she probably couldn't reach the top of his head. And she had no reason to kill him. No motive. You guys were friends, right?'

'Well, I like to think we were, but Sophie and me weren't really in that class. He was rich and we . . . well, it was more like we were followers. But he and Ellie were friendly to us. Always.'

'Did Nick ever, you know, play up to Sophie?'

'He sure looked, if that's what you mean, but so does every man in the audience every night. Did he ever make a pass at her? Not that I knew about. Not that she told me. But he was drinking a lot that night so anything's possible.'

'Why did she pass out? You said she was ill. She couldn't have been drunk. She told me she never had a drink before she sang. That's true, isn't it?'

'True? Yeah, well, yeah. She didn't like what it did to her range. But . . .'

My heart plunged to my feet. 'But what? She was drunk?'

'She had at least one drink from me. From my bar.'

'What?'

'Bee's Knees. With vodka.'

'One drink wouldn't get a baby drunk.'

'No, but there were two bars. It was a big party, so we

brought Doc with us. He's my best bartender here at Early's. He set up in the far end of the dining room, where all the food was laid out; I set up in the living room by the fireplace. She could've got a drink from Doc and I wouldn't know about it. Or from Stanley.'

'Who's Stanley?'

'The waiter who came with us. He's just a boy, but tall, so he looks older. He walks around with a tray of drinks so guests can swap their empties for a full one. Keeps 'em from having to stand in line at a bar. And I wasn't at my bar every minute, you know. She could've helped herself when I was out.'

'What do you mean, out?'

'The kitchen in the back of the house was our work area, where we stashed the extra booze, the ice, water, the clean glasses. The caterers used it, too. Me and Doc had to leave our stations now and then to restock. Sometimes, people don't want to wait for the bartender to get back and they help themselves. I don't like that, but I can tell when it happens.'

'And it happened?'

'Yep.'

'And you just gave her the drink?'

He bristled. 'Listen, Maddie, Sophie's her own girl. I don't tell her what to do. If she wants a drink, she doesn't get any lip from me.'

'So she could have been drunk that night?'

He gave a reluctant nod. 'I didn't tell the police that, though. I said she was ill.'

'But if they question Doc, or if other guests knew she was drinking, they'll find out. Nick was certainly drinking. If they learn Sophie had several drinks, they'll say Nick was killed in a drunken brawl.'

Thoroughly dejected, I made my way home without any awareness of the stream of bodies leaving the L or clogging the sidewalks. I believed Sophie. I still believed her. She didn't kill Nick. She couldn't have. But with most of the evidence pointing directly at her, I didn't know how to proceed. Questioning people straight up wouldn't work – who's gonna talk to the sister of the accused murderer? The police had it easy – they could go anywhere and ask anyone questions. I had to worm my way in with guile, and this was one of the ways I could do it. A lot of people open up when they think they're being interviewed by a girl reporter. And maybe the housemaid ploy would work again. I had to start somewhere, and fast.

FIVE

Dressed in a dirt-brown skirt with a yellow blouse, scuffed shoes, a cheap straw hat and a pair of snagged cotton stockings I'd been saving for just this sort of excursion, I came downstairs with Baby Tommy and plopped him in the kiddie coop in the parlor. Carlotta spotted me from the kitchen.

'Are you going out, dear?'

'Business, as usual,' I replied, placing Tommy's wooden farm animals and his alphabet blocks in the corner of the pen. 'Can you keep an eye on Tommy? He's got a clean diaper and won't need feeding 'til I get back. I shouldn't be long, but if he starts fussing, a bottle should hold him or there's an egg custard in the icebox.'

'Don't worry yourself about Master Thomas,' she said, wiping her hands on the apron as she stepped out of the kitchen. 'I'm happy to– Gracious, Maddie, you look like something out of the Oz book. What the dickins are you up to now?'

I had to smile. A casual observer would have pegged me for an immigrant, not destitute, but poor, someone employed in a menial capacity, which was exactly what I was aiming for. 'Just a bit of investigating,' I said as I pulled on a thick cardigan.

'Our new clients?' She'd given me several names the day before.

'Yes, Mr Rothfelder. And also one of Nick Bardo's daughters.'

'You think she could have . . .?'

'I don't think anything until I have some evidence, but it's possible that she and her husband have something to do with Nick's death. I have to start somewhere and they are as likely as anyone at this point.'

Market basket on my arm, I made my way to the library

branch closest to our house on the Near West Side. There I searched for the newspaper obituary of the deceased relative that Carlotta's newest client wished to contact, a Mr Jacob Rothfelder. After noting the particulars of his age, relatives, employment, address and other background information that would lead me to further personal details for Carlotta to sprinkle into her séance, I went to the reference section to look up the address of Mr and Mrs Warren Selinko, Nick Bardo's younger daughter, in Chicago's multi-volume *City Directory*. They lived on a street in the Near North Side, not far from Lake Michigan's shore. An easy trip by streetcar.

Within half an hour, I was standing in front of their house.

Built of pale gray stone with a dark gray slate roof, the Selinko mansion squatted behind a boxwood hedge like it was hiding from prying eyes. The wide ribbon of roses that edged the driveway and wrapped around the lawn testified to the presence of a skilled gardener, and sure enough, as I came closer, there was a man in overalls raking yellow leaves into a pile. He glanced up as I passed, and I saw that he was Chinese. People say they make the best gardeners.

I continued along the sidewalk past the house as if I had no interest in the place. The market nearest this neighborhood was three blocks further west, so I parked myself on a bench at the corner bus stop and pretended to wait for a bus.

No one thinks you're following them if you stay to their front.

Rich households with several servants usually send their cook or a young maid to the market every day or two for fresh meat and produce. I knew I might be wasting my morning, but the ruse had worked for me before. So when a middle-aged woman emerged from behind the Selinko house carrying a split-oak basket, I started off toward the market in front of her, glancing back every so often to make sure we were still going in the same direction.

We reached the market at roughly the same time, at which point I did follow her from stall to stall, discreetly of course, until she paused at the fruit vendor and picked up some bananas. I accidentally bumped her basket. I offered profuse apologies for my clumsiness. She excused me.

'I see you're buying bananas,' I said. 'I've never tried them. Do you mind me asking how you'll be cooking them?'

Of course I'd tried bananas. I liked them. I'd even mashed them for Baby Tommy to eat. But bananas had come to Chicago's markets only since I was a youngster and many people still considered them exotic. Or obscene.

'I'm making a banana cake. Just a regular yellow cake, really, with some mashed bananas stirred in the batter. My boss loves it . . . although why I'm still trying to please him, I don't know. Have you really never tasted a banana?'

'My mother refused to have them in the house. Said their shape was indecent!'

She chuckled. So did the fruit vendor. 'Here,' the man said, pulling the skin off the tip of one. 'Have a sample.'

I proclaimed it delicious and added a small bunch to my basket.

Her name was Andrea. She looked to be in her thirties, with olive skin, hair dark as mine, and a no-nonsense way about her.

'You mentioned a boss, so you must be a cook, right?' I guessed.

'I am.'

'I'm housekeeper for a German family over on Wells,' I lied. 'Been there nearly two years. How 'bout you?'

'I've been cooking for the same family three years now.'

'My family is good people and I like working there. Trouble is, they're leaving next month. Moving down to Springfield. You don't know of any jobs coming up in this area, do you? Anything where you work? I don't cook, but I'm good at cleaning and laundry, even babies and little ones. I got a good reference.'

She shook her head. 'No children at the house I work, but even if there were, I'll be honest, if you see anything on offer there, run in the other direction. Selinko is their name.'

'Gosh, if it's that bad, why don't you leave?'

'I would, but they're two months behind in my wages and if I go, I'm sure I won't see a penny of it. The mister says he's going to pay me – pay us all, there's a chauffeur, a house-keeper, three maids, and a gardener – as soon as money comes in from some business deal, but I'm getting pretty worried it's all a lie. I think he wants us to quit so he can start over with new help and get out of paying us anything.'

'That's awful!' And we both knew there was nothing she could do about it. 'Is he a gambler or something like that?'

'I've heard him talk about playing cards and betting on the dogs or horses, but I don't know how far gone he is in that. The man's in the hotel business with his wife's father who just got himself killed – maybe you read about it in the papers? Bardo his name was. I'm sticking around hoping there's some inheritance money she can pay us with. I don't trust him as far as I could spit.'

'What's she like? Mrs Selinko?'

Andrea gave it some thought. 'She doesn't treat us bad or anything like that, but she's a mousey thing. Doesn't know what she's doing from one minute to the next. No children, so she's got no one to think about but herself, but I'm pretty sure she'll pay us when she gets the dough.'

Not if what I'd heard from the lawyer's wife was true.

We gossiped a while longer and went our separate ways. Most of us are creatures of habit, and Andrea was no different. I learned she usually visited the market around nine, before the best produce and meats were gone, so it wouldn't be hard to meet her again. So much for my idea about getting a temporary day job at the Selinko house, but at least I had a contact inside if I needed to learn more. And a disgruntled contact at that, who wasn't shy about sharing information. The clock in a nearby church tower struck ten. I decided to take my chances at the jail. It wasn't much out of my way going home. Maybe they'd let me in to see Sophie. Maybe she had remembered something.

SIX

'I wanted to bring my little Tommy with me,' I told Sophie as the matron left us alone in the corner of the clammy visiting room. 'I wanted you to see him. He's so precious. But he's such a wriggling handful nowadays, not walking yet, and I knew I couldn't keep hold of him in my lap for more than a minute before he'd be squirming to get down on the floor, which . . .' I glanced down at a cement floor that showed smears of mud, tears, vomit, spit, sweat and God knows what else. 'Anyway, I wanted to stay the full half hour.'

Her dull eyes looked through me as she nodded glumly. I really do understand that not everyone thinks my son is the most precious boy the world has ever known, but I honestly thought my sister's spirits would get a lift from seeing him, maybe take her mind off her troubles for a few minutes. Carlotta was horrified when I'd mentioned the idea.

'Take a baby into that rat-infested cesspool of disease and filth? Are you mad?'

'I only want to cheer my sister up. And how do you know what it's like? You've never been inside the place.'

'I don't have to. I know what I know, and no baby of—' She caught herself. 'No baby from this house is going to be exposed to that, no matter what.' She was right and I knew it.

Sophie had not replied, so I continued in as cheerful a voice as I could muster. 'I brought you some things. Your brush and comb, some lavender soap, a linen handkerchief, these books, and some clean rags for your monthlies.' The matron had torn apart my meager stash and examined every item, confiscating the blue ribbon I'd brought so she could tie back her stringy hair. Probably feared it might be used around someone's throat instead.

My sister showed a flicker of interest in my offerings, fingering the hairbrush as if she'd forgotten what it was for.

The scented soap brought a tiny smile to the corner of her mouth.

'I thought these would help you pass the time,' I said, handing her the book of Irish fairy tales and a popular new mystery I hadn't read titled *The Mysterious Affair at Styles*. The matron had turned it upside down and shaken it in case I'd stashed a hacksaw inside. 'I won't ask how you are doing, Sophie; I know it's awful in here. Still, you've got to hang on until we can get you released. Don't give up! Everything's gonna be all right, you'll see. Meanwhile, you can help us by trying to remember everything you can about that night. Can you do that? For me? Please?'

She nodded.

'Copacetic! So . . . have you been able to remember anything more? Even the littlest thing would help.'

'Geez Louise, Maddie, I've been over it a hundred times in my head, and I just don't remember anything.'

'OK, let's talk about something else. Something happy. Tell me about when you and Sebastian played the vaudeville circuit. What was your act like? Where did you travel?'

Silence.

'What name did you call yourselves?'

She roused herself enough to reply. 'The Dales. Not very imaginative, was it?'

Finally! If I could get her talking about this, maybe I could shift the conversation to the Bardo murder.

'And you were singers, I gather, right?'

'It was a song and patter act.'

'What's that?' I knew, but I needed to draw her out.

'It's a light-hearted dialogue built around music. Seb was the straight man. I was the ditzy dame who confused words or took them too literally. We'd get a laugh, then sing something related, something with clever lyrics like from Gilbert & Sullivan, with updated words.'

'I wish I could have seen you perform! How about a sample?'

'Ah, no . . .'

'Oh, come on! I'd love to hear a snippet of one of your acts.'

Her brow furrowed for an instant then she continued, giving

the dialogue in a low voice for Sebastian's lines and a zany voice for hers.

'The telephone rings. Seb, you're wanted on the telephone.'

'Who is it?'

'I don't know but I think the caller is from Florida.'

'How do you know that?'

'He said he was Brown from the Morning Sun.'

My groan brought the ghost of a smile to her lips. 'You must have seen a lot of the country. I've never been out of Chicago.'

'We did travel a lot. All over the west, mostly on the Orpheum Circuit. Yeah, I've seen just about all the states west of the Mississippi River and some of the eastern ones. Even the Grand Canyon.'

'Do you miss it? The glamor? The travel? The applause?'

'It's not as glamorous as you think. Even when we were headliners and paid enough to stay in decent hotels instead of crap boarding houses, it's a rootless existence, living like gypsies, playing a town for a week and then hopping to the next town on Sunday and starting over. Week after week. The applause, yeah, that was nice. But I still get that at Early's.'

'When did you stop?'

'Almost a year ago. We were playing Chicago and Seb learned that Early's was for sale, so he bought it. I was glad to stay put.'

'And you still sing.'

Her face fell, and I could follow her thoughts: she wouldn't be singing anymore unless a miracle occurred.

'What did you sing for Bardo's party?'

'The first set was mostly popular songs, silly ones that made people laugh. The second set was going to be more jazz and serious. I sang a good first set: "Margie", "Bugle Call Rag", "I Wish I Could Shimmy Like My Sister Kate", that sort of thing. The pianist wasn't that great, but we managed.'

An inmate in the center of the room started sobbing. Bad news from the man across the table. Sophie and I ignored her.

'You remember arriving at the Bardo mansion, don't you?'

'Sure.'

'Well, tell me about that. When you arrived. What you did.'

'Seb and me, we came with Doc in the truck a coupla hours before the party was to start – start time was nine o'clock – so the boys could set up two bars. I helped a little, but they did all the heavy lifting. The bars looked nice. And the house was gorgeous, like something the Rockefellers would have. For someone who didn't grow up rich, Ellie Bardo sure knows how to spend money! She had filled the place with flowers, and she brought in this chocolate fountain thing, and Seb and Doc built one of those champagne glass tiers where you pour the champagne from the top and it trickles down. We snitched some of the food while the caterers were loading the dining room table and, man alive, it was divine! If I'd known that was the last good meal I'd ever get, I'd've eaten a lot more.'

'Don't talk like that, Sophie. There'll be plenty of good food in your future.'

'Yeah, sure. So anyway, I wore my new pea-green silk dress with sequins around the neckline and fringe on the hem and ostrich plumes in my turban . . . all that got taken away here. When I woke up here, I was wearing this sack. I don't know where any of my stuff is now.'

'I'll find out. Don't worry about it, I'll get it back for you.'

Her eyes focused on a point above my head where a high window let in the afternoon light as she continued her recollections. 'I never sang the second set.'

'Did you have a drink in between sets?'

'No, I don't drink when I sing.'

'Sebastian says you did.' I watched her closely.

'What?' She frowned at her hands for a full minute, trying to remember, then looked up. 'I had a drink from his bar but there was no liquor in it. Does he say different?'

'He says you had a Bees Knees with vodka.'

'I don't think so. I mean, I remember the drink he gave me, but I don't remember there being liquor in it.'

'Would you notice vodka?'

'Of course!'

I wasn't so sure. 'You didn't take a drink from Stanley's tray?'

'Stanley? Was he there that night?' She screwed up her face

and stared at a spot over my shoulder. 'I guess he was, wasn't he? Sweet boy, Stanley. No, I don't think I took anything from him.'

'Could your drink have been drugged?'

'Who would do such a thing?'

'Maybe by accident. A drink meant for someone else maybe. With laudanum, or something with opium that would make you sleepy.'

'I don't know. I didn't taste anything unusual.'

'You sang your songs and then what?'

'Applause, applause. I took a break. Ate some shrimp croquettes and oysters Rockefeller, meatballs and some little puffy pastry things. There was a monumental ruckus when Vivian and Gladys held a screaming match on the veranda. And then, everything stops.'

'You don't remember Sebastian and Ellie taking you upstairs?'

'No.'

'Tell me about the screaming match.'

'Heard loud voices. Couldn't see much, but we all knew who was quarreling. They'd gone outside for privacy. Some privacy – ha! We could hear them just fine. No words, just the nasty tone. Nick joined them and said something sharp and they quieted down, but Vivian stormed off.'

'And afterwards?'

She gave a fierce scowl that seemed to channel all her efforts to the fore, then dropped her head in her arms with a moan. 'I can't! I just can't!'

The matron signaled my time was up. No hugging was permitted so I patted Sophie's hand and promised to come back soon.

The streetcar stop on Dearborn in front of the jail was marked with the usual white-banded black pole and served by a single bench. I sat by myself to wait for the next car, dabbing my eyes with a handkerchief, feeling as helpless and hopeless as I'd ever felt in my life. During rush hour, the streetcars came by every minute or two, but this was just after midday, so it would be five or six minutes between cars. I hardly noticed when a middle-aged woman came out of the jail and crossed to my side of the street. I made room for her on the bench, but I didn't speak.

She did. 'Bad news, dearie? Your man in there?'

I looked up in some surprise and took stock of this brash female. She had big dark eyes and a round, friendly face, the kind you can't help liking from the moment you see her. She might have been in her forties, but her youthful skin, petite figure, and short bob made that a hard call. I can't say I admired all the autumn leaves and butterflies decorating her cloche hat, but I had to admit, her clothes came straight out of a ritzy shop. And those pearls! Two long strings and a choker with matching drop earrings. What on earth was a well-to-do lady doing at the jail?

'Not a man. My little sister.'

'Oh dear, and what did she do?'

'They say . . . they say she killed a man but she didn't. She couldn't have.'

'Have you spoken with the detective assigned to her case?'

'The investigation is over. He didn't believe her story.'

'Which is?'

'That she was unconscious on the bed when the man was murdered and remembers nothing about it.'

'Ahhh, might this be the Bardo murder?' I nodded glumly. Everyone in Chicago had read about the murder by now. The newspapers had sensationalized it mercilessly. 'I've read about it. I gather the evidence was pretty strong against her.'

'She was singing at his party and became ill. Her husband, the bartender, took her upstairs to a guest bedroom to lie down. Next thing you know, some guests came into the room and start screaming about a body on the floor.'

'And you sister said what?'

'She never woke up. The police found a bloody candlestick in her hand and carried her off to jail. She woke up in there, confused and scared. She's only twenty, really still a kid.'

'I don't blame her a bit. It's a pretty unpleasant place. Have you hired a lawyer?'

'John Farnsworth.'

'What does he say?'

'He'll plead self-defense, but it looks weak since she doesn't have any bruises or scratches from a fight. He hopes he can get her off with ten or twenty years. That's her whole life! She'll be an old lady by then. And she's innocent!'

'Why do you think that?' Some people have the ability to listen so empathetically that you want to pour your whole heart out. Her concern was so genuine and her eyes so kind, I held nothing back.

'For one thing, she's too small to take on a big guy like Nick Bardo. I saw him in the casket. He was hit on the head from behind. She's so short, I don't think she could reach the top of his head, even with a candlestick. And why was she unconscious? She doesn't drink when she's singing. Maybe some medicine caused her to faint or maybe a fever. Couldn't someone have entered the room, bashed Bardo over the head, wiped the candlestick clean of his fingerprints, and stuck it in Sophie's hand?'

'Wasn't there some idea that he was trying to attack her?'

'But she and her husband have known the Bardos pretty well for a year now, and Sophie said he'd never once made an improper suggestion.'

The streetcar rounded the corner a couple of blocks away and headed our way. I couldn't linger. 'I'm sorry to run on like this. I don't usually spill my guts to strangers, but I'm just so scared. I keep trying to think of something I can do to prove her innocence. But I know – I just *know* she didn't do this!'

'No apologies necessary, my dear. Your best bet is to trust in her lawyer. I'm sure he'll do all he can.'

It was becoming clearer by the day that whatever Lawyer Farnsworth did wouldn't be enough. The streetcar screeched to a stop. I climbed on and sank into a window seat. As the car rattled away, I realized the nice lady did not get on behind me. I caught a glimpse of her crossing Dearborn and heading back toward the jail.

SEVEN

'Maddie!' called Carlotta from the kitchen door. 'Telephone for you.' I was in back by the alley hanging diapers on the line. Drying wouldn't take long on a warm windy day like today.

Hoping it was Detective O'Rourke with some good news, I snatched the clothespins from between my lips and dashed into the house.

'Is this Madeleine Duval?' a female voice asked.

'Yes, but my married name is Pastore.'

'Ah, Mrs Pastore, of course. I'm Alice Clement. We met yesterday in front of the jail.'

The attractive woman who had spoken to me while we waited for the streetcar? 'Yes, of course. But how . . .?' How did she know my name? I know I didn't mention it. Or Carlotta's telephone number. Her own name sounded familiar, although I know she didn't mention it either.

'How did I track you down? You might well ask, my dear, but I'm a detective and good as such things. Detective Sergeant First Grade, I might add.'

Now her name rang a bell! Detective Alice Clement was in the newspapers quite often. A local celebrity, she was Chicago's first – and still only – female detective. Reporters loved this feisty woman, who, if their stories were to be believed, fearlessly faced down crooks of all stripes, even to the point of arresting them by herself. I'd not recognized her from her pictures in the papers – the petite woman sitting beside me that day bore little resemblance to the larger-than-life image created by the press.

'I wonder if you'd be interested in meeting me to discuss your sister's plight. There's a drugstore with a soda fountain across the street from the courthouse where we could talk.'

'Well, yes, of course I—'

'Good. Meet me there this afternoon at four o'clock.' And she hung up the receiver before I could respond.

'What on earth could she want with me?' I asked Carlotta. 'I had no idea I was talking with Detective Alice Clement yesterday. Do you know who she is?'

'You can't read the newspapers and not know who Detective Clement is.'

'I saw her come out of the jail yesterday. I told her about Sophie. After I got on the streetcar, she must have gone back inside to see if my tale rang true. She must have checked into Sophie's case. Maybe she talked with Sophie. Detectives can get in to the prisoners any time they like. Do you think she has some information for me?'

'I can't imagine she's wasting her time with a social call, dear. She must have something to tell you, something important. Maybe she's learned something that will make a difference. I do hope it's good news.'

Tommy woke up fussy from his long afternoon nap, so I dressed him in a clean linen gown and sweater, put his white bonnet on his head to keep the sun off his face, and plopped him in the buggy for the trip to the courthouse drugstore. He sat up most of the way, alert and curious, clutching the buggy sides with his tiny fingers, looking all about as I wheeled him out of our residential neighborhood and into the chaos of Chicago's hectic streets. His solemn eyes grew wide with wonder and his head bobbed this way and that as we maneuvered past blinking streetlights, honking cars belching exhaust, clanging streetcars, and the urgent shriek of the traffic cop's whistle. I couldn't help but notice the smiles people gave my boy as they passed us. He was such a handsome lad!

The drugstore was crowded, even at this odd hour in between lunch and dinner, and I wondered why she had chosen such a busy place for our meeting. I muscled the baby buggy through the door and up a few steps to a Formica booth across from the lunch counter where she was waiting for me. She stood as we came closer and shook my hand. Heads turned. Clearly, she was well known here.

'My, my. I didn't know you would be bringing your bodyguard,' she joked. 'A boy, right?'

'Tommy. Fourteen months.' After making sure my baby buggy wasn't blocking anyone's way, I removed my gloves and joined her at the table.

'How proud you must be. And yet you have a difficult job ahead, raising him without a husband.' She saw my surprise and said, 'Of course I know who you are. I remember the killings from a year ago last spring, when your husband and the others from the Outfit were gunned down. Terrible business.' That required no comment from me.

The soda jerk leaned across the counter and called, 'What'll you have, ladies?' I ordered a lemon ice cream soda; Detective Clement asked for a Champagne Freeze. I listened; she talked.

'I must say, my dear, the story you told me about your sister stirred my curiosity, so I returned to the jail and asked around, and lo and behold, your tale holds true! I spoke to your sister, too, and I agree that she likely didn't do this murder. Poor little mite. I think she was framed. Now you know me, hon, right? I been working for the Chicago police more than fifteen years, and I've cracked a lot of cases and pinched a lot of crooks, so Chief McWeeny gives me good deal of leeway in the cases I handle. I want a case, I get it. And I decided to take on this one.'

'Oh, thank you, Mrs Clem—'

'There's something fishy going on here, and I care too much about the welfare of Chicago's young girls to let it pass. That's what I do best: protect Chicago's young girls. That's what's most important to me. The evidence against your sister is just too neat. It looks to me like she was set up, but by who, that's the million-dollar question. Someone brained old Bardo – there's a piece of work for you – and set up poor Sophie, but who? You got any ideas?'

'Not really, I—'

'That first detective made up his mind without even questioning the main characters, you know what I mean? That's not the way I work. No, siree. That's not professional. Even back when I was patrolling department stores looking for pickpockets and shoplifters, I questioned all the witnesses.'

A man paused at our table and cleared his throat politely. 'Excuse me, ladies. Aren't you Alice Clement, the detective, ma'am?' She nodded graciously, like a queen accustomed to being interrupted by her adoring subjects, and flashed him a warm smile. 'I read about you in the papers last week, those girls you rescued from white slavery, well, that was brilliant work, ma'am. You're a credit to your sex, that's for sure.'

'I'd rather pinch a crook than eat,' she told him. 'It's the best game in the world.'

'And when you exposed that phony fortune teller last month? That one hit home 'cause my sister had been going to that very same faker, getting readings about her future, throwing hundreds of dollars down the sewer. I'd been trying to convince her the woman was a swindler, but there was no listening to me. Now she knows better. My family is grateful you shut that woman down. Saved us a lot of money.'

She nodded with satisfaction. 'Nothing easier than exposing these so-called spiritualists who prey on suckers. The most fun I've had in my career, and I love it, is cleaning out the clairvoyants in Chicago. Incidentally, it was the most dangerous thing I ever did, too. It made me resort to a different disguise every day. I've had my fortune told more than three hundred times to get the goods on these so-called mystics.'

Fortunately Mrs Clement was wholly absorbed with her admirer and not watching my expression, for when I heard her hold forth on fake spiritualists, I nearly swallowed my straw. I should have remembered that about her! I should have remembered that Detective Alice Clement not only targeted mashers and shoplifters, she had a particular aversion to anyone claiming to have spiritual powers. Now I recalled the case this gentleman was referring to. It had been in the newspapers a few months back. Some rich widow was being fleeced by a fortune teller. And there had been other occasions where Mrs Clement had exposed and arrested bogus mediums.

A cold horror swept over me. Was Mrs Clement honestly interested in Sophie's case? Or was she interested in exposing Madame Carlotta and using me to set her up? Did she even know about Madame Carlotta? She hadn't been to my house. She hadn't met Carlotta – not to my knowledge anyway. She couldn't have linked me to her, could she? She had certainly done enough research to link me to my late husband. She knew our telephone number. She could easily learn our address. Did she know who else lived there? Carlotta advertised in several newspapers, but the ad listed only her telephone number. She would assess prospective clients over the telephone to determine whether she could help them spiritually, and only then accept them as clients, set an appointment, and give out her address. And she never swindled clients like most mediums did. We made sure she never asked for money. Never even mentioned money. That was my job, to put a fin or a tenner in the basket as a suggested donation. Even if Detective Clement investigated Carlotta, she couldn't accuse her of any illegal activities, could she? I was pretty sure about that. But still . . . bad publicity alone could ruin us. And now that I knew what jail was like first-hand, I really wanted to stay out of it.

Mrs Clement dismissed her admirer with a patronizing smile and a coy turn of her head and continued to dictate her plans to me. I struggled to focus on what she was saying.

'I'm going to start by investigating the people closest to the accused and the victim: your sister's husband and Bardo's wife. I hear you've been doing some questioning yourself, so I thought you might like to tag along, just to see how the pros handle themselves.'

'I would, very much—'

'No time like the present, then. Let's get on over to the nightclub. Early's, isn't it? Things'll be slow this time of day and we can snag the husband, Sebastian Dale. See what he has to say. You can bring the baby along if you like. We won't be doing anything dangerous. But if the unexpected happens, I'm prepared.' She slid her hand inside her large purse and drew out a small gun. 'This baby is a .32-caliber hinge-break revolver. Reliable. So don't you worry about your safety when you're with me, hon.'

I nodded.

'You ready?'

I nodded again.

She dropped a silver dollar on the table. 'Let's go.'

Early's was a twenty-four-hour joint, but some of those hours were pretty thin on customers. By the time we arrived, it was almost five o'clock and the after-work office crowd would soon start to drift in. On the way over, I learned all about Mrs Clement's views on women's rights – she was passionate about the vote and a woman's right to divorce – and was treated to a lecture on the growth of brothels and white slavery in Chicago. She was bossy and opinionated and old enough to be my mother, so I went along respectfully, nodding my acceptance and now and then uttering a soft 'I see' or 'Oh my'. I would quickly learn that people usually went along with Detective Clement. She didn't give you any other option.

'Sebastian's office is through that door and up the stairs,' I told her as we entered the nightclub. 'We can ask one of the waitresses to let him know—'

'Nothing doing. We'll just go on up and surprise him. You don't want to give 'em time to think ahead about why you're here and how they're going to dodge your questions.'

Good to know.

Hoisting the baby buggy up that narrow flight of stairs wasn't going to happen, so I carried Tommy in my arms, feeling a little foolish about having him with me. But what else was I to do?

Alice rapped hard on his door. A muffled, 'Come in,' came from the other side. And yes, he was surprised, very surprised, to see me, the baby and the detective standing at the threshold.

'I'm Detective Alice Clement of the Chicago Police Department, Mr Dale, here to ask you some questions about Nick Bardo's murder.' She didn't show him a badge or any identification papers, presumably because she assumed everyone knew who she was. And in this case at least, it was true.

Sebastian raised himself from his chair behind the desk and looked about uneasily. 'Mrs Clement, I mean, Detective Clement, this is an honor. And Maddie? Good to see you again. Please, come in and have a seat. How can I help you?'

There was one chair in front of Sebastian's desk and a small sofa against the wall. Detective Clement took the chair. I sat on the sofa with Tommy on my knees. I expected Sebastian to ask about Tommy, who was, after all, a nephew he had never met, but he didn't.

'Did the police question you at the scene of the crime, Mr Dale?'

'Yes, they did. And a detective telephoned me the following day. I told them everything I knew.'

'Never mind that, now you can tell me. The whole story. No detail is too small. Let's start with your relationship with Nick Bardo and his wife.'

Sebastian leaned on his elbows and tented his fingers as if deep in concentration. 'Me and Sophie noticed the Bardos after they'd come to Early's a coupla times. We try to recognize our regulars. It keeps them feeling special. They were big fans of Sophie's and liked to request their favorite songs, sometimes buying her sheet music for new songs so she could sing 'em on their next visit. They were big drinkers but not excessive. Never excessive. Nick could walk out of here in a straight line after a long night of boozing. As I told the police, we were friendly, but I couldn't claim to be friends. Me and Sophie just don't run in those circles.'

'Was Nick a masher?'

'I never saw him come on to another woman. Not here at Early's.'

'But his wife was with him on those occasions, wasn't she? Did he ever come without his wife?'

'Not that I recall.'

'So you really wouldn't know if he was prone to pushing himself on other women when his wife wasn't present?'

'I guess not. But he adored his wife. He wouldn't have stepped out on her.'

'Tell me about this birthday party. How did they come to hire you?'

'Ellie – that's Mrs Bardo – she was planning a big bash for Nick's birthday. His fifty-sixth, I think. She went all out and it was a swell party – that is, it was swell until . . . well, you know what I mean. She asked me to handle the bars and hired Sophie to sing Nick's favorites.'

'So Nick didn't hire you. Ellie did.'

'I guess that's so, but it was no surprise party, if that's what you're thinking. Nick knew and approved. In fact, I think it was his idea. I suggested setting up two bars, considering the size of the guest list, and they told me to bring another bartender. Doc was hot to go, so I took him. He's my best.'

'You set up two bars at the Bardo house.'

'One in the living room, one in the dining room. We used the kitchen as a staging area. So did the caterers. It was Rose Catering. They're the best in town and probably the most expensive.'

'You and the caterers were in and out of the kitchen all night?'

'I can't speak for the food, just drinks. And yes, Doc and me went back and forth a few times to get ice or more mixers, olives, whatever. Not a lot.'

'Tell me how the evening went.'

'People were having a good time. Lots of drinking. Sophie sang her first set. Everyone loved it, as always. Some sang along with her. She doesn't like that, but . . . anyway, she came by my bar and asked for a Bee's Knees.' He looked at me then and added apologetically, 'I know she told you she didn't drink any alcohol, but she just didn't remember right. She got one drink from me. Then, one time when I slipped over to the kitchen for a few minutes, I came back and she was behind the bar helping herself to something. I didn't ask what. It could have been soda water.'

'But it could have been alcohol. When did she start to act drunk?'

'I didn't think she was drunk. I noticed her looking sick and I asked her what's wrong. She gets bad headaches sometimes and I thought maybe that was it. Next thing I know, she's having trouble standing up. I saw Ellie and quickly asked if there was a guest room I could use, to let her lie down for a bit.'

'Why didn't you take her home?'

'The party was barely half over. I couldn't leave Doc and Stanley alone to handle that many. I figured Sophie would rest an hour or so and then come back down to perform the second set. Don't you think I've been over this again and again? I wish to hell I had taken her home! Then none of this would ever have happened.'

'Bardo would still have been murdered, but not with Sophie in the room, is that what you mean?'

'Yeah, I guess.'

'So continue.'

'Next thing I knew, the police are raiding the place. I think it's some prohis busting up a booze party, but no, they go upstairs. I hear people saying Nick was hurt or dead, but the cops have blocked the stairs so no one can go up. I thought he'd had a heart attack or something. I see him go out on a stretcher, then I start up the stairs to find Sophie. That's when I see the cops taking her away. They're practically carrying her. She can hardly walk, she's so ill. I tried to go with her but they wouldn't let me near her. I didn't see her until two days later.'

'What was she wearing, your wife?'

Sebastian looked confused.

'A green silk gown with sequins,' I answered for him. 'I tried to get it back for Sophie but the jail matron said it was evidence. The cops have it by now.'

Detective Clement glared at me for interrupting. 'Sorry,' I mumbled.

'Did you see the dress?' she asked Sebastian.

'Yes. Why?'

'Was there blood on it?'

I hadn't thought of that. Surely there would be blood spattered on the dress of someone who'd stood inches away while they bashed in a man's skull. 'Not that I remember. Is that good evidence?'

'Could be. As long as some idiot doesn't clean it. Now, tell me about Sophie's health and how often she had headaches.'

On and on he went, answering the detective's questions in great detail, probably more detail than she wanted but she never interrupted, only nudged him a little when he got off track. She took notes without looking down at her pad of paper, keeping her eyes glued to his as if she could pull the truth out of him with sheer will power. He described the bedroom where Bardo was killed, the layout of the Bardo home, and the movement of various guests. It took far less time for him to tell what he knew about Bardo's wealth and position in the community.

'I don't know where he gets his money,' Sebastian replied. 'He has some hotels, that big one, the Adler, and some others I think. Nightclubs too.'

Tommy was getting restless. I bounced him on my knees and tried to keep him from disturbing the conversation, but it was getting harder. At last, Mrs Clement stood up.

'Thank you, Mr Dale. This is very helpful.'

'No, ma'am, it's me thanking you for taking on Sophie's case. We can never express our gratitude. With someone like you helping us, well, we can't ask for more, can we? I'm at my wits end here, trying to keep the club going but worrying all the time about Sophie. I've had to hire another talent and I need another bartender to take my place since I haven't been able to work the bar like usual.'

'I might be able to help with that,' I said. 'There's a boy – a young man – in my neighborhood who works the bar at his family's speakeasy, who'd be glad for a paying job.'

Sebastian's eyebrows rose. 'Yeah? What's his name?'

'Dan Ward. A good kid. Young, but a hard worker. And honest.'

'Send him over. I'll give him a try.'

'Meanwhile,' said Detective Clement, 'as long as we're here, I'd like to have a chat with that bartender who was working with you that night. Doc, you said his name was. Is he here now?'

'Working the bar right now. Go on, it shouldn't be too busy yet. He'll be happy to answer your questions. He'd do anything to help Sophie. Everyone loves Sophie.'

EIGHT

A serious young man, Doc had sad, dark eyes topped by bushy brows and a quiet, earnest manner that made him seem older than he probably was.

'Sure, I know who you are, Detective Clement,' said Doc earnestly. 'Everyone does. And you too, Mrs Pastore. I heard about Sophie having a sister. I don't think I know anything useful, but I'm at your service.'

I had retrieved the baby buggy and deposited Tommy in it, so I settled myself on a barstool and prepared to watch Alice handle the questions. Doc was thoughtful enough to offer me some bits of orange for the baby to suck, proving the old adage that the quickest way to a mother's heart is to do a kindness for her child. The gesture made me wonder if he had children of his own.

Detective Clement began by asking him to describe his actions that night, from the time he arrived at the Bardo house to the arrival of the police. His account was deliberate and started out much the same as Sebastian's.

'But you were in a different room, so you had a different perspective,' said the detective.

'That's right. I saw Sophie perform her first set. Nothing unusual about that.'

'She didn't seem ill or intoxicated?'

'No, she doesn't drink during a performance.'

'Her husband said she ordered a Bee's Knees from him and may have made herself another.'

'That's always possible. I made her a lime fizz, just lime juice and soda water. She seemed normal. Plenty of the guests were ossified by the time her first set was finished, but she was cool.'

'Which guests?'

'Bardo's daughters, for instance. They had a bust-up out on the balcony. They were snarling like cats in heat. Then there was the one's husband, Wilbur or Warren or something, who was downing whiskey like it was apple juice. Five at least. He was mad about something. Never even spoke to me, just came to the bar, slammed down his glass, and waited for me to fill it. Then he had a spat with his wife, the one they call the pretty daughter, although if you ask me, she's nothing to look at. They left together, before the birthday cake. Not a happy family, the Bardos.' He didn't look too sad about it.

'What about the argument on the balcony?' I asked, unable to keep quiet when I realized the detective wasn't going to pursue that angle. 'Did you see Nick go out there?'

Detective Clement stared at me like she wanted to order my immediate execution. I got the message – don't butt in on her interrogation again.

'Now that you mention it, he did. I didn't really pay attention.'

'And Ellie Bardo?' the detective resumed the lead. 'Did Warren or the daughters speak to her?'

'From what I saw, they all ignored her. Gave her a wide berth.'

'What do you remember about Ellie Bardo?'

A waitress came up to the far end of the bar to order drinks for a table of six. Doc excused himself to fill the order. I couldn't help but notice his hands as he worked. Those long fingers never wasted a single fluid motion. Reminded me of a pianist tickling the ivories. As soon as he'd finished, he returned to our end of the bar and resumed the conversation.

'I know Mrs Bardo from when she comes in here. Word has it she's a low-class showgirl who snatched a sugar daddy, but I go by what I see myself, not what other people say, and she's always been courteous to me and the waitresses when she's in here. Big tipper. Dresses stylish, not too flapper. I'd call her a class act.'

'What was she doing that night?'

'About what you'd expect. Mingling with the guests. Introducing people. I did notice she stayed far away from those Bardo gals, though.'

'Was she drinking?'

'Not from my bar.'

'How long have you worked here, Doc?'

'About a year. Mr Dale hired me when he came to manage the place. It's a good gig.'

'I thought Dale was the owner.'

I perked up. I'd thought he was, too. In fact, Sophie had told me straight out that her husband bought the place when they left vaudeville.

'Naw, he's manager. Frank Ricardo owns this place. He runs another joint on the south side. When he's here, he mostly stays in his office upstairs next to Mr Dale's.'

'This Ricardo, he didn't work the Bardo party?'

'Naw, there's no love lost there. Bardo was turning the screws on him, trying to force him to sell Early's.'

Alice and I exchanged glances. A possible motive?

She finished with Doc and motioned me closer. 'I'm going back upstairs to see if this Frank Ricardo is in. Your boy is getting restless, maybe you don't want to come?'

I wasn't going to miss this. At last, a bit of information that might help Sophie! 'I'll come. He'll be fine.'

It was getting on toward six and the tables were filling up. Meals weren't on offer here, but cocktails before dinner brought in the crowds and they had plenty of salty pretzels and popcorn to make people thirsty. Alice and I threaded our way through the tables and back up the stairs. At the end of the hall, past Sebastian's office, was the door I hadn't noticed earlier. An engraved brass plate read: Central Services Corp. This was the company that owned Early's. And other clubs, I gathered.

Sebastian had lied to us. He'd lied to his wife. Why? Male ego? Wanting to seem bigger in her eyes? But wouldn't she wonder who the man at the end of the hallway was? Perhaps not. Sophie seemed very trusting, not the sort to ponder inconsistencies or question what she was told. The opposite of me. And she worked at night when Frank Ricardo would be working during the day, so their paths would seldom have crossed.

Frank Ricardo was in. He was about to lock his door, but when he realized what the detective wanted and who she was, he welcomed us into his office. But he remained standing. The message was clear: this would be brief.

'So the famous lady detective is taking on this case because why? You think our Sophie didn't do the deed?'

'I have no opinion about her innocence or guilt, Mr Ricardo. I took the case because holes in her story were being ignored. More than that I cannot say. I've heard that Bardo wanted to buy Early's. What was your relationship with him?'

'I knew the fella. Came in here now and then. A real tough guy. Liked to get what he wanted. And yeah, he wanted Early's. Not just that, he wanted all three of my clubs.'

I knew it irritated Detective Clement but I couldn't help throw another question out. 'Was he part of Capone's Outfit?'

Ricardo ran his fingers through his thick grey hair until it stood up straight like a mad scientist's and chewed on the inside of his cheek while he considered his answer. 'Was he working *directly* for Scarface? I don't think so. But indirectly, everyone's working for Scarface, aren't they? Everyone in this part of town anyway. Everyone's part of the gang or cozy with the gang or they don't do business, see?'

I saw. The North Side Gang, the Outfit, the other smaller gangs, they supplied the booze you needed to stay in business. They dictated what you could serve, they set the prices, they collected their cut of the take. That had been my late husband's job, delivering bootleg hooch to the various restaurants, speakeasies, and nightclubs in Outfit territory. Fall behind in your payments, try to deal with a rival supplier, cheat on the protection payment, and watch your business go up in smoke. With you in it.

'Did you go to the Bardo party Sunday?' asked Detective Clement.

'Hell, no. Me and Bardo weren't exactly chums.'

'Where were you Sunday night?'

'Here, watching the cash register. All night until about four Monday morning. Sunday's a slow night, but even so, with both Seb and Doc out, I needed someone in charge that I trusted and that list is short. That's my alibi. You can confirm it with any of the waitresses. If you think they'll lie for me to keep their jobs, you're probably right, but you could also ask the performers or any of the regulars who were in here that night.'

'Thank you, I'll do that, Mr Ricardo.'

'I didn't like Bardo. Hell, I'll just say it right out: I hated his guts. He was a crook. I wanted him dead. I'm glad he's dead. But I didn't kill him. I was here all night. Now, the wife'll be waiting dinner, so if you're done asking questions, I'll be off.'

NINE

The shocking story of Nick Bardo's last will and testament made the front page of all the morning dailies in Chicago the next day. It was just as that lawyer's drunk wife had blabbed to me at the funeral: the revision left almost everything to his young wife, Eleanor Bardo, previously known as Ellie LaBelle on the burlesque stage. Reporters wrote with gleeful embellishment about the wife's former career, the daughters' feud, and how they loathed their greedy stepmother who had hoodwinked their father into turning against his dearest and only blood relations, depriving them of their rightful inheritance.

'Why are we going to the courthouse, Maddie? It's all here in the newspapers,' said Freddy after I'd finished reading the articles out loud. Freddy couldn't read. He'd tried to learn; I'd tried to teach him. He just couldn't make heads nor tails of the letters. But he wasn't stupid – he had a phenomenal memory, much better than mine.

'I still want to see the will for myself. You can't trust these reporters. They all exaggerate to make their stories more exciting. I swear, some of them make up facts out of morning mist. I need to read the actual will to know for sure who inherits what.'

'Follow the money,' said Carlotta, nodding wisely. 'I've heard that many times.'

Yes, following the money was a good way to learn who benefitted from a death. In the case of Nick Bardo, his wife, obviously. But *not*, I wanted to shout, my sister. The money trail did not lead to Sophie. She gained nothing from his death. She had no monetary reason to kill him. Perhaps others did.

The courthouse trip was not wasted. As it turned out, the reporters had summarized Bardo's will pretty accurately, leaving out only a few specifics they considered irrelevant, like his bequests to the Catholic Church, the Chicago Yacht

Club, the Salvation Army, and the YMCA. But the date on the will interested me: four months ago. This wasn't the impulsive result of some recent squabble. Nick had had plenty of time to reflect and change it back if he regretted his action. But he hadn't. Might he have changed it if he had lived longer? It was always possible. And what exactly was 'back'? What had the previous will said? I knew of no way to get hold of that.

'I think we should talk with the daughters,' I told Detective Clement on the telephone that day.

'I know they hated their father,' she said, 'but what would be their motive to kill him? They weren't going to inherit anything. It's rather the opposite, I would think: they would want him to live longer, at least until they could persuade him to change his will again.'

'But remember, they didn't know he had changed his will. They expected an inheritance.'

'Yes, of course, I know that. So, I've got a police car today. Where do you live? I'll come by and pick you up.'

'No!' I said, a bit too quickly and too loud. I couldn't risk Detective Clement linking me to a mystic. She'd be bound to shut Carlotta down and quit Sophie's case. 'I'll, uh, you don't need to go to the trouble. It's easy for me to get to the Adler Hotel. I'll meet you in the lobby. Just name the time.'

The last time I'd visited the Adler Hotel was on the occasion of our second anniversary, when Tommy's rising salary from his Outfit job let him splurge on an extravagant dinner at this glamorous wonderland. I had worn a new dress – a layered emerald chiffon with the upper part green and the lower parts in shades of pink – that still hung in my closet. I'd never wear it again but couldn't bear to part with it.

Vivian Bardo Wilcox, eldest daughter of Nick Bardo, lived in a penthouse apartment at the Adler, located in Chicago's Loop. A childless divorcée with no interest in a house in the country or a townhouse in the ritzy part of the city, she enjoyed a luxurious lifestyle with a minimum of servants' salaries to pay, thanks to the amenities of her father's prestigious hotel. I couldn't help but wonder if she'd be able to stay on, now that Ellie Bardo had inherited everything. Where else would she go? Without any inheritance, would she have to find work somewhere and earn her own living?

A butler answered the chimes, disappeared for several minutes, and returned to inform us that Mrs Wilcox would be pleased to grant Detective Alice Clement and her assistant a few moments of her time.

Vivian Wilcox greeted us in front of a large picture window that gave onto a sweeping view of the downtown and Lake Michigan beyond. The noise and fumes from the street seemed miles below us and the clouds only an arm's reach above. Lake Michigan's waters shimmered in the autumn sunlight as sailboats the size of toys glided along its glassy waters, their sails full of breeze. I tore my attention from the view and settled myself on one of two matching floral chintz sofas. Vivian Wilcox positioned herself across from Detective Clement, her fluffy pet poodle in her lap, and lit a cigarette. She did not offer us refreshments or a smoke.

'What can I help you with, Detective?' she began, ignoring me entirely. I was happy to be ignored. 'As you must know, I was not present when that woman murdered my father.'

'I want to understand what happened in the hours that led up to your father's death,' said the detective. 'Please tell me what time you arrived at the party and what time you left.'

'As I told the police, I arrived at about ten o'clock. I wasn't feeling very well, so I spoke to only a few people, had but one drink, and ate almost nothing. I wished my father a happy birthday and left after midnight.' She took a handkerchief out of her sleeve and dabbed her dry eyes in a lame attempt to exhibit grief. 'I couldn't know it would be the last time I would ever see him alive.'

'And was your conversation with your father cordial?'

She bristled. 'Of course.'

'And with your sister?'

'Of course.'

'What would you say, Mrs Wilcox, if I told you we have several witnesses who overheard you and your sister in a rather passionate quarrel on the veranda?'

'I would say they were exaggerating. My sister and I had

a brief disagreement. Nothing unusual in that. We seldom see eye to eye.'

'And what was the disagreement this time?'

She paused to fill her lungs with smoke and puff it back out in one long breath, cleverly giving herself time to think of her reply. 'That is none of your concern.'

'Begging your pardon, Mrs Wilcox, but everything related to your father's death is my concern. And there are witnesses who have described the argument to me, so this is your chance to give your version.'

'My *version*?' she replied scornfully. 'I do not have a version; I have the truth. Gladys had been spreading malicious lies about my art teacher's supposed estimation of my paintings at the Art Institute school. As Gladys has the artistic talent of a chimpanzee, she envies the abilities of others.'

'And your father's role in this?'

'His role? He had nothing to do with it.'

'I have witnesses who say your father went out on the veranda and joined the argument.'

She bristled. 'That's ridiculous. He came to call us inside, that's all. And it wasn't an argument.'

'What happened after this squabble occurred?'

'I left.'

'Immediately thereafter?'

'Not quite immediately. I finished my cocktail, complimented the pianist who was taking a break, and observed my sister's husband thrust his way to the bar to resume his journey toward complete intoxication. Then he turned on my sister. Watching him insult her was enough to keep me entertained for a few minutes. After that, I went to the hall to get my wrap.'

'And what was their argument about?'

'I've no idea what set Warren off. It happens frequently. He is easily prodded into rage over the most insignificant things, especially when drunk. Which is his usual state.'

'What time was this?'

'Let's see . . . I left at about one. The butler brought my wrap, I called goodnight and happy birthday to my father who was on the landing talking to Warren. Father ignored me. They both looked angry. My father continued up the staircase; Warren staggered after him. That would be my last glimpse of him alive.'

'So Warren was upstairs around one? Was it before or after Sophie Dale was taken to a guest room?'

'I've no idea.'

'And where was your stepmother?'

'I'll thank you to refer to Ellie LaBelle as my father's wife, not my stepmother. That scheming little tramp is no mother to anyone. Though I wouldn't be at all surprised if she didn't immediately bed the chauffeur and announce her pregnancy in an attempt to convince the world she is bearing my father's child.'

'Where was your father's wife during this time?'

'Why all these questions? I thought the police were satisfied that the singer from Early's had done in dear old dad.'

'We are simply trying to get a clear picture of the events surrounding his death.'

My mouth spoke before my brain could shush it. 'And we want to make sure there wasn't a second person involved.'

'I see. I hadn't thought of that.'

Neither had I, until just that moment. But it was possible, wasn't it? Two, maybe three people could have been in cahoots to bump off Bardo.

Detective Clement gave me a look that would freeze water before resuming her interrogation. 'Where was your father's wife during this time?'

'Oh, for heaven's sake, the little slut was flitting about the room, playing the role of adoring wifey. You don't think she had anything to do with his death, do you?' she asked, a hopeful note creeping into her voice.

'As I said, we are simply looking to understand the sequence of events.'

'She certainly had a motive – she inherits his entire estate, you know. You must've read that in the papers. But I also read they found fingerprints on the statuette or whatever it was that brained dad, and they weren't Ellie's, more's the pity.'

'There's always more to the story than what you read in the papers, Mrs Wilcox.'

Detective Clement probed for additional information, most of which seemed unrelated to me, but I wasn't the professional detective. I expect she was fishing, trying to uncover an angle that hadn't been explored yet.

'I'd like to talk with Warren and Gladys Selinko,' she said when we reached the hotel lobby.

'They live on the Near North Side. I've been by their house.' I told her the address. She didn't ask how I knew it.

'That's not far.' She glanced at her jeweled wristwatch. 'Plenty of time. Do you want to accompany me on this one as well? Same rules: you're my silent assistant. Stress on the word *silent*.'

'I'm sorry I spoke out today. If you're going there now, yes, I would. Thank you.'

TEN

As I rode with the detective in her police car to the Selinko house, I worked out several excuses I might use to decline her offer – if she offered – of a ride home afterwards. Then I warned her about my previous encounter with the Selinko cook and told her what the cook had said about overdue wages. 'Maybe I should stay outside.'

She dismissed my concerns with a shake of her head. 'That shouldn't be a problem, Maddie. The cook isn't likely to venture into the drawing room when her master and mistress are speaking to the police. Even if she does, I find that people don't tend to recognize others when they're out of context. She met you as a housekeeper, not a policewoman. Just look down and cough into a handkerchief if you see her.'

Good to know. I was grateful to be learning from a professional.

A pinched-mouth butler led us to a drawing room that had been decked out in the popular Egyptian style with exotic gold furniture, sand-colored upholstery, and hieroglyphics stenciled on the walls. Gladys Selinko rose from the sofa looking as if she'd stepped out of a scene from *The Sheik,* wearing a pleated, beige afternoon gown that matched the décor. I wondered how her exclusion from her father's will would affect her clothing allowance.

She wasn't rubbing red eyes today; she was smiling. 'Welcome, Detective Clement,' she gushed, sparing hardly a glance in my direction. 'Do have a seat. This is such an honor having you here. I must tell you how much I admire you and the amazing work you do. Such a voice for women's rights! And I loved your *Dregs in the City*! Such a wonderful picture! You've saved so many innocents from a life of shame.'

I'd forgotten about that. A few years back, there had been a great hullabaloo over the motion picture made by the Alice Clement Picture Company, starring Alice Clement, written by

Alice Clement, and directed by Alice Clement, in which a fearless female policewoman rescues a naïve country girl from the evils of white slavery and opium dens. When Chicago's movie censors banned the film, she set out on a highly successful lecture tour and showed it to audiences then. Tommy and I hadn't seen it, but the surrounding controversy certainly filled the newspapers. Nothing better for business than being censored!

Detective Clement simpered, 'I was put on Earth to guard the girls of Chicago and I intend to do my part. But right now, Mrs Selinko, I'd like to speak with you and your husband about events surrounding your father's death.'

'Oh, yes, of course. Warren is upstairs . . . indisposed. He'll join us shortly. What can I do to help?'

'Just tell me what you recall about that Sunday evening.'

'I told that other detective everything I know. He telephoned us the day after.'

'Certainly. But I'd like to go over it again, if you don't mind.'

So she dutifully outlined her actions that night, from her arrival at her father's home at about nine to her departure with her husband after the police allowed everyone to leave, and I could see that the detective was trying to get a clear picture of who, besides Sophie, was upstairs when Nick Bardo was killed. Someone who might have killed him or at least seen someone suspicious. Like Warren Selinko.

'Now tell me about this quarrel with your sister.'

'What quarrel?'

'Several people have said they overheard you and Vivian quarreling on the veranda.'

'Oh, that. It was nothing. She puts on such airs with her silly paintings. Ridiculous.'

'What about your husband? I've heard that he was angry about something.'

'I can't say for sure what. I guess he was angry, though.'

'Angry with you or with someone else?'

She looked down at her hands and fidgeted with her flashy rings. 'I, um, I don't remember. It was nothing important. It was probably my fault anyway.'

'Your husband went upstairs that night. Do you know why?'

'I think to see my father.'

'And did he?'

'I don't know. Probably.'

'What time was that?'

'Oh, let me see . . . about eleven. Or maybe, no, I think midnight. Actually, closer to one.'

'Was he drinking excessively that night?'

'Well, not really, not any more than usual. You'll— Oh, here he comes,' she sighed with relief. 'Here you are, darling. Look, it's Detective Alice Clement come to ask about Dad's death.'

Warren Selinko stopped with a jerk when he realized who was sitting with his wife and blustered, 'What in hell's name's going on here?'

Detective Clement stood. 'Good evening, Mr Selinko. I'm here to ask some questions of you and your wife, questions about the party. I appreciate your—'

'What have you been blabbing about, Gladys? What kind of moron are you, talking to a detective without me in the room? Whatever she's been saying to you, lady, is completely unreliable since she was drunk out of her mind that night and doesn't know up from down even when she's sober,' he said, clenching his fists as he spoke. 'You got nothing on me or you'd arrest me, so get the hell out of my house.'

'Warren, dear, Detective Clement only wanted—'

'You shut your face. You've said more than enough already, I'll wager. Mitchell!' He called to the butler who was hovering around the doorway. 'Escort these dames out. Now. And don't come back if you know what's good for you.'

This sort of thing must have happened to Detective Clement every day of the year, because she appeared entirely unruffled by the bully's rudeness. Without a word, she allowed the butler to escort us to the door.

'He's right,' she admitted once we were back in her police car. 'We don't have anything on him. But he knows more than he's saying. I'll have to think about this a bit. Meanwhile, there's one more person I need to see.'

'Ellie Bardo.'

'She's at the center of all this.' She started the car. 'I have another engagement now so it will have to wait. Where can I take you?'

'If you would be so kind as to drop me near the Maxwell Street Market, I have some shopping to do before I go home.'

Later that evening, after I'd fed Tommy and put him down for the night, Carlotta and I sat on the back porch while I summarized the day's events. 'Warren Selinko certainly acted guilty of something. He was hiding something. But what? Did he have anything to do with his father-in-law's death? Did he see something when he was upstairs? I know he's short of cash – could he have killed Bardo so his wife would inherit sooner?'

'But you told me she was cut out of the will.'

'He didn't know that then. He didn't know that until the will was read several days later.'

The telephone bell rang. Carlotta went into the back hall to answer. I could hear her soft voice, but not the words. It sounded like a new client. Her next scheduled séance was Monday night and I had some work to do for that. For one thing, Freddy and I hadn't planned the enhancements yet. For another—

'Maddie, we have two new clients who want to come as soon as possible. Do you think you can investigate these right away? One man's name is Daniel Raymond and he wants to contact his deceased brother, Pete. Peter Raymond, who died three years ago. The other is a woman, Daisy King. Young, by the sound of her voice. Wants to contact her roommate who died suddenly last week. A Miss Eileen Perry. Can you work on those quickly?'

That wasn't much to go on – and with Miss Perry's death so recent, there would be no will or even a burial to investigate – but I usually managed to dig up something, even under the worst of circumstances. I was proud of how well I did my job, even if it was a little on the shady side. 'Sure,' I said confidently. 'I'll get on it first thing in the morning.'

ELEVEN

D aniel Raymond's brother, Peter G. Raymond, Jr., passed away three years ago, in September of 1922. His obituary in two Chicago newspapers touted accomplishments well beyond what one would expect in someone who had died at the young age of thirty-four. Peter Raymond had been a Chicago fireman for ten years and was awarded a medal for having fought his way into a burning house to rescue two small children overcome by smoke. Cancer took him. As the saying goes, only the good die young. He was mourned by a wife (but no children), a mother and father (Mr and Mrs Peter G. Raymond, Sr.), two sisters and a brother. It was the brother who had contacted Madame Carlotta to arrange for a séance.

He had left no will. Young people seldom write wills because they own little and think they have plenty of time for such things. I visited the Raymond family plot and picked up a few facts about his deceased relations including a baby who had lived only two days. The dates suggested the baby could have been his and his wife's. Peter's brother Daniel wanted to contact his spirit. About what, he didn't say.

I next turned to check into the surviving brother to see if I might find something about him that would give us any bit of concrete information to use in the séance. A visit to the newspaper morgue turned up two short pieces, each buried in the back pages, about a person by the name of Daniel Raymond. The name was not terribly common, but with two and a half million people living in Chicago, there were surely many who used it. I couldn't be sure if this Daniel Raymond was our man. One article mentioned his arrest, along with three other men, in a jewelry store heist. He was sentenced to four years in the state pen for that crime. The other concerned a robbery in a liquor store just before Prohibition started. Arrested again, he was found guilty and sentenced to five years this time. The arithmetic told me he'd recently been released. Clearly not a hero.

There were seven Daniel Raymonds listed in the current *City Directory* and only one Peter G. Raymond, Sr., and – lo and behold – two addresses were the same so I knew I had the right Daniel Raymond. Recently released from Joliet prison, he had evidently gone back to live with his parents. I took a quick trip to their Near South Side neighborhood to snoop around. Bringing Baby Tommy along always helped lower people's guard – no one is suspicious of a mother with a baby in tow. Following my usual tactic, I kept an eye out for For Sale or For Rent signs stuck in nearby lawns.

The Raymond house sat in the middle of the block. It reminded me of the one Tommy and I had owned: one-and-a-half story brick with four rooms down and two up. Judging from the runabout at the curb – the cheapest vehicle Mr Ford made – someone was home. I knocked.

A plump older woman answered the door.

'Hello. I'm Anne Holloway,' I said. 'My husband and I are considering making an offer on the house at the corner there, and I wonder if you could tell me a little about the neighborhood.'

'Why, of course, dear,' she said, smiling self-consciously – her hair was in curlers and wrapped with a blue scarf. 'Excuse me . . . hair-washing day. Would you like to come in for a moment?'

While I told her about my baby boy and made up some questions about nearby parks and churches, motherly Mrs Raymond went on about how they'd raised four children in the house. Their living room, which was the only room I saw, had a piano in the corner and a curio cabinet full of porcelain angels. She needed no encouragement to talk about her four now-grown children, except for poor Peter who died three years ago from cancer. No grandchildren yet but she had hopes since both daughters were married. She didn't mention the son who had spent years in the hoosegow – no surprise there. She enjoyed playing the piano and earned pin money giving lessons to neighborhood children. 'Of course, I tried to teach my own too. My girls took to music more than my boys. They were more interested in baseball, playing it in the park and going to Cubs games.' She was so sweet, it made me sad to think cancer had stolen her hero son and left her with the felon. But I gleaned a cornucopia of information which I passed on to Carlotta and Freddy as soon as I got home.

The second name was harder and so took less time. Eileen Perry had no obituary but her death was mentioned in last Sunday's newspaper. A very short piece on a back page mentioned the death from typhoid fever of Miss Eileen Perry, a girl of seventeen or eighteen years, who had come to Chicago just six weeks ago to look for work. No known surviving kin. The death of an unimportant person like Miss Perry, about whom little is known, would not have rated newspaper coverage at all but for the disease that robbed her of her life. Typhoid fever. The words alone brought chills to the back of my neck. The disease brought rising temperature, severe aches and pains, diarrhea, and rashes. There was no cure for typhoid fever and it was almost always fatal.

With all other research avenues blocked, I could only hope that meeting the young woman who had lived with Miss Perry would give me something to go on, something we could use at a subsequent séance. I'd spend the minutes between her arrival and the start of the séance to try to talk with her. Freddy and Carlotta would have to work up some soothing words from the spirit world.

Carlotta liked to schedule her séances to begin at twilight, a moving target that depended upon the season. Her next session a few nights later was set to start at seven, and clients began arriving fifteen minutes before. Tommy was safe in his kiddie coop upstairs, sound asleep. Freddy and I had worked through his role upstairs with the enhancements. I was needed in the séance room where we had already drawn the velvet draperies to block the remaining light. A floor fan provided a soft hum to cover up any of the tiny noises sharp ears might pick up, such as when Freddy lowered the speaking tube from the ceiling or when he closed a hidden peephole in the wall.

Someone coming to a séance for the first time might be feeling confused or even frightened, so part of my job was to reassure guests that they were not going to encounter anything evil or alarming. I played the role of a grieving widow – which required no pretense on my part since I was still reeling from my husband's murder a little more than a year earlier. That night, like others, I dressed in severe half-mourning attire with no jewelry, and I pulled my long black hair into a tight bun covered with a silver net. Madame Carlotta, dressed in a swirl of colorful ruffles and a bangling of gypsy bracelets, greeted her guests. Her gray hair was tucked tight under a ruby red turban, except for one visible lock that she blackened with shoe polish 'to make me look younger,' she would say.

That night, the first to arrive was a middle-aged couple, Mr and Mrs Frank Gentry, who were coming to see if they could get any information about their missing fifteen-year-old son, Frank Junior, who had disappeared – run away? – several months ago. Then came Miss Barbara Joyner, a frequent visitor whose contacts with her mother always brought her joy. Tonight she'd brought a friend, Miss Francine Waleston, who claimed she had no interest in contacting anyone; she just wanted to observe. That wasn't unusual, but it always made us nervous because the observer could change her mind in a flash and make some request that we'd not planned for. One of the hazards of the job. Next came Miss Daisy King, the roommate of the typhoid fever victim. As Carlotta had surmised, she was young, perhaps eighteen or nineteen, gaunt, and wore ill-fitting hand-me-downs. The last to arrive was Mr Daniel Raymond.

Carlotta began as she usually did by introducing everyone.

'May I leave my pocketbook here on the divan?' I asked as a way of suggesting the other women do the same.

'Yes, of course, my dear. Hats and coats too, if you like, on the hall tree. No distractions in the séance room! Your belongings are quite safe in my parlor. We have a full table tonight,' she continued in a low, whispery accent she considered her gypsy voice. 'Seven spiritual travelers into the Great Beyond. And one guide – myself!' She clapped her hands with genuine glee. She couldn't wait to begin. Helping people was her all-consuming passion, and she was convinced that her spiritual efforts steered her clients toward happier emotional lives. 'Come into the Spirit Chamber, ladies and gentlemen. Come take a seat, everyone, but first, feel free to look about the room. You must reassure yourselves that there are no hidden compartments under the chair seats or secret drawers beneath the table. Take your time. And each of you must have a look inside the Spirit Cabinet in the corner to verify that it is empty. Sadly, there are so many fake spiritualists out there that I feel I must prove my own impeccable bona fides.'

Seating arrangements seldom mattered as long as I got the chair on Carlotta's left, so I could free up my right hand when we were all holding hands. The electric fan was already circulating air in the room. As everyone began rapping on the table for hollow compartments that weren't there and peering into the empty Spirit Cabinet, I said in a clear voice, 'Pardon me, Madame Carlotta, may I be excused for a moment to powder my nose?'

'Certainly, my dear. Up the stairs and straight ahead.'

I closed the séance room door behind me so no one could see that I did not go upstairs, rather tiptoed through the hall back into the parlor to rifle the women's handbags. It didn't happen every time, but sometimes I came across a clue that would give Carlotta or Freddy, working above us in the enhancement room, a trivial detail that could be woven into their patter during the séance. A locket, a photograph, a theater ticket, a foreign coin, an addressed envelope – any of those might allow us to salt the gold mine, so to speak. If I found a nugget, I would sneak upstairs and tell Freddy or use some ruse to draw Carlotta aside for a moment to whisper what I'd learned. But tonight the cupboard was bare. I returned to the séance room where Madame Carlotta was ushering clients to their chairs.

'Mrs Pastore, you haven't had the chance to examine the Spirit Cabinet,' she reminded me, waving her beringed fingers toward the ornate antique cupboard in the corner.

'Oh, you all have already done it so I don't think . . . well, maybe I should.' Positioning my body so no one could see my hand, I laid an 1860 Indian-head penny inside the box for Miss Joyner to find later. It was minted the year of her mother's birth, something I'd learned from the old lady's tombstone, and it would mean a lot to her daughter as a message from the Great Beyond. 'Yes, it's empty,' I said, taking my seat as, with a magician's flourish, Madame Carlotta closed the door to the parlor, switched off the electric chandelier, and took her seat next to mine at the round table.

'Now let us all join hands to unite us in the circle of life . . . and bow our heads in prayer,' she said, after lighting the scented candle in the middle of the table. 'Dear Lord, who commands the day and night, the heavens and earth, the past and future, look with favor, we beseech thee, on our work tonight as we pierce the dark veil of death and commune with those who have crossed over to thine everlasting glory. Amen. Now, as our savior Jesus Christ has taught us to say, Our Father, who art in heaven . . .' Carlotta liked to start with a prayer to reassure her clients that they weren't participating in devil-worship or anything so sinister.

As the soft chant filled the air, I took stock of the clients in the flickering candlelight. Mr Daniel Raymond bit his lips nervously while his eyes darted about like he expected a ghost to materialize in one of the corners. The Gentrys stared intently into the flickering flame while Miss Joyner and her friend Miss Waleston kept their eyes closed tight. So did Daisy King, who was holding my left hand. It didn't take long for Carlotta to fall into her trance. After a long silence, she spoke in a low, raspy voice, '*Ave verum corpus natum . . . vere passum immolatum in cruce pro homine . . .* O Michael, prince of the angels, greatest of the angels, deign to visit us tonight, I beseech thee . . . We are all believers tonight, believers who wish to commune with the spirits of our dear departed loved ones . . . You who escorts the souls to Heaven, you who commands the spirits . . . favor us tonight with the blessing of your presence. Are we not all believers?'

'We are,' I said, prompting others to chime in.

At that moment, Freddy opened the small trap door concealed in the ceiling medallion above the electric chandelier and used his bellows to send a strong gust of air down toward the candle, extinguishing the flame and prompting a faint cry of alarm from one of the ladies. We were left in darkness so black you couldn't see your hand in front of your face. Which was, of course, the point. The muffled sound of a bell floated above us. One of the men – I couldn't tell which – murmured nervously. I gave Daisy King's thin fingers a reassuring squeeze.

'Welcome, Michael, beloved of all angels,' continued Carlotta in her mysterious voice. 'We beseech thee, blessed archangel, bring us the spirits of those who we wish to commune with tonight . . . *cuius latus perforatum* . . . *fluxit aqua et sanguine* . . . favor us with a visit from the spirit of Tommaso Pastore, beloved of his wife who is with us tonight . . . can Tommaso Pastore be found, O great archangel of God?'

Carlotta liked to position me first so the evening would start with success and encourage others to hope for the same. I'd played this part often. The first time, I confess, I almost believed it really was Tommy back from the dead, so convincing was Freddy's hoarse whisper through the speaking tube above our heads. Tonight, Carlotta began with me and for a few minutes, I was the forlorn widow speaking to her husband's spirit. I asked the questions we usually used and Freddy provided the expected responses.

Then Carlotta took over from Freddy, using her gravelly voice. After a stream of Latin gobbledygook, she called on the archangel Michael again, asking if he would bring the spirit of the Gentry's son. 'O powerful archangel, can you bring us the spirit of Frank Gentry Junior? His mother and father miss him very much.'

This case had been a tricky one. The parents of fifteen-year-old Frank were hoping Carlotta could tell them if their son was still alive and if so, where he was. The boy had disappeared after a fight over his behavior – late nights, coming home drunk, sometimes not coming home at all. Had he run away? It seemed likely. That's what they'd thought at first, but it had been several months now, and they had heard nothing. Naturally they feared the worst. The police seldom bothered searching for runaways unless they came from very wealthy families and certainly not any who were older than fourteen. The Gentrys had already checked the records of unclaimed bodies at the Chicago deadhouse, so I hadn't needed to do that. I'd tried to find an answer to their unanswerable question but luck was against me. Freddy often had more success in cases like these: he'd put out feelers to prostitutes, hobos, and scavengers he'd known when he lived a beggar's life in Chicago's alleys to see if anyone knew of the boy, and he'd asked the men at Carl's chess club where he was a regular, but he'd come up empty, too. We couldn't hope to find the lad – it wasn't at all certain he was still in Chicago. We couldn't tell the parents whether their son was alive or dead. Carlotta felt the kindest thing she could do in cases like this was to give them hope.

'He isss not here,' said Carlotta, changing to her version of a Middle Eastern accent she believed came straight from Archangel Michael. 'He isss not here.'

'W-what does that mean?' asked Mrs Gentry.

'If Junior isn't there, Enid,' her husband answered, 'he must still be alive somewhere on Earth. We must have faith that he'll come home to us one day.' This is what Carlotta would usually say to people searching for lost relatives. It was hardly a satisfactory conclusion, but it was the best we could do. Hopefully the missing person was alive and would contact his family someday soon. But this time, Carlotta hadn't finished. She cleared her throat and continued. 'He will come home to you . . .'

'Oh my!' cried his mother. 'When? Do you know? Can you tell us when?'

'He will come home . . . in fair weather . . . not this year . . .'

I nearly gasped. Carlotta never made predictions. 'I am no fortune teller,' she would insist scornfully. 'I'm no charlatan swindling people out of their money, no palm reader telling bogus futures.' Yet here she was, prophesying like some ancient Greek soothsayer. What was she thinking?

But I could say nothing in front of all these people. She had moved on to the next client.

'I sense . . . I sense another . . . O blessed Michael, prince of angels, there is one among us who wishes to contact his brother Peter Raymond . . . *tantum ergo sacramentum* . . . can Peter Raymond be found?' Carlotta hummed her one-note tune and mumbled more Latin, until at last, she broke off. 'I sense the spirit of whom we seek . . . he is among us . . . he is here . . .'

A long wait drew the tension tight as a drum. Carlotta murmured more Latin in a soft growl. In the room above, Freddy ran a bow across some violin strings, sending an eerie, forlorn, almost human cry floating through the air. At that moment, I let go of Carlotta's hand and laid my right arm on the table in front of me, releasing a stream of water through a tube in my sleeve that came from a rubber sac under my arm. This was a good enhancement for drownings or people lost at sea. It never took long for someone to notice.

'Wh-what's that?' said a voice.

'What?'

'Something wet.'

'I think it's water,' I whispered helpfully. Once when I did this trick, someone thought it was blood, so now I guided their thoughts in the right direction.

I moved my hand slowly from side to side until the water reached every hand. Of course, no one could see my arm in the dark. Carlotta, or the archangel Michael, interpreted the symbol. 'Fire and water . . . provide us with both life and death . . . a spirit is with us . . . one who knows the life and death cycle of fire and water.'

'It must be my brother Peter! Is that really you, Pete?'

Through the speaking tube that brought Freddy's words down to a point just above our heads came his lowest tone of voice intended to mimic the deceased fireman, Peter Raymond. 'I am with you, brother.'

'Are you really Pete? Prove it! Prove you are Pete!'

'Our little white house . . . porcelain angels in the corner.' The voice came slowly, with a pause after each word as if the labor to speak was crushing him. 'Ma . . . music lessons. Old piano . . . every night . . . thirty minutes . . . baseball . . .'

Daniel nearly came out of his chair with excitement. 'You remember the Cubs games at Weeghman Park we used to go to, you and me?'

'I remember.'

'The pitching duel in '17 with the Reds?'

I held my breath. I knew nothing about baseball; neither did Carlotta. This could trip us up big time. But Freddy was not a Cubs fan for nothing. 'The great Hippo Vaughn,' he replied. I let out a sigh of relief.

'It *is* you, Petey. It really is! How are you, brother? Ma misses you something terrible.'

'I miss Ma . . . miss you . . . and Becky and Lily . . . Marjorie.'

'I'll give them all your message. They'll be so glad to hear from you. All of 'em. Are you in heaven? What's it like where you are? What shall I tell them?'

'Send them my love. Tell them forever . . . no pain . . . no hate . . . love of God . . . no old . . . no young . . . no sick . . . the Lord is on his throne and angels like stars gather round . . . God wipes away every tear . . . no death, no sorrow, no crying . . . No more pain, for all former things have passed away . . . will meet again.' The voice grew increasingly feeble. I knew Freddy was done. Daniel was not. He pressed for more, but his brother Pete had returned to the Great Beyond.

Carlotta took over with a growly hum deep in her throat, something that meant she was preparing to speak for a spirit. I squeezed her hand for encouragement. It was time for Miss Joyner's mother to appear.

'I . . . am . . . with . . . you, daughter,' she breathed at last, her voice little more than a whisper.

'Oh, Mother! I am so glad you've come tonight! I have so much to tell you.' And for the next ten minutes, Miss Joyner did all of the talking, keeping her mother current on her sister Fay's oldest boy who was starting first grade at St Norbert's School this September; a distant cousin who had won a blue ribbon at the Illinois State Fair for her Double Wedding Ring quilt, and Uncle Albert's arthritis which had gotten so bad he now had to use two canes to hobble around. I waited for her friend, Miss Waleston, to surprise us with a request to contact a long-dead relative, but she remained the silent observer that Miss Joyner had promised. I thought it likely we would see her in the future, though.

Daisy King had not moved her hand an inch throughout the entire séance, but now, realizing that she was the only person who hadn't been contacted, she tensed, squeezing my fingers hard. Carlotta coughed and cleared her throat, then called the archangel Michael.

'Blessed archangel, can you bring us the spirit of Eileen Perry, who has just crossed over into your sacred realm? Her friend wishes to speak with her. She wishes to know if she is safe and happy in the Great Beyond. Can Eileen Perry join us for a brief moment?'

Freddy's natural voice was rather high-pitched, so it required only a minor adjustment to raise it enough to sound like a girl's. 'I am with you . . . I am here . . . I am part of the eternity where I have always been and always will be . . .'

'Eileen? Eileen, is that really you?' Daisy King said. 'I'm so sorry I wasn't there when you needed me. When you were sick. I came home and you were . . . you were hardly breathing. I tried my best, honest! I got that nurse from across the street and she came and said you were beyond all hope. She made me leave so I wouldn't catch it. I didn't mean to desert you. I'm so sorry!'

'Do not berate yourself . . . You were a good . . . a good friend . . . no one could have done more. It was my time. I am content.'

'I didn't know what to do. You never told me about your family or who to get in touch with in an emergency! Can you tell me now? Who should I notify about your passing? You said you had no family, but now, surely, there is someone who will want to know about your passing. And your things. What shall I do with your dulcimer? Your jewelry? The other things?'

'I am content . . . There is no one . . . You have done everything I could have wished. Farewell, dear friend. We will meet again one day.'

Daisy King sniffed loudly, trying to hold back the tears. I dropped her hand and pulled a clean handkerchief from my dry sleeve to pass to her.

The séance had ended.

We were a sober group, filing out of the room into the parlor. I waited for the right moment – a moment when the others would notice what I was doing – and placed a tenner in the basket in the parlor, thanking Madame Carlotta profusely as I did so. Just a suggestion, of course, but it usually brought similar donations from others. If not, Madame Carlotta bore no grudges. 'If someone can't afford a donation, it makes no nevermind to me,' she would say. 'My clients are welcome to my services for free.' I had not yet been able to adopt her charitable attitude toward freeloaders, but tonight, I sidled up to Daisy King, who clearly could not afford to part with a nickel, and whispered, 'That ten was for the two of us.'

She thanked me with a tremulous smile. 'I'm glad you were able to reach your husband. I wish Eileen had stayed longer.'

'Those of us who come several times often find the second or third visit is better.'

'I'll remember that.'

And I needed to dig up more information about Eileen so we could perform better next time. I wanted to be able to tell her where Eileen came from, and not just for her sake. For Eileen's sake too. And for her relatives, if there were any. The idea of a young girl dying without anyone knowing about it offended my sense of right and wrong.

As always, I left Carlotta's house when the clients did. Usually I just walked to the corner as if I was going to a parked motorcar or the bus stop and then used the darkness to shroud me as I circled around to the back door. But tonight, I walked out with Daisy King. 'It looks like I'm headed in your direction, Miss King. Would you mind if we walked together for a while? Are you going far?'

'My rooms are just a few blocks over on Clark Street. That's how I picked Madame Carlotta. She was the closest spiritualist I could find.'

'What a coincidence! That's near where I live.' We reached the corner stop sign and turned left before I launched my first question. 'I was very sorry to hear about the death of your friend Eileen. How did she die?' I knew the answer from the newspaper article, but had to get started somehow.

'Typhoid fever.'

'How very sad you must feel.'

'Sad? Yes, of course. She was so young. But to be honest, I hardly knew Eileen. She moved into the boarding house with me on the recommendation of the landlady acquaintance just six weeks ago. She was a sweet girl but very shy. Didn't talk much about herself – didn't talk much about anything really. All I knew about her relatives, if there were any, was that they must be living far away. She seemed estranged from her family, if you know what I mean.'

'I do at that.' Except for my sister, my own family relations were similarly strained.

'I didn't press her. I always figured we'd get to know each other and eventually she'd trust me enough to tell me where she was from and why she came to Chicago.'

'Did she have a job?'

'She worked a few weeks at a furniture factory, stuffing horsehair cushions, but the foreman fired her when she didn't act friendly enough toward him – you know how that goes – so she was looking for something else. I just wish I knew more about her so I could notify her relatives that she had died. Surely there's someone who deserves to know her fate! Actually, there was one person who visited her, an aunt. But I never met her or even got her name. I was at work when she dropped by to see Eileen.'

'An aunt? That's interesting. Someone local?'

'No idea. Eileen didn't say much about her. Just that an aunt had dropped in. She was surprised but pretty happy about it, as far as I could tell. I had the impression the woman came from far away and happened to be in Chicago, so she found Eileen and stopped by to say hello, but I could be wrong.'

'When was this?'

'A little more than a week ago, I think. Here we are. I mean, this is where I live. Fourth floor. Would you like to come up for a cup of tea?'

I'd been hoping she'd invite me inside, so I agreed with pleasure.

Daisy had two rooms in the boarding house. Tiny but spotless: one room with two narrow beds and another slightly larger with a sink, a table and two chairs, and a ragged sofa. A shared toilet and washroom down the hall rounded out the amenities. 'It's not much,' Daisy began apologetically, 'but it's home.'

'It's very cozy. I like your art.' Several canvas paintings covered the plaster cracks on the walls.

'Thank you. I painted those.'

'Did you really? My word! Are you a professional artist then?'

'Hardly. It's a hobby, that's all. I work at the soap factory around the corner.'

'They're very nice. I wonder that you couldn't sell them.'

She set about heating water on an electric hot plate and scooping loose tea into a tea ball. I sat at the table.

'I don't mean to be presumptuous, but have you looked through Eileen's things? You might find some information there.'

'I did take a look. Found nothing.'

'Do you mind if I . . .?'

'Be my guest. Eileen sure won't mind. Her drawers are on the right side. Her half of the closet is the right. The bookcase is all hers.'

While Daisy waited for the water to boil, I stepped into their shared bedroom. With no idea what I was looking for, I started with the bed, checking under the mattress and inside the pillowcase for anything Daisy might have missed. Hanging in the closet were four simple cotton day dresses, a green overcoat that she wouldn't have needed until the cold weather hit, three pairs of shoes, an umbrella, three cheap hats, and a pair of rubber galoshes. Nothing hidden in any pockets or stuffed inside any footwear. A gray bath towel hung on a nail beside her bed. Her drawers held undergarments, stockings and garters, a pair of tan gloves, and two sweaters. Most girls have an 'everything' drawer and Eileen's was a jumble of lipstick, rouge brushes, eyebrow pencil, kohl, keys, rubber bands, papers of needles, spools of thread, scissors, safety pins, pencils, a small penknife, and some jewelry in little boxes. Unlike the rest of her belongings, the jewelry looked nice. As in 'real'.

'What do you make of this jewelry?' I called to Daisy. One by one, I picked up three rings, two with stones that could have been real, one a signet ring with some sort of engraved emblem, a choker necklace of pearls – I ran the edge of my front teeth across them to test for that gritty feel and found to my surprise that they were genuine – a silver chain had a clasp marked STER and a heart pendant, and a gold chain marked 14K had a disk engraved with a date: January 2, 1907.

'Some of it, maybe all of it, was her mother's. That much she told me. I assumed that her mother was dead, or why would she have her jewelry? But I don't know that for a fact.'

'What about the date on this gold charm?'

'Huh?' Daisy joined me in the bedroom and examined the disc. 'I've seen her wear that but didn't know it was engraved. Maybe her birthdate? That would have made her eighteen.'

'Probably.'

'Tea's ready.'

'I'll be right there.'

A bookcase stood beside her bed. On its top shelf, snug inside its leather case, lay a dulcimer, a long, four-stringed instrument. I had once seen someone play such a thing with his fingers and a pick, so I knew it sounded sweet, like a harp or violin. This was worth something. Daisy was an honest girl not to have sold it and the jewelry to the pawn shop right away. I closed the case and turned my attention to the lower shelves that held a dozen books. A thrill surged through me when I spied a diary, but it quickly ebbed when I found she hadn't yet written the first word.

Eileen may not have been a writer but she was a reader. She liked romances, like *Flapper Wife* and *Hollywood Girl* by Beatrice Burton, and adventure stories: Jules Verne's *Journey to the Center of the Earth* and *Mysterious Island* were on the shelf. She had a serious side too, I realized, as I picked up a copy of *All Quiet on the Western Front* that lay on top of the stack. Idly, I ruffled the pages, only to find an old vaudeville playbill for a bookmark stuck at page ninety-four. She hadn't finished. She never would.

On impulse, I picked up the other books one-by-one to see if there was any bit of paper between the pages. Inside *The Little Yellow House* I hit paydirt: a letter had been inserted between the cover and the first page, a single sheet of pale blue paper still it its thin envelope.

The letter was brief, written by someone whose penmanship

looked feminine and who signed his or her first name as 'P'
then the last name starting with T, then 'A' (or 'O'?), an inch-
long squiggle, and finally a cross mark like a 'T' or an 'X'.
It could still have been a relative, of course, but the person's
last name wasn't Perry. The message was brief.

> Dear Eileen,
> I am sorry to be the bearer of sad news but must inform
> you of your father's death. He passed away on May 15th
> of a weak heart the doctor said, but you know of his
> other problems. We buried his earthly remains beside
> your mother and ordered a simple headstone to mark
> both graves. May they rest forever in peace in the arms
> of the Lord,
> Yours,
> P. Ta-----x

The paper bore no engraving, but the envelope had a two-cent
stamp that had been postmarked in 1925 in San Francisco – at
last, a clue to the girl's origins!

'Daisy, look at this,' I said, waving the envelope. 'Did Eileen
ever mention San Francisco? There's no return address but the
postmark says San Francisco and the date is this year.'

'Does that help find Eileen's family?'

'This letter brings news of her father's death by heart attack.
It mentions "other problems" too, probably drinking or drugs.
And your guess was right – her mother is dead. But now we
have something to go on. I know a detective – she's a woman
detective, maybe you've heard of her – Alice Clement?' Daisy
looked blank. She must have been the only person in Chicago
who didn't know the detective's reputation. I went on. 'She
can notify someone in the San Francisco police department
and have them look up in the newspaper obituaries for a man
named Perry who died last May fifteenth. It will probably be
in the papers on May seventeenth or eighteenth or nineteenth
. . . they'll find it. Then we'll know Eileen's father's real name
and any surviving relatives, like Eileen. Maybe she had a
brother or sister; maybe this aunt you mentioned will be listed.
And also, Detective Clement can ask someone to look up in

the San Francisco courthouse to see if Mr Perry had a will. That's another way to learn the names of relatives or anyone he left his worldly goods to.'

'And then I'll know where to send her jewelry. And the dulcimer.'

'I think so, yes. I'll contact Detective Clement first thing tomorrow morning.' The publicity-hungry detective might be peeved at me for asking questions during her interrogations, but this was exactly the sort of case she relished: one involving a poor young girl struggling to survive the ruthless jungles of Chicago. She couldn't bring Eileen back, but she could at least bring a fitting resolution to the mystery that was her death. Maybe she wouldn't drop Sophie's case if I handed her this one.

By the time I had returned home, Freddy had come downstairs for our regular review of the evening's events. I was eager to talk to Carlotta about her unprecedented foray into fortune telling.

'Carlotta, are you aware that you made a prediction during your séance? I don't recall you ever doing that before.'

'A prediction? When was that, Maddie?'

'When you told the Gentrys that their son would be coming home. "Not this year", you said.'

'Did I?'

'"In fine weather", you said. That could be any time of year, of course. Even winter has days of fine weather, but still . . .'

'Well, if Archangel Michael is comfortable passing along the future through me, I can't complain, can I?'

Predictions were uncomfortably easy to verify. This new turn of events made me uneasy.

TWELVE

I telephoned Detective Clement the following morning to see when we might call on Nick Bardo's widow, Ellie. She, in my view, was critical to our understanding of events that night, and I thought the detective must have a good reason for leaving her for last.

'I talked with Mrs Bardo yesterday,' she told me.

'What? Without me?'

She bristled. 'I am not obliged to take you with me on my investigations, Maddie. That was just a favor to you. I work best alone, without interruption.'

She must have been more annoyed with me than I had realized for her to cut me off completely. I hoped I could win her back with the Eileen Perry investigation. 'I know, I know, of course. And I'm sorry about that. It was unforgivable and it won't happen again, I promise. But I . . . I really wanted to hear what Ellie Bardo had to say.'

'And I took careful notes, as always. Mrs Bardo itemized her whereabouts that evening, accounting for every moment and sharing names of guests who could corroborate her story. She was always in the front hall greeting people as they arrived or, after the rush was over, in the dining room or living room. She went upstairs only once, when Sebastian Dale came to her about his wife's sudden indisposition to ask if there was a guest bedroom where she could lie down for a time. She said Sophie looked pale and kept putting her hand to her head, as if she had a headache, and that she was unsteady. So dizzy, in fact, that she couldn't walk unaided, so she and Dale got on each side of her and guided her up the stairs. She said she offered Sophie a drink of water and a cold compress for her forehead, but she declined both and just collapsed on the bed before they could even pull back the spread. She said she offered to call a doctor – there were none at the party – but in the end, she and Mr Dale decided to let Sophie sleep and check back in an hour to see if she was feeling any better. This was about one o'clock. Mrs Bardo returned to her guests and thought nothing more about it – if Dale went back to check on his wife, she wasn't aware of it – until she heard hysterical screams coming from the second floor. She was in the hall at that time; it was about two o'clock. She ran upstairs, nearly colliding with the couple who had stumbled, quite literally, on the body of her husband.

'This couple, name of John Angioti and Angela Horowitz, were married, just not to each other. Eager to pretend they had been taking an innocent tour of the mansion to admire the art, they told the police that they didn't see anyone else upstairs before discovering the body. I'll be getting their stories next.

'Mrs Bardo followed the screams upstairs and ran into the bedroom where she found her husband on the floor. She turned him over, thinking he had fallen or was drunk, only to find the top of his skull covered in warm blood. The murder had just happened. She said she knew at once he was dead. No one could survive that deep a headwound. Initially she suspected Angioti and Horowitz, but they were clearly traumatized, and when she saw the bloody candlestick on the bed in your sister's right hand, well, that clinched it for her. And for the police who arrived minutes later.'

This all matched the testimony of others. So did what Ellie Bardo told Detective Clement about the arrival of the police, their brief questioning of the guests who were then sent home, the removal of the body, and the escorting of Sophie to a paddy wagon while her husband tried unsuccessfully to ride along with her.

'What about her relationships with her husband and her stepdaughters? Did you ask about the arguments? What about the will? All that inheritance was surely a strong motive!'

'Mrs Bardo's manner was calm and serious. She had recovered from her earlier shock, but was still shaken. Murder is so unexpected. I can always spot fake tears, Maddie, and she didn't try to pull any of that stuff. She said she knew very well what people were saying about her and her marriage to a man so much older and richer, but that she and Nick were genuinely in love and his friends would tell me the same. She said he was generous to a fault, to her and to his daughters, always giving them presents, trips, money, jewelry, whatever they wanted. She never asked for anything, never expected anything but his love. He was faithful to her and she to him, and she had looked forward to decades of marital bliss. "I miss him dreadfully", she told me – several times.'

'What about her relationship with his daughters?'

'She was well aware of the animosity the girls felt toward her and she understood it. She said it was quite normal that they would draw the wrong conclusion and exhibit hostility toward a second wife who was younger than they were and who had, in their eyes, usurped their mother's place at the dinner table, even though their mother had been dead for years. Both she and Nick were prepared for that in the beginning. But they were sure they could win over the daughters as time passed and the girls realized that their father and stepmother shared a genuine fondness. As the months went on, Nick became increasingly annoyed at their constant belittling of their stepmother, their refusal to speak to her except in an insulting manner, their criticism of her every purchase, her make-up, her clothing, her hairstyle. When he first mentioned cutting them out of his will, she had begged him not to, saying that would only make things worse, that they would come around in time. And she was sure they would have, eventually, because she was never going to give up. Even now, she vowed that after letting them stew for a few months, she was planning to offer to pay off their debts and work out some basic allowance so the two would not suffer an embarrassing decline in their standard of living. How's that for decent?'

I thought of the Selinko servants and their unpaid wages. 'Very decent. And who's going to check back later and see if she keeps her word?'

'She said she understood how people would think badly of her, a former showgirl, inheriting such a large amount of money and property, and how they might think she was responsible for his death or at least gratified at the outcome, but she claimed she had no motive at all. "I already had everything of his", she told me. "I already had the use of all his money, his house, his cars, his servants, his fine life. It was already mine. He gave me everything I could ever want and plenty more I didn't want. I didn't need his death to get what I already had." She was very convincing.'

'Remember his daughter said she expected Ellie would bed the chauffeur and claim the baby was Nick's. Did she say anything about being pregnant?'

'I asked. She said she had no reason to think she was pregnant yet, but she would know for sure in a couple of weeks. She said she fervently hoped she would have Nick's baby to love, now that he was gone forever, but that she didn't need a baby to claim any of his wealth. And that's true. I've seen the will. It's not like Nick left money to an unborn child. He wasn't thinking that far out when he rewrote it. She's probably right – he probably would have changed the will again after the girls became more tolerant of his new wife. Which would remove them from any suspicion of involvement.'

'Except they didn't know they'd been cut out of the will when he died. They could have done it or paid someone to do it, only to find out they'd destroyed any chance they had of inheriting anything.'

'True. But do you really think those two sisters could cooperate long enough to order from a menu, let alone plan something like their father's murder? Where's your evidence?'

Ah, evidence . . .

All of this testimony was well and good, even touching, but without having seen Ellie Bardo's facial expressions, her hesitations, her nervous hands or fidgeting, her tone of voice, how was I supposed to evaluate whether or not she was telling the truth? Maybe the detective got something more out of the interrogation, but her report was worth little to me.

Time to butter up the famous detective so she wouldn't dump Sophie's investigation.

'Have you heard about the young girl who died of typhoid fever a few days ago? It was in the papers.'

'The mystery girl?'

'That's the one. Eileen Perry. She'd lived in Chicago for only six weeks and even her roommate knew nothing about her background. Well, I've met the roommate and come across a letter Eileen kept, a letter notifying her of her father's death in San Francisco.' Briefly I sketched the details of my find and what information I hoped she could uncover through her police connections. Detective Clement was all ears.

'Right up my alley, yes siree. I know of someone in San Francisco, Kathyrine Eisenhart, a female cop – there aren't many of us, you know. She's not a detective like me, mind you, just regular police, but she'll do me a favor just as I would for her. I'll send a telegram right away. I'll do whatever it takes to help Chicago's young girls,' she said, climbing back onto her soapbox. 'Even when they're dead, it's never too late.'

THIRTEEN

The doorbell chimed. I was up in my room, changing a messy diaper, when Carlotta's voice floated up the stairs. 'A gentleman caller for you, Maddie.'

Something in her tone told me she was teasing, so I wasn't surprised when I came downstairs to see a boy waiting in the hall. A Negro boy. He pulled the soft cap off his head when he saw me and said, 'Good morning, ma'am. I'm Stanley Jones from Early's. Mr Dale told me bring these things to you for Miss Sophie. He said you be going to the jail today and could get them there sooner than he could.'

This was the boy Sebastian had brought to the Bardo house to help with the cocktails. Tall enough to be a grown man but skinny as a kid, he had wide, dark eyes and ears like jug handles. No one to my knowledge had questioned him about what he might have seen or heard that night. That gave me an idea.

'Do come in, Stanley,' I said, reaching for the towel-wrapped bundle in his hand. 'What's in this?'

'Stuff for Miss Sophie. Some soap and baking soda for her teeth and fancy shampoo. I sure hope she come home soon, poor lady. She always real nice to me.'

'Can you sit a moment and have a glass of cold milk and piece of cake or something to eat?' There was one thing about living in a house with a teenage boy I could be sure of and that was Carlotta's never-ending supply of home-baked cake or cookies. Growing boys, she liked to say, were always hungry. Stanley didn't have to be persuaded. I led him into the kitchen and bustled about pouring milk and setting a plate of fresh oatmeal cookies in front of him.

'Now I remember who you are. Sebastian said a young man was working with him as a waiter at the Bardo's house that night. That was you, right?'

'Yes, ma'am.'

'What were you doing? I mean, what does a waiter do at a party like that?'

'I take the tray and put six highballs on it. Then I walk around the room so's folks can switch glasses with me. That way they don't hafta wait in line at the bar.'

'I wonder . . . did anyone from the police talk to you about that night?'

His mouth full of cookie, he could only shake his head. No surprise there, the police would not have considered a young colored boy worth interrogating. In any case, his race meant he wouldn't be allowed to testify in court.

'I wonder . . . did Miss Sophie take any of your drinks?' His eyes grew wary so I hastened to reassure him. 'She's my sister, you know. I'm trying to help get her out of jail, so if you can tell me anything about that night, I'd appreciate it. So would she, even more.'

He nodded so I continued.

'How old are you, Stanley?'

'Thirteen. Fourteen come Christmas.

Younger than I thought. 'What sort of job do you do at Early's?'

'Most anything. Take out trash, deliver packages, set up tables and chairs, take messages, sweep the floor . . .'

'And serve as a waiter. Do you tend bar? Mix drinks?'

'Not yet, but Doc say he'll teach me when I'm older.'

'Did you see when Miss Sophie went upstairs at the party?'

'Yes, ma'am. Mr Dale and a pretty lady help her up the stairs. She look really tired. Mr Dale say she'd rest a while and come back down soon to finish singing.' He reached for another cookie.

'The pretty lady, was that Mrs Bardo?'

'Who?'

'The hostess. The woman who owns the house.'

'Oh, yeah, that's her. She went up with Mr Dale and Miss Sophie.'

'Did you see her come back downstairs?'

'Yeah, she came right back down while I was in the big hall. I remember 'cause she took two highballs off my tray – my last two – and gulped one down right there in one long guzzle like it was water and she was real thirsty, and then she walked off with the other.'

'What did you do after that?'

'Well, like I said, my tray was empty so I went to Mr Dale's bar but he wasn't there, so I waited around, but he didn't come and he doesn't like it when I help myself behind the bar, so I went to Doc's bar and he filled me up.'

'And then?'

He shrugged. 'I just kept on doing what I was doing, walking around with the tray of highballs 'til they was gone.'

'Did you happen to hear any arguments?'

'Whoa yes, ma'am, there was a lot of arguing going on at that party. A lot of mad people. And when a mad person's drinking hooch, they get louder and madder.'

'Could you hear what any of them were saying?'

'Well, those two women who went outside were yelling like cats, something about a painting, and insulting each other with words my momma would wash my mouth out with soap for saying. Then Mr Bardo, the man who was killed, he came out and yelled at them to shut up and act nice to Ellie. That's Mrs Bardo. Mr Dale told me those daughters don't like her at all 'cause she's younger than them and prettier. Then later I saw the yelling on the stairs.'

'What was that about?'

'Money. That's what most yellin's about, isn't it? Money or women. Anyway, I was in the front hall, carrying around that tray, when Mrs Bardo went up to Mr Bardo and said how Miss Sophie had to go upstairs and lie down. She said could he go upstairs and have a look in on her to make sure she all right? So he gave me his drink to hold and went up the stairs. He never come back for that drink, no he didn't. That's when another man, that I don't know his name, followed him and they stopped on the stairs where the steps turn and they stood there a minute.'

'Could you hear what they were talking about?'

'Some of it, yeah. I came to the bottom of the stairs so I could hear better 'cause it sounded like another fight. And it was a doozy! Other people stopped to listen, too. You know, how folks pretend to talk but get all quiet so they can really listen? Something about the man wanting money 'cause Mr Bardo said, "Another loan? You ain't paid me back the last two!" And whew! That made the man madder than all hell – 'scuse my language, ma'am – 'cause his face turn red as a tomato. Then Mr Bardo he say something about how the man should make his wife be nice to Ellie. He say something about no money in his will 'cause they so mean to his Ellie.'

'Mr Bardo said that? He told the other man he had cut the girls out of his will?'

Stanley nodded and reached for a third cookie.

'What happened then?'

'The two men look down and saw people listening, so they went on up the rest of the way. Mr Bardo, he went first. The other man followed him. Do you think that man killed Mr Bardo? Lots of people saw them go upstairs together. Maybe he did the killing and not Miss Sophie.'

'Maybe. Did you see that man come back downstairs?'

'No, ma'am. I had to go to Mr Dale's bar then to turn in the empty glasses and get six more highballs. But Mr Dale wasn't there, so I waited a while, but he still didn't come. So I left the empties and went to Doc's bar and worked in that room until the police come.'

'What happened then?'

'The police, there was two at first, then more and an ambulance. They push everyone into the dining room and say the party's over, and we could leave as soon as they ask us a few questions. Only they say I could stay since I was working.'

'Then what?'

'I was in the dining room and they closed the doors, so I didn't see anything else until they let me go.'

'Where did you go?'

'I stayed with Doc and packed up both bars and everything and went back to Early's. Mr Dale, he disappeared. Doc say he followed Miss Sophie to the jail. She a nice lady, Miss Sophie. I'm sorry she in such trouble.'

'Me too, Stanley. Me too.'

I thanked Stanley and showed him out. Then I poured myself a glass of cold milk and picked up a cookie and thought about what he'd said.

Warren did it. Warren was upstairs with his father-in-law. Warren was angry. Warren needed money. Warren was the perfect suspect. There was no one else. I wanted to believe Warren did it. Desperately.

There was only one fly in the soup, as my French grandmother would say. If Warren knew that Nick had altered his will to cut out his wife and her sister – and he had just been told that on the stairs in front of many witnesses – then he had every reason *not* to kill Nick. In fact, Warren Selinko would be the person most interested in keeping Nick alive, so that he could persuade Gladys to behave in a civil manner to Ellie and worm her way back into her father's good graces. And into his will. Now, with Nick dead, it was too late.

FOURTEEN

I t was way too late for a telephone call – almost eleven o'clock. Carlotta had gone to bed, Freddy was holed up in his room, and I had just turned off the light when a harsh jangle from the back hall shattered the silence. I dashed downstairs on soft bare feet to catch it before it could further disturb the house. The last thing I needed was for Tommy to wake up and start crying.

'Good evening. Madame Carlotta, Spiritual Advisor. Madeleine speaking,' I spoke into the mouthpiece, hoping my irritation wasn't audible.

A man's voice replied. 'Hello. I, um, I saw your ad in the newspaper and, um, was wondering if you, I mean, if I could come to one of Madame Carlotta's séances.'

'I'm afraid she's asleep right now, sir, but I'm sure she'd be delighted to talk with you in the morning about your wishes, if you'll give me your name and telephone number.'

He should have apologized for disturbing us so late. He didn't. 'Um, no, in the morning, I'll be asleep. I work nights. Could I just make an appointment now?'

'Certainly. Let's start by getting your name, but oh dear, if you work nights, that's when Madame Carlotta holds her séances so—'

'I don't work Sundays, so Sunday night would be good.'

'All right, Mr . . .?'

'Makepeace. Howard Makepeace.'

I wrote this down on the pad of paper Carlotta kept beside the telephone. 'Can you tell me a little about what you hope to achieve at a séance? Who you want to contact, for instance?'

'Oh, yeah, sure. My parents. Either one or both.'

'And their names?'

'Dorothy and Elmer Makepeace.'

'Have they recently passed away?'

'Mom died three years ago. Dad went a year later.'

That would be 1922 for her and 1923 for him. It would have made my job easier if he'd given me a date or at least a month, but to push for specifics might raise his suspicions.

'And what is it you hope to achieve at a séance?'

'Well, I guess I just want to contact them and let them know I'm doing fine.'

No doubt there was more to it than that, but I wasn't as adept as Carlotta at prying helpful information out of prospective clients. This taciturn man was serving me up a challenging case. 'All right, Mr Makepeace. I'll put you on the schedule for this Sunday – whoops! No, I'm sorry, Madame Carlotta's table is full Sunday. It will have to be a week from this Sunday. Will that work for you?'

'I suppose there's no rush.'

'Good. The séance begins at seven o'clock. Please be a little early so you can spend a little time talking with Madame Carlotta first.'

'Will others be there?'

'There is no one else on the schedule at the moment, but it is likely that by then, yes, there will be one or two others. Is that a problem for you, Mr Makepeace?'

'I guess not.'

'If it is, Madame Carlotta can work out a time for a private séance.'

'No, Sunday is fine.'

'Then Madame Carlotta will look forward to meeting you then. Good night, sir.'

I was halfway up the stairs when the damn thing rang again! Cursing Mr Makepeace under my breath, I snatched up the receiver and prepared to give him a big piece of my mind.

'What is it now?' I growled.

It was not Mr Makepeace.

'Who is this?' a man on the other end demanded.

Without thinking, I replied with my full name. 'Madeleine Pastore. Who is this?'

'I'm calling with a message from Mr Hymie Weiss who wants to meet with you. Tomorrow at the florist. You know which one.'

'What? What do you mean Mr Weiss wants to see me? I don't even know him. What on earth for?'

'Business.'

'What sort of—'

'You'll find out when you get there, lady.'

'I have no intention of—'

'Be there at ten.'

'I'm not available—'

'Sharp.'

'I can't—'

Click.

Hymie Weiss wanted to see me? Hymie the Pole, the murderous boss of one of Chicago's biggest, most vicious gangs, the man whose thugs had murdered my husband last year, that man wanted to see me? I froze, shivering in my bare feet, my cold fingers gripping the receiver, staring down the hall to the exact spot where, last winter, Hymie Weiss and one of his thugs had held me and a friend hostage as they emptied their guns through our window at the police outside. It was almost as if it were happening all over again. I could feel his rough hand pulling me by the hair to the open door, then holding me in front of his chest like a shield as he made his way to the getaway motorcar, at the last minute flinging me into the gutter so he could flee. And now he wanted to see me? At ten o'clock tomorrow?

I could refuse. But he knew where I lived. He and his gang could come and shoot us all with impunity. I could call Detective O'Rourke who had helped me out in the past. He would send guards to our house, maybe come himself, and they would stay for a day or a week or even a month, but they couldn't stay forever, and Hymie Weiss would wait until they had gone. I could grab Baby Tommy and run. Where, I didn't know, but I could never come back to Chicago, not if Hymie Weiss was still alive. I had no friends or relatives outside Chicago who might take me in, no money to buy more than a couple of nights at a hotel, and no way to get a job with a baby to care for. What did Hymie Weiss want with me? I was nobody. An unimportant widow. What had I done? Or what hadn't I done?

Maybe I hadn't done anything. Maybe he just wanted some information. I knew nothing about anything, but maybe that was all this was. Maybe he'd ask me a few questions and let me go home. It was only a straw but I clutched it.

I must've stood there trembling in the hallway for half an hour, maybe more, scrolling through all the miserable options I had, until the sound of a faraway police siren snapped me back to reality. There was only one option, really. I knew that. Sleep was out of the question, but I returned to my bed and lay there, planning for my meeting with the North Side Gang's murderous boss.

FIFTEEN

Widows don't usually wear mourning for more than a year after their loved one dies. Sure, I've known some to wear black the rest of their lives, but I was only twenty-eight and black was too dreary for me to go that route forever. It had been a year and four months since the North Side Gang had put a bullet in Tommy's forehead, and I had set aside my mourning clothes, if not my mourning, months ago. But I put them on the next day hoping they would make me look more respectable in Weiss's eyes. More sympathetic. A pitiful widow.

Schofield's Florist sat at the corner of State Street and Superior on Chicago's Near North Side, directly across from Holy Name Cathedral in the heart of North Side Gang territory. The area bustled with motorcars and pedestrians all day long but particularly in the mornings when shoppers surged into stores, telegram delivery boys bicycled about, and runners rushed documents from office to bank to courthouse. A streetcar carried me most of the way. My sturdy black shoes brought me the last block.

I'd left Baby Tommy with Carlotta and Freddy along with instructions to call Detective O'Rourke if I hadn't returned by noon.

'Tell him where I went. I don't know that he'll be able to do anything, but there's no one else who has a chance of getting through to Hymie Weiss.' I didn't need to remind them that Kevin O'Rourke's twin brother was reputed to be an enforcer with the North Side Gang. We had known the charming Liam O'Rourke rather well last winter when we believed he was a starving-in-the-garret artist. Then I'd learned about his real job.

Carlotta was terrified. Her memories of that cold night in December were all too vivid. Freddy wanted to come with me. 'Absolutely not,' I said. 'I'll need you to take care of Baby

Tommy if I don't come back. Which I will, of course, so try
not to worry. I'm sure I'll come home safe and sound. Hymie
the Pole doesn't want to call attention to himself with the law
by bothering a poor widow.' Confidence is everything.

I had steered clear of Schofield's Florist ever since the day
– November tenth, 1924 – when Dean O'Banion had been
gunned down on the premises by members of Capone's Outfit.
Oh, it was Johnny Torrio's Outfit back then, but everyone
knew it had been his second-in-command, Al Capone, who
had ordered the O'Banion killing, dispatching four thugs to
surprise O'Banion, who used his florist as a sometime meeting
place. They caught him completely unawares in the back room,
his hands full of chrysanthemums, and plugged him with six
shots, point-blank range. Supposedly it was revenge for an
earlier attack that nearly killed Torrio . . . These payback
murders went on and on until no one could remember who
had actually cast the first stone. As if it mattered.

Evidently Weiss was continuing the O'Banion tradition of
holding meetings at Schofield's. Ever mindful of last year's
surprise attack, he had stationed several beefy men outside the
shop, men absurdly dressed in overcoats on a warm autumn
day as if they could hide the obvious. I spotted one on the
corner, another across the street on the cathedral side, and
another by the florist's door, leaning on the door jamb trim-
ming his fingernails with a knife. No doubt there were more
well-armed thugs around back.

They were expecting me. The leering brute at the front door
gave an ironic bow and held it open as I approached, the
parody of a gentleman.

Buckets of gladiolas, roses, lilies, asters, lavender and carna-
tions lined the floor while the shelves sagged under the weight
of so many potted orchids and ferns. The pungent scent of
hundreds of cut flowers failed to calm my nerves, but the sight
of six or seven customers made me breathe a bit easier.
It looked like a normal shopping day at a busy Chicago florist.
Surely Hymie Weiss wouldn't attempt any violence with so
many witnesses. Surely he couldn't kill all of them, too.

'I'm here to see Mr Weiss,' I said to the colored man at the
desk. As if he didn't know. It was as if everyone was acting

a part in a play, pretending to be oblivious to what was really going on around them. With a jerk of his head, the man indicated the door to the back room, the room where O'Banion had been murdered.

Like most of Chicago's top-shelf gangsters, Hymie Weiss was young, somewhere in his twenties, with clear skin and thick dark hair in that popular style where the sides are shaved close but the top grows longer. If you'd just met him in a park or at church, you'd think he was a nice-looking young man, maybe someone a girl would like to get to know during a stroll by the lake. He was seated in a corner – always a corner – his back to the wall and his legs stretched out long and crossed at the ankles in a relaxed pose, reading a morning paper like a respectable businessman without a care in the world. Two of his gang stood beside him, fists in pockets. To my relief, no one moved to search me.

Weiss's manners didn't include standing when a lady entered the room. 'Well, well, Mrs Pastore,' he began, uncrossing his legs and dropping the paper on the petal-strewn floor. 'We meet again. Under far more pleasant circumstances, huh?'

'I hope so.' I dared not meet his eyes for more than a second in case he should see how afraid of him I was.

'You're probably wondering why I asked you here.'

'I am.'

'You know what? I'm an admirer of yours, Mrs Pastore. I admire how you conducted yourself during that unfortunate incident last winter. Most dames woulda fainted dead away at the sound of the first gunshot or gone all hysterical when the police arrived, but you? You kept your wits about you. That's rare in a female. You got good nerves. I remember that.'

'You didn't ask me here to pay compliments.'

He barked a laugh. 'No, no, you're right about that, Mrs Pastore. Right as rain. Thing is, I think you're the sort of person I can work with. The steady sort who doesn't shy away from hard work. Someone who can tell it like it is. We can be straight with each other, can't we, Mrs Pastore?'

'We can try.'

'Ha! "We can try", she says.' He looked at the two bodyguards and grinned, a signal that they too could afford a little chuckle. 'Well, that's just dandy. Now that we're all friends here, I can tell you how I need your help.' That was a good one. The North Side Gang boss needed my help? 'You're gonna help us rub out Scarface.'

My eyebrows shot up. I could think of nothing to say.

'We're gonna hit him at your house during one of that gypsy woman's séances,' he said. 'When he's holding hands at that round table and his goons are in the front room. The details' – he waved his hand dismissively – 'that's for us to worry about. Your job is simple – get Capone to the séance.'

The plan was a resurrection of an idea Weiss had flirted with last year, modified to suit changing circumstances and to sidestep Capone's uncanny ability to scent a trap. No way would it work. I had to make him understand that.

'No way will he come to a séance at Carlotta's. I promise you, no way.'

'He came once before. To speak to his dead brother, Frank. A worthless piece of shit, if I can speak ill of the dead.'

'He wanted to speak to his brother, yes, but there was no contact. Madame Carlotta couldn't reach his brother's spirit because the archangel Michael said Frank wasn't there. His soul wasn't in heaven. Capone was furious and stormed out. No way he's ever coming back.'

'So Frank's in hell, huh?' He smirked at the thought. 'Tell him Frank's been promoted to heaven and wants to talk to him. All those paid-for masses the priests said for his soul musta done the trick, right? Whatever you come up with, I don't give a damn. That's your job, Mrs Pastore. You're a smart dame. You think up a way to make him come back and try again. Think it up fast, because we're in a hurry here.'

'Even if he would come again, there's no place to hide in that séance room.'

'I beg to differ, Mrs Pastore. You see, I had one of my men check out your séance room on the sly, so to speak, to learn how these things work. You may remember him: "Slats" Raymond contacting his fireman brother?'

With a sinking heart, I nodded. Of course I remembered Daniel Raymond, the felon, and his hero brother Peter. I don't know how I could have known that he was a spy. Maybe I should have been more suspicious when I learned of his prison sentences.

'So Slats gave us the layout of the house and the room where the gypsy does her spooky stuff and told us how the séance goes so we could make our plan. There'll be a guy behind the curtain. Maybe two for luck. Maybe another one under the table. By the way, Slats was impressed with your gypsy. Said she was the real deal, calling up the spirits like she did. Good to know there are some honest people left in this crazy world. You understand everything I'm saying, Mrs Pastore?'

'But I'm absolutely certain that no invitation is going to make Capone return.'

'Failure is not an option here, Mrs Pastore. There would be consequences. Serious consequences. I'll be honest with you – our code is not to harm women and children. You know that, right? But understand, though, that's an aspiration, not a rule.'

I understood.

'Show Mrs Pastore out, Dicky. And give her a bouquet of roses to remember me by.'

No part of the journey home pierced my consciousness, so thoroughly absorbed was I in my quandary. Go along with Weiss's plan and spark an indoor massacre when the North Side gangsters opened fire on Capone and his confederates. I could visualize the carnage: men firing from behind the curtain, another bursting up from under the table, pistols blazing. Carlotta and I and anyone else in the room would perish in the slaughter accidentally or on purpose if the gang wanted to eliminate witnesses. They would probably find Freddy upstairs and shoot him too when they realized he'd seen them from his post above the chandelier. And Baby Tommy? Even a bloodthirsty gangster wouldn't kill a baby, would he? The best I could hope for would be an orphanage for Tommy and a grim, lonely childhood without a single family member. He'd never remember me or know how much I had loved him. If I was wrong and we were lucky enough to survive the massacre, our lives would be worthless anyway because Capone's goons would know exactly who had helped his mortal enemy, and his successors would hunt us down and take their revenge.

The other option – betray Hymie Weiss and throw in with Al Capone – was no safer. As soon as he learned I'd defied him, Weiss would follow through with his threat to kill me and Tommy and maybe Carlotta and Freddy too, for all I knew. My husband once told me that Hymie Weiss was the only man Al Capone feared, and for good reason. Tommy said Weiss took great pleasure in watching his victims die and preferred to take his time doing it himself rather than delegate to underlings.

There was always an appeal to the police. My friend Detective O'Rourke would arrange for short-term protection, but Hymie Weiss was a patient man. However, even police protection wasn't very reassuring when you knew most of the force was on the payroll of at least one of those gangs.

No matter how many ways I rewrote the story, Carlotta and I always ended up dead.

SIXTEEN

You didn't just pick up the telephone and ask the switchboard gal to put you through to Al Capone. I had to find a way to send him a message, and it wasn't easy bypassing the layers of protection the Outfit boss had built between himself and the public. Face to face was the only way I could come up with.

I headed to his office at the Metropole Hotel on Michigan Avenue the following day, bringing Baby Tommy with me. Seeing as how my son was Capone's godchild (heaven help us both), it was the closest thing I had to a plausible excuse for a social call. I'd been to the Metropole before to see Johnny Torrio when he was the Outfit's boss and another time to meet Capone. I knew that their offices jumped around inside the building as a safeguard against enemies knowing which window the sniper should aim for, and I knew that Outfit headquarters might well have moved out of the Near South Side altogether to a building somewhere else in the city or to Cicero, the town just west of Chicago where Capone owned the police and the politicians. The only way to find out was to pay a call.

Since he'd inherited the organization from Torrio, Big Al had gone crazy over security. No wonder – there had been so many attempts on his life, it was a miracle he could still draw a breath. Some said he had divine protection. Hymie Weiss wasn't Capone's only rival, not by a long shot. Just last month, another mob boss tried to bribe the chef at Bella Napoli Café to put prussic acid in Capone's soup, which would have been fatal had the chef not alerted Capone to the plot. Capone's revenge included bombing several of the gangster's buildings, killing all the people inside, and personally beating three others to death with a baseball bat. When the loyal chef was found days later with his throat slashed, no one wondered who was responsible. Then a different gang leader choreographed an elaborate assassination attempt, luring Capone to the window of Hawthorne's Restaurant and blasting through the plate glass with more than a thousand bullets from shotguns and those new-fangled Thompson submachine guns. Capone narrowly escaped that one. Several other diners weren't so lucky. The moral of such stories never changed: help one side and the other side will get you.

The row of black limousines lined up along the curb beside the Metropole suggested it was still Outfit headquarters. Men with bulging pockets lounging awkwardly in the lobby reinforced the view.

'I'm here to see Mr Ross,' I said to the wizened desk clerk, using Capone's secret alias, which couldn't have been too secret if I knew it. 'I'm Madeleine Pastore with Tommy Pastore, his godson. If he's not too busy, I'd like to say hello.'

Two thugs approached and wordlessly searched me, my bag, Tommy and his baby buggy. Finding nothing, they motioned me to an armchair beside the elevator to wait.

Minutes later the desk clerk received word from upstairs. 'I'm sorry, madam, but Mr Ross is not in.'

I had anticipated that. 'Never mind, I'll leave a message.' Drawing a letter from my purse, I handed it to the man and left the hotel for home.

As I stepped off the streetcar a block from our house, I nearly collided into young Dan Ward who was heading in my direction.

'Hello, Mrs Pastore! And hello to you too, Tommy,' he said, patting my boy's head. 'How are you?'

'Fine,' I lied. 'How's your job going at Early's?'

'That's the best job ever, Mrs Pastore. In fact, I'm heading to work now. I can't thank you enough for recommending me to Mr Dale. I get a good salary and tips are great, Ma's over the moon, and Sis is holding her own at our bar.'

'That's wonderful! Yes, I've seen her there. She's learning the ropes. And Mr Dale? He's good to work for?'

'I guess so. I really work for Doc. He's my direct boss. Do you know him? Doc Makepeace, Early's head bartender. He's training me. I thought I knew a lot about mixing drinks, but he knows tons more and he's a good teacher.'

Makepeace! That was the name of the man who had reserved a place at Sunday's séance. Detective Clement and I had questioned a bartender called Doc about his activities at the Bardo party, but I'd never caught his last name. Or his real first name, for that matter. 'Yes, I know him. He was at the party when Nick Bardo was killed. What was his first name, do you know?'

'Doc.'

'No, his Christian name.'

'Oh, um, I think it's Howard, but everyone calls him Doc because he used to go to medical school before he became a bartender. And before that he was a medic in the war. He's a swell guy.'

'Really? How interesting! A doctor working in a bar?'

'He's not a real doctor. He dropped out of school after a year. But folks still call him Doc, and he's good at bandaging cuts and stuff.'

'I guess he didn't like doctoring as much as he thought he would.'

'I think he was sorry to quit but he didn't have the money to keep going. Something about he had to take care of his parents when they tanked.'

'Tanked?'

'Lost their business. Went bankrupt. And gaga.' He twirled his finger around his ear.

'What a shame!'

'Yeah, I guess. But not for me. I'm glad he's there. Ma always says, every bad thing that happens has something good come of it. She calls it a silver lining.'

'She's right. Pay attention and learn as much as you can from Doc.'

'Sure will, Mrs Pastore. And thanks again. Bye for now. Bye, Tommy.' And with another pat on my boy's head, Dan Ward loped off to work, the proud family breadwinner at fifteen. And I had a clue to Howard Makepeace's identity. Now I knew enough to investigate his parents' former business and dig up some pertinent facts for Carlotta before Sunday's séance. But the coincidence in all this nagged at me: was it just chance that Doc Makepeace had picked Carlotta's advertisement from the newspaper, or did it have something to do with Sophie and the Bardo murder? I couldn't see the connection, but I'm suspicious of coincidences.

Carlotta met me at the kitchen door with an ear-to-ear smile and a newspaper in her hand.

'Look, Maddie, look!' she said, pointing to the front page, lower left-hand corner. It was a small piece and the headline said it all. *Selinko Arrested for Bardo Murder*. 'Good news at last! Will they let Sophie out now?'

The short article credited Detective Alice Clement with cracking the case. 'I wasn't gulled by the sham evidence Selinko cooked up, putting the murder weapon in an unconscious girl's hand,' the reporter quoted her as saying. I winced as I realized how this would go over with the male detective who initially worked the case. Alice Clement might be the darling of the newspapers and a favorite with the public, but I suspected her grandstanding ways were much resented by her peers in the police force.

'Isn't it wonderful?' persisted Carlotta.

I sank to the kitchen chair with Tommy on my lap. 'Not as wonderful as it seems. That colored boy, Stanley Jones, who was here yesterday, can testify that Warren Selinko knew about the changes in Bardo's will, which makes it highly unlikely that he would have wanted him dead. He was asking for money that night, but he sure wouldn't get it from a dead father-in-law.'

'But no court will allow testimony from a Negro.'

'Even so, plenty of other guests at the party overheard Selinko's argument with Bardo and will understand what it means, that Selinko had every reason to want Bardo alive, not dead. I'm afraid the charges won't hold up when all that comes out.'

'Oh dear. Will you tell the detective?'

Tell the detective the information that would prevent my sister from being released? That was a tough one. I heaved a deep sigh. She'd get it sooner or later anyway. 'I'll suggest Detective Clement talk with Stanley Jones. She can take it from there.'

Carlotta busied herself with adding bits of sausage to a

kettle of potato soup while I gave Tommy some bread and butter.

'Oh, Maddie, it slipped my mind, you had a telephone call from Sophie's husband, Mr Dale. I told him you would return his call as soon as you came home. Maybe he has some news.'

I hoped it was good. I'd had my fill of bad news today. 'Probably about Warren Selinko's arrest, in case I didn't know. But I'll call right now.'

It wasn't about Selinko. 'I heard from Farnsworth, our lawyer,' Sebastian told me. 'He said the trial date has been set for October fifth. That's a little more than two weeks from today.'

'What! Two weeks? I thought lawyers got more time than that to prepare their cases.'

'Evidently not in this instance. But he didn't know about the Selinko arrest. That should allow the charges to be dropped, so it doesn't matter.'

'I'm afraid the charges against Selinko won't hold up once some new evidence comes in, but we can always hope.'

'What new evidence?'

I told him.

'But isn't it possible Selinko lost his temper and struck his father-in-law without thinking of the consequences?'

'Yeah, but what were they both doing quarreling in the bedroom where Sophie was lying? Look, I hope it's Selinko too, and maybe it is. I just don't want to tell Sophie yet so she doesn't get her hopes up, only to have them dashed.'

'Yeah, you're probably right about that.' He sounded like death warmed over.

I changed the subject. 'On another topic, what do you know about Doc Makepeace?'

'Doc? Why, he's a swell bartender. I hired him right when I started at Early's.'

'You mean, when you bought Early's? Sophie said you bought the place.'

He sounded embarrassed. "Well, yeah, that's what she thinks, you know, and I didn't, you know, want to disappoint her. I'm planning to buy it, one day."

'I see. Do you know anything about Doc's family?'

'Well, he's not married, but other than that, can't say as I do. Why?'

'Probably no reason. I'm just curious about something. I'll keep you up on developments.'

SEVENTEEN

I couldn't sit around twiddling my thumbs while I waited for Capone to answer my note. Whatever my own problems, Sophie was still in dire straits with her trial looming and Carlotta had a séance fast approaching with a new client to investigate. Something told me the two events might be related.

The place to start was with Doc's background. Because I didn't have a firm death date for either parent, I began at the library with a stack of back issues from Chicago's three biggest English newspapers from the year Doc's father, Elmer, died – 1923. His mother, Dorothy, passed away the previous year, but women seldom rate an obituary. More often they get a death notice, which isn't as useful because it gives only their name and the funeral specifics. His father was the better bet. Flipping quickly to the M's in each obituary page took mere seconds, so I was able to race along through January's *Daily News Tribune*, and *Sun* in little more than half an hour. No luck, so on to February, praying he hadn't died in December.

Eureka! The May twenty-eighth, 1923 issue of the *Chicago Daily News* reported that Elmer Makepeace had died two days earlier at the age of fifty-nine. No cause of death. Survivors included his son Howard; two sisters, Rebecca and Geraldine; and several nieces and nephews. He had been predeceased by his wife, the former Dorothy Mae Allen, and a daughter who died in infancy, both of whom were buried in St Mary's Catholic Cemetery on 87th Street. Elmer, however, was interred at Rosehill Cemetery on North Ravenswood. Not with his family. Only one explanation came to mind.

My eyes grew round when I read this paragraph:

> Mr Makepeace is fondly remembered by his many employees at the Adler Hotel, originally built by his father, the late John D. Makepeace, after the Chicago Fire of 1871 and greatly expanded by Mr Elmer

Makepeace in 1918 with a nightclub, health club, ballroom, swimming pool, and two additional restaurants. A
kindly boss who knew the names of every employee and
most of their families, Mr Makepeace was known to
enjoy a stroll through the public rooms every evening
to satisfy himself that the hotel's exacting standards were
being upheld.

But Nick Bardo owned the Adler – or did until his death gave
it to Ellie. Elmer Makepeace must have sold the massive
complex to Bardo shortly before his own death, although
the obituary made it sound as if he still owned it at that time.
Maybe it was sold shortly afterwards by his only son and heir.
Regardless of when the sale took place, Doc Makepeace must
have inherited a small fortune. Why had he left medical school?
Why in heaven's name was he working in a bar? Surely the
answer lay deep inside the *Tribune* morgue.

There was something else I wanted to look into, as long as
I was up to my elbows in newspapers. Leafing through papers
four days before and four days after Eileen Perry's death, I
came across no other mention of Chicagoans dying from
typhoid fever.

Odd, that.

I hurried home to relieve Carlotta, who was taking care of
Tommy. Lately she had been spending more and more of her
day looking after him, and although she doggedly swore she
was not put out in the least and I could see that she doted on
the boy, I was wary of taking advantage. It was a lucky decision. The moment I walked in the door, the telephone bell
rang. It was Detective Alice Clement.

'I have in my hand a telegraph from Officer Eisenhart in
San Francisco,' she reported officiously. 'We were right to be
suspicious! She found Miss Perry's father's obituary right
where you said it would be. His survivors are his daughter,
Eileen Perry, and his sister, Jane Perry Brent. That must have
been the woman who visited Eileen two weeks before her
death. But here's the kicker: Officer Eisenhart looked up the
man's will and what do you think she found? He didn't own
much, a few dollars that disappeared, probably went to pay

for his funeral, but . . . get this, he had some land in Colorado. Land he left to his daughter.'

'That letter I found telling Eileen about her father's death doesn't say anything about land.'

'Precisely,' she said.

'Whoever wrote it – and it wasn't Mrs Jane Perry Brent because the illegible signature scrawled at the bottom doesn't come close to matching that name – either didn't know about the bequest or was concealing it.'

'All of which is highly suspicious, I'd say.'

'I've been thinking about typhoid fever. It comes from contaminated water.'

'Everyone knows that, Maddie. That's the main reason they reversed the Chicago River back in 1900, to flush the polluted water away from Lake Michigan so Chicagoans could have clean drinking water and quit dying from typhoid fever.'

'I was just a kid, but I remember when they opened the river and people lined the banks to watch the water flow in from the lake.'

'So what's that got to do with the price of bread?' she asked.

'Just this: this afternoon I checked the newspapers during the time around Miss Perry's death and you know what? No other deaths from typhoid fever were recorded that week. The only typhoid fever deaths in recent months were traced to oysters shipped in from the east coast. If there had been some contaminated water coming into their building or into any of the tenements around Clark Street, wouldn't others have sickened and died? That's how typhoid fever usually works, isn't it? Why was Eileen Perry the only victim?'

'Now that you've brought that up, I'll admit, it is unusual.'

'Could it be the coroner was mistaken about cause of death? Or maybe he was paid to be mistaken. Now that we know about the land in the father's will, Eileen Perry's death is starting to look suspicious.'

'Like someone gave the girl a bad oyster?'

I had one more suggestion. 'I have an idea.'

'What?'

'If your Officer Eisenhart will perform one more task for us . . .'

'She's eager to help. I'd do the same for her.'

'Would she go to the current *City Directory* and look up the aunt, Mrs Jane Perry Brent?'

'What will that tell us? Supposing she's even listed.'

'She may not be listed at all, of course. She may not live in San Francisco. But if she's a widow, she may be there and we might learn an address.'

'What good does that do?'

'With an address, Officer Eisenhart could drop by her home and see if she was the aunt who visited Chicago a few weeks ago. What was she doing here? Telling Eileen about the land her father left her? In any case, as Eileen's aunt, she'll want to know her niece is dead. If she's not the aunt, well, we're no further away from the truth than we were.'

'Hmm, good thinking. I'll telegraph Eisenhart at once. Oh, and by the way, Maddie, about your sister, I talked to two of the Bardo party guests yesterday and found out they over-heard Selinko arguing with Bardo on the stairs as they both went up. Something about a loan. We confronted Selinko in his cell with this information and he broke down and bawled like a baby. I've seen it before: stand up to a bully and he blusters and threatens until all of a sudden, he deflates like a popped balloon. He confessed he was deep in debt – evidently he's got the gambling fever – and had been begging his father-in-law for another loan. Bardo refused, saying there would be no more money until Selinko persuaded his wife Gladys to make nice with Ellie. Said he'd already cut the daughters out of his will for that very reason. Selinko swore they'd parted in the hall, right at the moment when Bardo put his hand on the doorknob of the guestroom where your sister was. He swore he hadn't killed Bardo. Said he had every reason to keep him alive because he was going straight to his wife and beat her black and blue if she didn't change her tune about Ellie. Bardo's death lost him his only chance of paying back his gambling debts and he's frightened out of his wits at the consequences. I'd leave town if I was him. Those loan sharks aren't playing tiddlywinks when it comes to deadbeats.'

Just as I'd feared. Warren Selinko hadn't killed Bardo. He'd been the last to see him alive, though. 'Did you ask him if he saw anyone else upstairs in the hallway?'

'Of course we did. He said the hall was empty. We have a few more things to check, but I believe he'll be released tomorrow. I'm sorry that doesn't help your sister, my dear, but that's how the evidence breaks.'

EIGHTEEN

Every time the telephone rang or the doorbell chimed, I jumped, but no word came from Al Capone. Saturday crawled by. And Sunday. Surely he wasn't so cocky as to ignore my message.

Shortly before sunset, a paunchy tough in a black-and-gold striped suit pounded on the front door. I struggled to keep a straight face – he looked like a bumble bee in that getup.

'You Madeleine Pastore?'

I looked past him to an unusual dark green limousine idling at the curb and my grin fell away. A black Cadillac coupe sat behind the limo and a Cadillac sedan waited across the street. The windows of the limousine were obscured but I could make out the faint outline of a driver at the wheel and someone in the back. Capone? Or Weiss? Or another of the myriad gang leaders who infested Chicago?

'Who's asking?'

'Mr Alphonse Capone.'

'I'm Mrs Pastore.'

A jerk of his head indicated I was to follow him to the curb. With a sweep of his arm, he opened the back door. Al Capone sat on a buttery leather seat smoking a cigar.

'Good day to you, Mrs Pastore. Won't you join me?' he said, patting the empty place beside him in a friendly manner that made my skin crawl. Once I had climbed inside and arranged my skirt to cover as much of my legs as possible, the bodyguard slammed the door with a solid thud and click that made me think of a bank vault. Then he took his place up front with the driver. 'Drive on, Lou,' ordered Capone. Lou pulled away from the curb. Capone craned his neck to peer behind us, making sure the two Caddies were following close like some army convoy.

'Where are we going?' I asked, glancing at Lou's hands on the steering wheel. He was missing several fingers.

'Out for a scenic Sunday drive along beautiful Lake Michigan. That will be nice, don't you think? How do you like my new motor? It's a McFarlan. I've got a second one on order.'

I feigned interest, like this was a normal conversation between casual acquaintances. 'McFarlan? I don't think I've heard of that make.'

'Me neither until I did a look around. When that sonofabitch Sloan at General Motors snubbed me and then so did Henry Ford, I found McFarlan in Indiana who wasn't so snooty. This model usually costs seven thousand five hundred, see? But I paid twelve thou five for this baby. Why do you think I did that, huh?'

That kind of money would buy three nice houses. 'It's very pretty leather,' I ventured weakly, stroking the soft upholstery and remembering the motorcar Tommy and I bought the year we married, a Ford runabout. Two hundred ninety dollars.

'It's what you can't see that counts. Take a good look at these windows? That glass is an inch and a half thick. No bullet can pierce it. I know, I tried. You can't see too good out of 'em, but no one outside can see inside too good either. And the sides are reinforced with steel plates. Has a custom heavy-duty frame and truck-quality springs. Damn thing weighs a coupla tons! Of course it has special tires to hold that extra weight, and if they're pierced by a bullet, they have an inner tire that lets 'em keep rolling for a while. Long enough to get outa range.'

'My word.'

'You know who else has got one of these McFarlans?'

'I can't guess.'

'Jack Dempsey, that's who. And Fatty Arbuckle from the pictures.'

'How interesting.'

'Ever since January when I first got a load of those new Tommy guns, when Moran and Drucci ambushed me, well, I knew it was past time to buck up my game. Those babies can pierce regular cars like they was tin cans.' He knocked on the side of the motorcar with his knuckles. 'This'll stop anything they can fire at me.'

Big Al's attention shifted to the driver. 'No, Lou! Take a left up there! Jesus H. Christ, don't you know the way to Lake Shore Drive? Shit, my old driver didn't need a map to get around his own city!' Then under his breath to me, he added, 'But he was snatched up and butchered by Hymie Weiss's goons. A big loss to me, I can tell you. A big loss. But now, the small-talk part of this conversation is over. What's this about a life-and-death problem? *My* life and death, your note said.'

I swallowed hard and launched into the story I'd rehearsed in my head a dozen times. 'It's about Hymie Weiss. He wants to kill you.'

'And that's news to who?'

'He wants me to help him.'

That got his attention. Capone's eyes narrowed to evil slits. The man was ugliness personified with his stubby neck, fleshy jowls and thick lips always twisted into a sneer. A receding hairline aged him far beyond his twenty-six years. It was all I could do not to recoil in disgust at the two great scars on his cheek. People said there was a third scar on his neck, but he took pains to cover it with his collar or a scarf. Nothing, not even the make-up he used, could obscure the other two. Folks had started to refer to him by the nickname Scarface. He hated it. Wanted to be called Snorky on account of his flashy dressing.

'It's a simple plan, really. Weiss wants me to convince you to come to another séance. I'm supposed to tell you that your brother, Frank, has contacted Madame Carlotta and wants to talk to you. We set the day and time for the séance and you show up at my house, where he'll have some of his men – and maybe himself – waiting to ambush you, hiding under the table and behind the curtain. Or so he said.' Even someone like me, inexperienced in the fine art of assassination, could figure out that Weiss was likely to change the details of the plan he had divulged to me.

Capone's cigar had shrunk to one-third of its size. Ignoring the ashtray built into the side of the car, he dropped the stogey on the floor and crushed it with his heel, then reached into a small compartment and pulled out another. As if he hadn't a care in the world, he took his time peeling off the wrapper, lighting a wooden match and toasting the end of the cigar. As it smoked, he took a few short puffs to get it going. It was a struggle not to choke.

'Well, well, Mrs Pastore, this is a most interesting turn of events. Your late husband, God rest his soul, would be proud of you for coming forward with this information. I am sure we can deal with Mr Weiss and his foolish plan. Let us set a date for the séance. I think September thirtieth would be a good day for Mr Weiss to meet his maker. And the time will be six o'clock.'

'Madame Carlotta's séances are usually scheduled for sunset. Seven o'clock would be normal.'

'You know best, Mrs Pastore. Seven o'clock it is.'

'What will you do?'

'Simplicity is always the best strategy. You'll tell Weiss the séance is at seven and he'll want to be there at six. But we'll be there at five and he'll be the one who's ambushed. Simple.'

'What about us?'

'You?'

'Me, Baby Tommy your godson, Madame Carlotta, and the boy who lives with her, Freddy. What do we do?'

'You get out of the house when the Outfit welcome committee arrives.'

'And afterwards? Weiss probably won't come there himself. He'll send his men. They'll get killed. He'll know I double-crossed him and come after me. All of us, including my baby. He promised as much when he gave me these orders.'

'We'll set up protection around your house.'

'You know as well as I do that an arrangement like that can't last as long as Weiss's memory.'

'Move to Cicero. You'll be safe there. I own that town.'

'I'm afraid Weiss has proven that he can find ways to get at your people, even when they're under your protection.' I didn't say it but I was thinking about the torture of his previous driver, the murder of his brother Frank, the death of the chef who warned him about the poisoned soup plan, and all the others whose loyalty to Capone and the Outfit cost them their lives. 'I have another idea. On the day of the séance, I take Baby Tommy and Madame Carlotta and Freddy and leave Chicago for good. No one knows where.' I gave him some time to mull this over, then when I saw him nod, I added, 'But I don't have enough money to keep us out of the poor house.'

'How much?'

'We can all live a year on two thousand.'

He reached into his coat pocket and pulled out a wallet. Without comment, he peeled off twenty hundred-dollar bills from a thick wad and handed them to me.

'Thank you.'

He didn't really give a damn about Carlotta and Freddy, what would happen to them. He didn't care about me and Baby Tommy either, not really. We were just props to show others how good he was at 'taking care of our own'. My plan was simple enough, although I hadn't told Carlotta or Freddy yet. They had no choice but to come with me, at least until the dust settled. We could plan how they could start over later in another town if they wanted. It would be easier for them to relocate and blend into the scenery. The targets painted on their backs wouldn't be as large as mine.

Lou drove us in silence for a few minutes while Capone puffed and I pretended to look out the window at the blurry landscape. My heart pounded and my thoughts raced. Two thousand dollars would keep us all safe in a boarding house in Aurora, a town about fifty miles west of Chicago, for more than a year, time to find a woman to look after my boy while I went to work. I couldn't type so office work was out, but good recommendations from my years at Marshall Field's would get me retail jobs. Carlotta could change her name again – Madame Voronika? Madame Zuzana? – and start up her séances. Freddy would never leave her.

Big Al was talking again. 'Lou, spin around.'

'There's something else I wanted to ask you,' I said as Lou deftly turned the heavy motorcar in a wide circle. 'I saw you at Nick Bardo's funeral.'

'Why didn't you speak?'

'You were in and out before I had a chance. You looked

like you had something on your mind and I didn't want to disturb you.' He grunted. 'Besides, I was incognito. The sister of the accused murderer would hardly be welcome at the victim's funeral. Not that many people know I'm Sophie Dale's sister, but still.'

'So what?'

'Did you know Nick Bardo?'

'Lotta people knew Nick Bardo.'

'Did you do business with him?'

The long, speculative look he gave me convinced me the conversation was over, but I was mistaken. 'He had some night-clubs. And a big hotel. He bought our beer and booze. You could say I was interested in owning his nightclubs and eliminating the middleman, so to speak.'

No way would I risk asking if he'd eliminated Bardo. I danced as close to that idea as I dared. 'My sister is accused of Bardo's murder.'

'That I am aware of.'

'She didn't do it.'

'I figured as much.'

'I'm trying to save her by finding out who did.'

'And you think I had something to do with it?' There was no response possible, so I just clasped my hands in my lap and tried to look innocent. 'Bardo and me would've come to some amicable agreement about his nightclubs. I didn't need to kill him to get those. I got a reputation I don't deserve, you know that, Mrs Pastore? I'm a simple businessman, and like businessmen everywhere, I prefer to do business peace-fully rather than with guns. He woulda listened to reason.'

Meaning he'd have threatened Bardo to get what he wanted. Scaring off the victim usually worked. Murdering a busi-nessman, as opposed to a rival gangster, would have been a last resort for Big Al. Not to mention that braining a guy with a statue was hardly the Outfit enforcers' preferred means of disposal. No, they used guns and dumped bodies in the Chicago River.

'You wouldn't have any idea who might have done him in, would you?'

There was another long silence before he answered, sort of,

in a roundabout way. 'You know what, Mrs Pastore? Bardo's killing was interesting. Sloppy. Not a professional job. Embarrassing, truly. Lou, head back to Mrs Pastore's house. I believe our business here is finished.'

NINETEEN

The very next morning after my ride with Capone, I stepped out back to the clothesline with a load of wet diapers only to feel the sting of winter on my cheeks. Chicago's seasonal fluctuations had been happening so far outside my notice that I might never have put on a coat that day but for Carlotta's remark. 'Better bundle up our young man this morning. The mercury reads thirty-nine degrees.'

With Tommy looking like the winner of a Cutest Baby contest in his almost new sailor suit, we set off in the baby buggy for the *Chicago Tribune* morgue to figure out the puzzle that was Doc Makepeace. Sophie's trial date loomed, and I'd have to flee Chicago on September thirtieth, so it was important to do this last thing for my sister while I could. After this, I had nothing left to offer.

Before leaving home, I made a telephone call to the number that Hymie Weiss had given me. An old woman with a quivering Irish accent answered, making me think the operator had connected me to the wrong number; but no, it was correct. I repeated my name and the pre-arranged message, 'Appointment made', so Weiss would know that I'd met with Capone. The ball was in his court now. I could do nothing but wait for him to contact me about the details.

The brand-new Tribune Tower on Michigan Avenue looked more like the pictures I'd seen of French cathedrals than a workaday office building. Over the past two years, I'd watched it go up, stone by gray stone, marveling at its soaring pinnacles and intricate traceries and carvings. Every day would find Chicagoans clustered at the street corners, craning their necks to gawk at the wonder of it all. I made my way through the arched entryway and across the polished floor to the elevators, steering Tommy's buggy onto a car going down. The elevator boy remembered me, for he asked, 'The morgue, miss?' and rode me five floors below ground to Mrs Waterman's windowless realm.

Mrs Waterman was helping a reporter when I arrived, so I
sat on a bench and jiggled the buggy a bit to pacify Tommy.
When it was my turn, I presented her with my problem: 'I
need to learn everything I can about the Adler Hotel's previous
owners, the Makepeace family. Not the current owner who
was just murdered, but Elmer Makepeace. Oh, and guess what?
Tommy walked for the first time on Wednesday! He was
holding on to the coffee table and just turned and let go and
walked four whole steps without touching anything. You
should have seen his face – he looked so surprised.'

Wordlessly, she disappeared into the bowels of the archives,
returning ten minutes later with a stack of newspapers. Handing
me the bundle, she lifted Tommy from his buggy. 'You go on
with your work. I'll mind this one. I want to see him do his
new trick.' And to my astonishment, she sat right down on
the cold tile floor and set Tommy in front of her on his tiny
feet, each little hand clutching one of her large, ink-stained
fingers, and gently let go of him. He wobbled a bit before
taking three shaky steps toward her outstretched arms, then
dropped to his hands and knees for the old reliable way of
getting about. 'Come on, big boy, let's do it again,' she crooned,
lifting him up. Clearly, this woman should have been a nanny,
not a newspaper archivist. Taking advantage of the diversion,
I spread out on one of the library tables, hoping no other
employees would bother us for the next hour or so.

It took many issues and much skimming to make sense of
what had happened at the Adler Hotel. The original had been
built by Elmer Makepeace's father (Doc's grandfather) in the
1880s. Its fancy restaurant and elegant ballroom quickly
earned it a reputation as one of Chicago's grand hotels where
the wealthiest families gathered to celebrate milestones
and the most successful business tycoons met to hammer out
important deals. Sophisticates like that demanded fine food
and fancy surroundings. Elmer Makepeace inherited the property at his father's death and ran it competently for years.
During the first two decades of the twentieth century,
Chicago's population swelled, first with immigrants from
Europe and later with Negroes from the South, and the city
grew in importance as a major international port, the hub of

a dozen railroad lines, and the heart of the nation's meat-packing and grain industries. In no time, Chicago could boast more millionaires than any city in the world, bar New York. After the Great War ended in 1918, Elmer made an astute business decision to expand, adding an enormous nightclub with a hundred showgirls, several themed bars featuring the hottest jazz and dance bands, a theater that seated almost a thousand people, and an indoor swimming pool and spa, all connected by atriums big enough to drive a tank through. The Adler was the talk of the town.

Then came Prohibition and the world turned upside down. The Adler suffered from the sudden withdrawal of liquor sales just as thousands of bars, saloons and taverns all over the country did. The enormous loan Elmer had taken out depended on revenue from alcohol beverages to cover payments. Every facet of his business took a nosedive during the first years of Prohibition, leaving the Makepeaces drowning in debt they could not begin to service.

I gathered that Elmer was too much the straight arrow to do business with bootleggers, or maybe he did but it still wasn't enough to save him. In any case, balancing on the knife-edge of bankruptcy, he made a deal with Nick Bardo for partnership, which allowed him to limp along for another year or so. Even still, he couldn't cover his own half of the debt. In 1922, Bardo forced a sale of Makepeace's half for peanuts, at which point, as sole owner, Bardo entered into business with Capone to supply liquor and began to revive the hotel's shaky fortunes.

The story begged for details only Nick Bardo or Elmer Makepeace could have supplied. Since both were dead, my only recourse was Ellie Bardo. Would she know anything about her husband's business during those years?

Only one way to find out.

Last year I'd met a reporter from the *Chicago Tribune* while I was investigating one of Carlotta's spirits who turned out to have died of a highly *un*natural cause. Lloyd Prescott and I worked together on that case for several weeks, during which time I'd studied his methods and learned how reporters use their moxie and their press credentials to gain access to places others couldn't go and how to worm information out of people that others didn't dare try. He referred to me as his stenographer or assistant often enough that I almost came to believe it myself! In point of fact, girl reporters were rare, but the *Tribune* did have a few on staff to handle the society column and the homemakers' pages, so the thought of me masquerading as one of them seemed plausible. Lloyd Prescott went along because the stories that came out of our investigations won plaudits from his newsroom bosses. He was willing – even eager – to team up with me as long as he got the rights to the story. In short, any time I wanted to pose as a girl reporter and say I was working with Lloyd Prescott from the *Chicago Tribune*, he would confirm my claim. It was a scam, but it was my way in.

Taking advantage of Tommy's long afternoon nap, I dressed in what I imagined looked like professional girl-reporter clothing – my gray plaid, drop-waist coat-dress with matching cloche hat and gloves, an outfit that was stylish three years ago – and set out for the Bardo house. No guarantee the missus would be home, but bereaved widows seldom venture beyond the front door, so it was a good bet.

After I told the butler I was a reporter for the *Tribune* doing research for an article on the Adler Hotel, he allowed me to come into a marble-floored entrance hall as big as Texas. 'I'll see if Mrs Bardo is in,' he intoned.

She was.

The dour man led me a long dance up two flights of stairs and around several corners until we arrived at an intimate parlor decorated entirely in pink like some little princess's bedroom in a fairytale castle. Ellie Bardo was seated at a dainty writing desk by a window draped with pink lace curtains, her head bent over her work as she scratched away on pink stationery. She did not look up when her butler announced me so I waited in awkward silence, shifting from one foot to the other as I examined the fanciful designs in the pink Persian rug and the pink cabbage-rose wallpaper. It was probably only two or three minutes, but the wait seemed longer. At last she set down her gold fountain pen, blotted the ink, folded the letter carefully, and placed it in a matching envelope which she addressed and sealed with pink wax. Laying it on a silver tray with several others, she acknowledged me at last.

'How can I help you, my dear?' This from a woman younger than myself, but I suppose wealth confers some of the benefits of age.

Ellie Bardo may have begun her career as a risqué burlesque dancer, but there was no denying her poise and beauty. From her corn-silk hair to her painted toenails, she radiated money. It was not hard to imagine how she'd caught the eye of Nick Bardo, a wealthy widower, but no ordinary woman, no matter how pretty, could have snared such a man with looks alone. There was steel in her backbone and a spark from hard flint in those wide eyes that all her efforts to play the gracious lady could not disguise. Ellie Bardo was the sort of woman who got what she went for.

I repeated the story I'd given the butler about writing an article on the hotel. 'I realize you're in deep mourning, Mrs Bardo, so I'm most grateful for a few moments of your time. I had planned to interview your late husband for this, but . . .'

'It will be my pleasure to help you in his place. There is never too much good publicity when it comes to promoting a hotel. It will be *good* publicity, will it not?' she said archly.

'Of course. I've done my homework on the subject of the hotel's early years, when it was built, how it was expanded—'

'With my late husband's money.'

'Precisely. I understood that he first invested in the hotel in 1920?' She confirmed this with a nod. 'Buying half interest in 1920 and the rest in 1921?' She nodded again. 'I wish I could interview Mr Makepeace or your husband about the details, but perhaps you can help me understand how that came about. I've read all the past articles in the newspaper and it seems the hotel fell on hard times when Prohibition struck.'

'I was not married to Mr Bardo then, but I was seeing him and I do recollect the circumstances surrounding the sale of the Adler. The owners, Mr and Mrs Makepeace, had expanded recklessly, taking out huge loans to add amenities and renovate rooms. They overestimated the ability of hotel revenues to repay the debt, and my husband rescued the hotel just in time, saving it from bankruptcy.' She tapped her long fingernails on the desk as she relayed her story.

'That was in 1922?'

'Correct.'

'And the Makepeaces died shortly thereafter. What do you remember about that?'

'Very little. The old woman was a lush. Drank herself to death.' In case that sounded too harsh for a quote she quickly added, 'Poor dear.'

'And Mr Makepeace died the following year?'

'Tragic,' she sighed without the slightest trace of sadness. 'Shot himself, they said. Put a pistol in his mouth and bang! Poor thing. Couldn't take the shame of losing his family's hotel.'

'Weren't there children?'

She shrugged. 'I think so. A son anyway. Lucky for him, the law says you can't inherit the debts of your parents.'

'What do you mean?'

'I mean they didn't just die poor, they died in hock. What's this got to do with the hotel?'

I'd learned what I needed to know, so my questions shifted to something less suspicious. 'Oh, just curiosity, I suppose. Tell me about what your husband did after he took complete ownership of the hotel. What improvements did he make?'

I pretended to take notes as Ellie prattled on about gold-plated silverware in the Regency dining room and the third tap for ice water in each guestroom sink, but my mind had taken a sharp turn toward the crime's solution. Doc Makepeace had to drop out of medical school when Bardo drove his parents so deep into debt they couldn't escape. Both his mother and father were suicides: his mother by liquor, his father by gun. His future ruined, his parents dead, and with no legal remedies available, Doc had taken revenge where he could – by persuading Sebastian Dale to let him help work the Bardo party where he could sneak away from the bar, follow Nick Bardo upstairs, and kill him, laying the blame for his gruesome death on someone else.

TWENTY

For someone looking for personal information about Elmer Makepeace, Ellie Bardo was a poor source. She had known him only superficially, so, still in my reporter guise, I headed to the one place guaranteed to be full of people who had once known him very well: the Adler Hotel.

Two crimson-coated doormen sprang to attention as I climbed the stairs. They swept open the heavy brass doors, bowing as I walked through. The main lobby gleamed with polished brass and white marble floors overlaid with blood-red Persian rugs. Red marble columns reached to the ceiling where they branched out like real trees. I waylaid the first red-jacketed bellhop I saw.

'Can you tell me how long you've worked at the Adler?'

'Three years, madam.'

'I need to speak to someone who has worked here for many years. Ten at least, or twenty. Can you suggest anyone?'

He paused not a second. 'That would be Ben Boardman.' Looking about the cavernous lobby, he soon spotted the man he wanted. 'That's him, there, with the luggage cart. He's worked here since it was built, I think.'

Thanking the bellhop with a quarter, I made my way toward the elderly gent and caught him just as he was about to push his cart into an elevator. Before the doors could close, I slipped in beside him.

'Hello, Mr Boardman, isn't it?'

Surprised eyes raked my figure as if they could identify me by my clothing. 'Yes, madam. Can I be of assistance?'

'I hope so. I'm Phoebe Dressler, a reporter for the *Tribune* working on a story about the old Adler, back in the day when Mr Makepeace ran it. I'm told you've been working here for many years.'

'Twenty-one, madam,' he said with pride.

'Then you are just the person I need to see. Might I have a few minutes of your time?'

The elevator doors opened and we stepped out into a smaller lobby on one of the higher floors. There was no one in sight, no one to disturb us.

'Of course, madam. How can I help?'

'Did you know Mr Elmer Makepeace personally?'

His chest puffed out. 'He was the very one who hired me. I was proud to work for him.'

'And I'm sorry I won't have the chance to interview him myself. His death was so sad. What was he like? As a boss, as a man?'

A faraway look came over his face. 'He was a good man, Miss Dressler. Honest. He demanded hard work from his people but no one worked harder than him. He was here fourteen or fifteen hours a day, seven days a week. I never worked a day that I didn't see him walking through the lobby or taking his meals in one of the restaurants, checking up on everything and everybody.'

'Can you describe him for me? I'd like to include some personal details in the story. Something that would make readers feel like they knew him.'

'Well, he was a good dresser but not showy, if you know what I mean. He greeted me by name every time he saw me and asked how the job was going, how my family was, even remembering the name of my wife. He'd walk the halls every day, and you could tell where he'd been by the scent of his tobacco.'

'Cigarettes?'

'A pipe.'

'He smoked a pipe, did he? Did he favor a particular tobacco?'

'Three Nuns was his preferred. I'd give him a tin for Christmas every year, sort of a thank you, you understand.' He sighed. 'Nothing against Mr Bardo, mind you. That poor fella didn't deserve his end. But you know what they say in the theater world, he had "a tough act to follow". Nowadays, I dunno who's the boss.' His eyes narrowed in speculation. 'Some say it's Al Capone.'

Referrals to a chambermaid on the fourteenth floor and a waitress in the Lakeview Lounge resulted in a few more personal details. Mr Makepeace wore a red carnation in his lapel every day. He never swore except when very angry, at which point he would say 'Shucks' or 'Dang it'. He always carried a pencil and a small notepad to jot down his observations as he walked the hotel corridors. A thoroughly decent man, according to his employees.

TWENTY-ONE

The house I lived in was a simple one, typical of those built just before the turn of the century in Chicago's Near West Side neighborhoods, where houses were planted two together with passageways in between that were barely wide enough for a thin man to walk through. It had three rooms on each floor: a parlor, dining room, and kitchen on the first floor, and three bedrooms and a bathroom on the second. The cellar had a coal furnace at one end and a laundry sink at the other, where I spent many hours scrubbing diapers on the washboard before hauling them up to the kitchen to boil them on the stove – how I wished we could afford a washing machine! (And believe you me, as soon as I could save up ninety dollars, we'd have one.) We'd tricked out the dining room for séances because it gave us access from four sides. Freddy or I could work our magic from the room above, from the basement below, from the kitchen in the back, and from the outside window that opened to the alley. In short, it was the perfect mystic's house.

Which was why I couldn't invite Detective Alice Clement there, lest she realize what Carlotta did for a living. All it would take would be one glance around the parlor with all of Carlotta's crystals, angel figurines, charms, fortune-telling globes and otherworldly bric-a-brac to launch her into another campaign of anti-spiritualist shutdowns, although being out of work might be the least of our troubles. Detective Clement hated spiritualists something fierce. She'd jailed many of them. It terrified me to think that she might find out about my investigations and how Freddy and I bamboozled people into believing they were really in contact with their loved ones.

So when I needed to tell her my suspicions about Doc Makepeace, I didn't dare ask her to my house. Instead I arranged to meet her at that same drugstore by the courthouse where we had met before. I arrived first and snagged the private corner table.

She had news for me too. 'Officer Eisenhart in San Francisco telegraphed this afternoon. She couldn't find our Jane Perry Brent in any city directory. A thorough woman, she even checked outlying cities. No luck.' She sipped her cup of Java and toyed with her long pearl necklace. Real pearls, no doubt. 'I'm afraid we've reached a dead end, Maddie.'

'Not quite. I'm going to check the Chicago area directories just in case Mrs Brent is local.'

'But that roommate told us she came from out of town.'

'The roommate didn't meet her. She just heard about her visit from Eileen Perry. It could have been something she assumed, seeing as how Eileen was from somewhere out west, or it could have been a mistake or even a deliberate lie. It's no trouble for me to check. I go to the library a lot.'

'I suppose there's no harm in it.'

'And I have some news – really good news, I think. I hope. I've discovered something about the second bartender at the Bardo party – Doc, remember him?'

'Yes.'

'His real name is Howard Makepeace, and he's the son of Elmer Makepeace who used to own the Adler Hotel.'

'And?'

'Guess who swindled the Makepeaces out of their hotel? Nick Bardo!'

'And?'

'After Bardo forced Elmer to sell his half interest and then got the other half for a pittance, Mrs Makepeace drank herself to death. Shortly thereafter, Elmer shot himself in the head. Their son, in a riches-to-rags story, had to drop out of medical school and take work as a bartender at Early's. How's that for a revenge motive?'

She turned the idea over in her head for a few minutes.

Impatient, I continued. 'Don't you see? Doc works at Early's. The Bardos come in often. He wants revenge for the theft of his family's hotel and the deaths of his parents. He learns about the Bardo party and asks to work it with Sebastian. During the party, he comes and goes several times from his bar to the kitchen. One of those times, he sees Bardo heading upstairs. There's an argument on the stairs with the son-in-law. Doc follows him up the stairs and into the bedroom where my sister is sleeping. Bardo was supposed to check on her, that's all. He wasn't trying any funny stuff. Doc comes in behind him, grabs the nearest deadly object, and whacks him over the head. Then he goes back to his bar in the dining room.'

'No one saw him go up the stairs.'

'Waiters and waitresses are part of the furniture. No one notices where they go. So, what do you think? A pretty good hypothesis, huh?'

'It certainly is. Good sleuthing, Maddie. I admit I was running out of leads, but this one's worth looking into. I sure would like to be the one to solve this murder. And exonerate your poor sister who's been languishing in jail for far too long.'

'I was turned away the last time I tried to visit her. There wouldn't be any way you could get me past the front desk, is there?'

'I'm afraid not, but I can visit her, and I will. Young girls in trouble are my specialty.'

'Thank you. I appreciate that more than you know.'

'Which is why I'm going to pay a call on that roommate of Little Miss Eileen Perry. What did you say her name was?'

'Daisy King. On Clark Street. When were you thinking about going?'

'Tomorrow. Noon.'

'Daisy won't be there then. She works at a soap factory. Evening would probably find her home. In fact, right now would be good, and we could go together. I know the way.'

Within minutes, we'd paid for our coffee and were on the way in the detective's police car. My prediction proved true – Daisy King answered our knock. We'd disturbed her supper. And an odd supper it looked to be – a plate of delicate, bitesize pretties, little stuffed pastries, and bits of cheese, like you'd serve at a fancy party.

I introduced the two women and was gratified to see that Daisy had remembered what I'd told her about Chicago's famous female detective. 'Detective Clement has taken an interest in Eileen's death,' I said. 'She'd like to ask you a few questions.'

'Gosh, sure, but I don't know what I can tell you. Like I told Mrs Pastore here, I didn't know Eileen very well. She lived with me for only a few weeks.'

'That aunt of hers, what did Eileen tell you about her?' asked the detective.

'Gosh, nothing really. Just that her aunt was in town and came to visit. It was the only person who ever visited Eileen. I was at work at the time, so I didn't meet her.'

'Was Eileen happy to have seen her aunt? Or fearful?'

'Gosh, I didn't notice. I think she just told me she'd had company, that's all.'

'Do you mind if I have a look at her belongings?'

Daisy pointed toward the pile of things on Eileen's narrow bed, her clothing, her jewelry, her books, her knickknacks, and of course, the dulcimer. Detective Clement picked the items up one-by-one and examined each closely while I chatted quietly with Daisy.

'We're closer to learning more about Eileen,' I told her. 'We've discovered her mother died years ago and her father was buried beside her last May. Eileen was their only child. It looks like her father left her some land. Did Eileen ever say anything about any land? It's in Colorado. Did you ever hear her mention Colorado?'

'No, ma'am.'

'We're hoping to find this aunt or some other relative to notify about her death and to send her things, if they want them.'

'If no one wants her things, what would happen to them?'

'I'm sure Eileen would approve of you keeping them.' Daisy's honesty impressed me no end. Anyone else would have sold the dulcimer and jewelry by now. She was the rare sort who gazed unflinchingly at the world and saw only what was decent.

Detective Clement's voice rang out sharply from the other room. 'Look at this, would you?' When Daisy and I came closer, she pointed to the dulcimer strings. When I put out my hand, she snapped, 'Don't touch it!'

She picked up the instrument and carried it close to the one electric lamp in the apartment. She ran her fingers along the three strings. 'Look, there's crust on these strings.' She looked at her fingers. 'It feels rough but there's no rust.' Taking her magnifying glass out of her pocketbook, she looked closely at the strings for a full minute. Straightening up, she turned to Daisy.

'I haven't touched it since she left,' said Daisy with a worried frown. 'I didn't get it dirty.'

'No one's accusing you of anything, dear,' said Detective Clement. 'I need to wash my hands. May I use your sink?'

'Certainly.'

'Did you ever see Eileen play this instrument?'

'Yes, ma'am, several times. It gave her such pleasure. She could sing real pretty too.'

'How did she play it?'

'How? Well, like on her lap, and she didn't use a pick much, just her fingers.'

'Very well. I'm taking this in to the microscopist. What we've got here is a murder case, and a good one. The only thing we're missing is the murderer.'

TWENTY-TWO

The murder of Eileen Perry had nothing to do with my sister's predicament, but if it meant keeping Detective Clement interested in Sophie's case, I'd do anything she asked. It wasn't like I didn't care about poor little Eileen, who after all was just a kid trying to survive in the harsh world of gangland Chicago, but I had enough trouble of my own without adding Eileen's death to my crisis list. I'd been in her shoes, though, so I understood the dangers better than some.

So I plowed ahead with my investigation of Eileen's aunt, Mrs Brent, by scouring the *Chicago City Directory* for her name. And I found her, but only after I'd exhausted the Chicago books and moved to the outlying towns. Daisy was right in her impression that Eileen's aunt had come from out of town. She was listed in the Cicero directory, the town at Chicago's western edge.

City directories usually give the person's address and occupation: painter, tailor, nurse, foreman, salesman, cabinetmaker, clerk, plasterer and so forth. Married women were seldom included and they had no occupation; widows and spinsters usually were. Mrs Brent's inclusion suggested that she was a widow. And indeed, there she was at the very bottom of the page, Mrs Jane Perry Brent, USPHS. It took me several minutes to run down a librarian who could tell me what USPHS stood for.

That haughty man glared past the spectacles at the end of his nose and gave me a lecture about the United States Public Health Service, implying that I was something of a moron for not having known about it all along because it had played such an important role in the reversal of the Chicago River back when I was a child. Seems the agency originated in the early years of the United States when the government set up marine hospitals for sick seamen in major port cities, including Chicago. Their job was noble: to thwart the spread of diseases like yellow fever, smallpox and typhoid fever that are often carried into the United States by sailors from foreign ports and spread through domestic ones. At the turn of the century, Congress expanded the service to include research surrounding the safeguarding of clean public water supplies and the disposal of sewage, all vital to a city's health. And Mrs Brent worked there.

Back home, I asked the operator to connect me to the US Public Health Service building. Yes, said the switchboard girl who answered, Mrs Jane Brent had been employed there for seven years. In the laboratory. Did I want to be put through?

No, I didn't.

I was beginning to follow Detective Clement's train of thought. She had given me the idea; now I could give her the evidence.

'Wonderful sleuthing, Maddie!' she exclaimed when I relayed the information. 'And here's the kicker: the microscopist examined the residue on the dulcimer strings and what do you think he found? Typhoid fever. No wonder Eileen Perry was the only victim of typhoid fever that month – no one else played her dulcimer. Now that I know that the substance came from the USPHS lab, I can arrest Mrs Brent, posthaste. We'll just see what that lady has to say!'

I expressed my delight, careful to play down my own part. 'No doubt this will result in another series of articles in newspapers all over the country,' I said, pouring on the flattery as thick as cream. 'Such fine detective work! I only hope you can work your magic with my sister's case as well.'

'Yes, yes. I am busy pursuing leads there too, especially the one you referred to me about Doc Makepeace. Your theory is certainly valid – many guests noted his trips to and from the dining room bar to the kitchen – and now you've supplied the motive. If I can find a witness to say that he went upstairs after one fifteen, after Nick Bardo and his son-in-law argued, I'd have enough to arrest him. Never a dull moment in fighting crime in the Windy City!'

I had my own idea about cornering Doc into a confession. His séance was coming up on Sunday night.

Last year, when Detective O'Rourke was still Officer

O'Rourke, he visited Carlotta to ask for her assistance in solving murders. Himself a fence-sitter when it came to spiritualism, he couldn't deny her past success at sorting natural deaths from murder, and he became convinced that Madame Carlotta's séances could provide the police with helpful information. I was careful to steer him toward the idea that it was Madame Carlotta who called all the shots, and that I was merely an occasional onlooker at her séances. He knew nothing of the special enhancements Freddy and I provided because we had minimized the spooky parts during the one séance he had attended. O'Rourke was far too perceptive to fall for stunts like the crow on a string or the ghostly violin music. Freddy and I had sworn we'd never host him at another séance – it was too nerve-racking. But now I needed him at a séance. Sunday evening's séance, to be exact.

'Carlotta has a new client,' I told O'Rourke over the telephone. 'Someone who approached her for an appointment, and she thinks he's involved in the murder of Nick Bardo. The man is coming to Sunday's séance and, if she can get him to confess, we want somebody in law enforcement there to witness the confession and arrest him on the spot.'

'I see. And who is this person?'

'Howard Makepeace, also known as Doc. He's a bartender at Early's and worked the Bardo party that night.'

'Makepeace . . . it's a familiar name.'

'His father owned the Adler Hotel until a few years ago when Nick Bardo cheated him out of it. The loss of the hotel caused Doc's mother to drink herself to death and his father shot himself shortly thereafter.'

'Now I remember. They were deep in debt. Bardo owned lots of watering holes that threw off enough income to buy the Adler. For a song, if my memory serves.'

'It serves. Doc had to drop out of medical college when the family went under. He had at least three reasons to kill Bardo: to avenge the loss of his parents, his medical career and his inheritance.'

'You say he contacted Madame Carlotta to arrange for a séance? Does that seem rather suspicious to you?'

'I admit it's a coincidence, but Madame Carlotta does

advertise in three newspapers. So do other fortune tellers and spiritualists, but Makepeace said he chose her because she was the closest mystic to where he lives. There's a slim possibility he's setting her up for something, but I think he's legit. He wants to contact his parents, probably to let them know he's avenged them. And if he says anything like that during the séance, I'll need you there with your handcuffs. He won't know you're a cop until the end, or not at all if things don't go as I think they will.'

'And if you're wrong?'

'You've wasted an hour.'

'What if he doesn't connect with the spirits?'

'Carlotta will make sure she puts on a convincing performance in order to draw him out. She'll have some eerie candles and some extra features that'll add to the supernatural atmosphere. You know, this is just the sort of thing you asked Carlotta to help you with, and the results should put a murderer behind bars. Are you game?'

'What time?'

TWENTY-THREE

The following evening, after I had put Tommy down at his usual seven o'clock bedtime, finished ironing his clothes, and pinned the day's diapers on the line outside, I heard the clock strike eight. I was tired but restless and not ready for bed. I'd've considered a game of chess with Freddy but he was already at Carl's, playing against skilled opponents who could give him a more challenging run for his money than I ever could. Carlotta and a neighbor were knitting mittens in the sitting room, giggling like girls over some neighborhood gossip.

'Carlotta,' I said, throwing my coat on over my plain skirt and cardigan. 'I think I'll pop over to the Greengrocer's for a bit. I won't be long.'

'Have fun, dear.'

The convenience of having a speakeasy at the end of your block was indescribably comforting. The Greengrocer's was a cozy place that drew neighbors from several blocks, and I always seemed to know someone there, no matter the time of day or night. It was safe too. No long walk in the dark, no boisterous strangers, no chance of accidentally drinking deadly rotgut, and Mrs Ward wasn't harassed by police or gangsters because she never bought any liquor. She was still working off the supply her late husband had laid up before his tragic demise. She expected it to last for years.

'Got the baby to bed, did you?' called Molly, a cheerful mother of six who lived two houses down from us. She was there with her husband, a foreman at a pants factory.

'I sure did. And finished the laundry.'

'You've earned your drink, hon.'

'I agree.' I laughed, and stepped to the little bar where one of the Ward girls was mixing drinks. 'Tommy started walking this week.'

'Now that's something worth celebrating! Hey, you'll be

needing shoes for him now, won't you? Our Johnnie has grown
out of his two-year-old shoes – his feet grow so fast, I don't
think he wore those more than ten times. They're nearly new.
Can Tommy use them?'

'Thank you, yes. That's very kind of you.'

'Oh pooh, it gets 'em outa my house, that's all! I'll put 'em
on your front steps tomorrow.'

I ordered a lemonade with gin. Next to me at the bar were
Ed Gilligan and a man I didn't recognize, slumped on their
elbows congratulating themselves on the Cubs' victory over
the Brooklyn Robins in the twelfth inning.

'Petey's arm was hot, that's for sure. And for him to
get the winning run! Man!'

'And Staley. No one's better than him. Oh, good evening
to you, Maddie.'

'Good evening, gentlemen.' Ed Gilligan was a freckled
young man with a new wife and a baby on the way. I liked
them both, but being around them reminded me of how Tommy
and I were, not so long ago, and that made me sad.

'You don't know Ray here, do you? He's my cousin who
just moved to Chicago from the farm in Moline for a job. Ray
Miller, meet Maddie Pastore from across the street.'

'Welcome to Chicago, Ray. Where will you be working?'

'Ed got me a place at the Kraft factory. Fifty cents an hour
to start.'

'He's staying with Marge and me 'til he gets his feet on
the ground,' explained Ed. 'That way he can save up a few
bucks for a place of his own.'

'Good luck to you, Mr Miller. I hope Chicago living agrees
with you.'

'It ain't the farm, and that sure agrees with me.'

When at last I sat down with my drink, it was with Jenny
and Louise, spinster sisters in their forties who taught fifth
and seventh grades at the local school. The two women couldn't
have been more different in appearance: Jenny was tall and
thin with dark, gray-streaked hair and a hook nose; Louise
was short, fair and plump with a perpetual smile. Some whispered that they weren't sisters at all, but I had too many secrets
of my own to be nosing into whatever others wanted to keep

quiet. We had an unspoken agreement: they didn't pry into my life and I didn't pry into theirs. It was always comfortable in their company.

I mostly listened as they recounted their day at school, making the children's antics and lessons sound funny and fun. Clearly, they enjoyed their work and their pupils – the kind of teacher every mother wishes for her children: kind but firm. I hoped they would still be teaching when Tommy was old enough to start school – then I remembered that we wouldn't be living here by then. All at once, the two women stopped talking and looked up at something – or someone – behind me. I turned around.

'Why, Detective O'Rourke! Fancy seeing you here! I didn't know you frequented the Greengrocer's.'

'Good evening, Mrs Pastore. It's my first visit. Madame Carlotta told me you were here and I decided to have a look at the place. I've heard about it.'

I introduced the teachers who invited him to join us, but he declined. 'I'll just get myself a drink and make myself at home over there,' he said, indicating some empty seats near the bar.

Clearly, he had come down into the speakeasy looking for me. He must have had something to tell me. Good news, I hoped. 'Excuse me, please,' I said to the teachers. 'I need a refill and I see the detective has come to talk.'

The women exchanged meaningful glances that told me exactly what they were thinking. They were wrong, but I could hardly contradict them without looking silly. 'Shoo, then, Maddie, shoo,' said Louise, waving her hands like she was shooing chickens. 'We'll talk another time.'

'What are you drinking?' asked O'Rourke when I joined him.

'Lemonade with gin.'

He motioned with one arm and pointed at my glass. The Ward girl got the message and brought another drink to the table. 'Nice place, this,' he began.

'Yes, it opened last year after Mr Ward died and his wife found a huge stash of liquor – every bottle legal – behind a false wall. But you didn't come to see the Greengrocer's. Do you have some news for me?'

'Nothing of substance. While I was at the jail today on other business, I stepped over to the women's side to check on your sister.'

I envied detectives and police officers who could come and go at the jail whenever they liked. 'How did she seem today?'

'She's coping, but, well, it's a miserable place to be. I was able to bring her a newspaper, for what it's worth . . . Not much.'

'That was very kind of you. Thank you.'

'You might get her lawyer to bring her a sweater. The night air has turned pretty cold and they haven't turned on the heat yet. The inmates are walking around wrapped in their blankets.'

'I will. Right away.'

'Are you and Detective Clement making any headway on her case?'

'No stirring successes so far, but I'm optimistic.'

'She's a good investigator. One of the best.' But he said it grudgingly.

'You don't sound convinced.'

'Not at all. I'm plenty convinced. Alice has nabbed an impressive number of crooks in her day and she doesn't get the vapors when the going gets tough. She was on the force when I first joined, eleven years ago. She was already a detective then, so she has far more experience than I do.'

'But?'

'She has precious few friends on the force. Her manner is, well . . . you've seen her. She's boastful and theatrical, always snatching at publicity and putting others down. Whenever the Lady Detective solves a case, it's front-page news plus a photograph in every Chicago newspaper and half the papers around the country. When a male detective solves a big case, it might warrant two column inches on page fourteen. And that moving picture she made!'

'You're envious.'

He winced at my accusation. 'I don't like to think so, but there could be something to that. We all like to be recognized for good work. Anyway, she's pushing the limits of Chief McWeeny's patience.'

'You just don't want to see a woman in a man's job.'

'On the contrary, I'd like to see *more* women officers and detectives on the force. They can often do things the men can't, and they relate better to female suspects, not to mention children. If anything, being less unusual would pare back Alice's pretensions, which might result in a longer, happier career for her. But McWeeny isn't keen on welcoming another Mrs Clement onto his force, so I'm thinking it won't happen any time soon.'

We sipped our drinks in silence and listened to the jazz piano music coming from the radio. The announcer said the time was nine o'clock.

'Why did you join the police back then? Eleven years ago, you said.'

'Well, let's see now, I'd graduated from high school and gotten a job in a bicycle factory that was owned by the uncle of a friend. I worked there for two years give-or-take, when it went bust.'

'What a shame!'

'The guy was a drunkard and a bully and dumb as a brick on his best day, but we made good bicycles until we didn't. My friend started his own business repairing bicycles and invited me to partner with him, but I was ready for something else. That was the year the Great War started in Europe. Another friend told me the police department was hiring, and there was a lot of appeal for me in that. I envisioned myself as being one of the good guys, protecting the public from crooks. A genuine hero.' He smiled at the boyish vision.

'And it didn't work out that way?'

'Reality beat out romance. When America joined the war in 1917, my brother Liam was drafted. I tried to volunteer to go with him, but my job was deemed an "essential occupation". So I did not serve my country.'

I thought of my husband's short stint in the army. He'd been drafted, trained and shipped to France with a unit that arrived two weeks before the armistice, so he never saw combat. Never felt he deserved the parades that marched every Armistice Day. I put a flag and poppies on his grave last November for Armistice Day, and I was determined to do so again with little Tommy every year until I died. He had earned a parade.

'Yes, you did. Just not in France. You are still serving.'

He grinned and ran his fingers through his curly hair. 'The job sure is different from when I started.'

'I guess so. Prohibition has turned Chicago into gangland. "Square Deal" Dever promised to clean up the city if he got elected mayor, but I don't see a shred of improvement over Big Bill Thompson and he's had two years to wash the filth away.'

'At least Mayor Dever is honest. The gangs don't control him. But that's why he won't be reelected. Thompson was in cahoots with Capone. They say he's still on the Outfit payroll. They're scheming to get him back into office in '27 and they'll do it too.'

'It's disgusting.'

'Mind you, there was crime before Prohibition. But it was mostly gambling, prostitution, robberies, fistfights and such – all bad things, for sure, but not terribly violent. And not organized beyond a few local toughs working together. With Prohibition, it's torture, gruesome murders, gun battles in the streets and a level of violence we just didn't see before, all run by gangs made up of hundreds of men with tentacles that stretch across the country. Even overseas. With so much money in play, they can control the politicians and the police and we can't touch 'em.'

That part I knew. The gangs had controlled my husband, luring him into their spider web of crime by offering three times what he was making at his honest delivery job.

'I estimate at least half the Chicago force gets gang money. Probably more like two-thirds. Think about it – they offer a cop a month's pay *not* to walk down a certain street of his beat at a certain time of night; he'd be a fool not to take it.'

And O'Rourke was no fool.

TWENTY-FOUR

'Now we'll all join hands to symbolize the circle of life,' intoned Madame Carlotta as she reached out, 'and we'll begin the never-ending journey toward spiritual fulfillment offered to all souls but accepted by few.' And with that she bowed her head and began chanting the Lord's Prayer. Except for the bayberry-scented candle burning in the center of the table, the room was dark.

'Wait.' Howard 'Doc' Makepeace interrupted the prayer. 'I want to change seats.'

Ah, suspicion. He had already thoroughly examined the chairs for false bottoms and the table legs for secret compartments, and he'd established that the spirit box in the corner was empty. He didn't find the trap door in the floor because we had covered it with a large rug. He wouldn't see the sliding door in the ceiling medallion where the electric chandelier attaches because no one ever thinks to look up when invited to search the room. He didn't notice the pinhole openings in the wall separating the séance room from the kitchen because they were obscured by the busy floral wallpaper. He wouldn't hear any of the tiny scratching noises that came from movements Freddy or I would make because they were obscured by the hum of the electric fan. And not once had anyone suspected a shill was sitting beside them. Moving seats was Doc's last-ditch attempt to forestall any prearranged tricks that might be targeting him in some way, and it was fine with me. We didn't care where anyone sat as long as I was beside Carlotta.

'Certainly, Mr Makepeace,' Carlotta said without any indication that his request ruffled her feathers. It didn't. Amenable as always to her clients' whims, she offered the chair on her right. 'Why don't you take Mr O'Rourke's chair. You don't mind, do you, Mr O'Rourke?'

'Happy to oblige.'

Doc's move put him and me on either side of Carlotta, leaving O'Rourke seated between us at the small round table we used when there were four or fewer clients. Carlotta resumed her prayer, her voice growing softer and breathier with every passing minute until it matched the pitch of the electric fan on the floor.

'Dear Lord, who commands the day and night, the heavens and earth, the past and future, look with favor, we beseech you, on our work tonight as we pierce the dark veil of death and commune with those who have crossed over to your everlasting glory. I call on the archangel Michael to bless us with his presence tonight . . . *Esto nobis pregustatum in mortis examine.* Are you there, most beloved of all God's angels? Can you hear my voice, sense my plea? Come to us tonight . . . communicate with us mortals . . . forge the bonds that link us to our loved ones who dwell within your realm.'

No response from the Great Beyond. She continued, adding to her string of Latin gobbledygook to up the ante.

'We beseech thee, blessed archangel, bring us the spirits of those to whom we wish to commune tonight . . . *Ave verum corpus natum* . . . Favor us with a visit from the spirit of Tommaso Pastore, beloved of his wife who is with us tonight . . . *vere passum immolatum in cruce pro homine* . . . Can Tommaso Pastore be found, O Great Archangel of God?'

The candle flame flickered wildly and was snuffed out by a gust from Freddy's bellows, plunging the room into pitch black. O'Rourke's fingers squeezed mine – was the brave cop perhaps a bit nervous or was he trying to reassure me? This was only his second séance and we'd kept the first very tame. It felt too awkward to return the gesture, so I kept my fingers still.

Evidently the archangel Michael had decided to join us but not to speak, for the next voice we heard was Freddy's through the speaking tube he'd lowered under cover of darkness. His hoarse whisper, eerily similar to my late husband's, floated down as if from a cloud.

'I am heeeere.'

'Tommy? Tommy, is that you?'

'I am here, beloved.'

'Oh, Tommy, I am so happy to hear from you. I've missed you so.'

'And I you.'

'Every day, every night, I think of you and wish you were here with me. With our son.'

'Our boy . . .'

'I named him after you. He looks like you . . . especially his eyes. Sometimes, when I hold him close and look deep into his dark eyes, I see you.' My voice cracked a little. I cleared my throat and reminded myself sternly that I wasn't talking to my husband. I knew that very well, but somehow, tonight, in the dark, I could almost believe he was there, above me, beside me, listening to me, understanding how much I had loved him. And loved him still.

'He started walking this week. His first baby steps. He was holding onto the coffee table and scooting along when all of a sudden, he let go and took four steps – four! – toward me. You should have seen his little face! His eyes went wide like he knew what he'd done. He looked so proud. And a bit stunned too. I thought of you, and how you would have been proud to see his first steps.' I tried to blink back the tears that pooled in the corners of my eyes, but one trickled down my cheek, and I couldn't release the hands I was holding to brush it away.

'I am proud of him,' came the ethereal voice. 'And of you, my own dearest heart.'

That stiffened my spine – Tommy would never have called me 'my own dearest heart'. I'd have to coach Freddy in some more appropriate phrases.

'And he's so good. He hardly ever cries, just smiles and laughs when I tickle his tiny little toes. You would love him so much.'

'I do love him. And you . . .' The voice faded to a whisper and was drowned out by the purr of the fan.

Carlotta filled the stillness with more Latin, then concentrated on Doc.

'Dear Michael, there is one with us tonight who would commune with his parents. Can you bring Elmer Makepeace to his son tonight? Or his mother, Dorothy Makepeace?'

I could sense Doc squirming in the chair across from me. I tensed. I was about to learn if I'd brought O'Rourke here on a fool's errand.

'There are two possibilities as I see it,' I'd told O'Rourke earlier that evening. 'Why did he call Madame Carlotta for a séance? He said he wanted to reach his parents. Sure, lots of her clients want that. But why? He didn't say, but I believe there are two possibilities. One, he wants to know if his father really is in heaven.'

'Why would he doubt that?'

'His father killed himself.'

'Who told you that?'

'I figured it out. He died shortly after his wife's death and his bankruptcy, and he wasn't buried with his wife and their small child. Those two were interred in a Catholic cemetery. He wasn't.'

O'Rourke's lips tightened. He was raised Catholic too. 'And self-murder is a mortal sin, so he couldn't be buried with his family.'

'In which case, Carlotta's intermediary, Archangel Michael, wouldn't be able to find him in Heaven, just like he couldn't find Capone's brother Frank last year.'

'And the other possibility?'

'That he wants to tell his parents he's avenged them by doing away with Nick Bardo.'

'If that's true, he's hardly going to blurt out in the middle of a séance, "I brained Nick Bardo with a candlestick."'

'Probably not, but he'll at least allude to it, hopefully with enough detail that you can take him in for questioning, if not arrest him outright.'

I never knew what Carlotta would do during her séances. She didn't either. I could only coach her so far, give her what information I'd uncovered, and hope her instincts would carry the day. So I waited, my heart in my throat, and prayed Freddy's quick reactions would fill any holes. After a long minute, Carlotta broke the silence. With the gravelly voice she thought passed for something angelic, she intoned, 'The holy spirit of Elmer Makepeace has come to speak to his son.' Then she lightened her tone and whispered, 'I am here.'

Freddy's timing was dead on. He'd lit up a pipe full of Three Nun tobacco and as soon as Carlotta began channeling Elmer, he sent its smoke gusting down to the séance room through the speaking tube. Doc didn't react but he couldn't have missed the familiar scent.

'Dad? Is that you?'

'I am here.'

'And Mother?'

'We are here. Beside you. Our beloved son.'

I let go of Carlotta's hand and raised my own up as high as I could reach, palm out, so the glow of the Undark paint would be visible. Freddy had drawn a face on my palm, one that tried to resemble the photo we had of Elmer Makepeace from the newspaper that showed a thin goatee and pencil mustache. Of course it was nowhere close to a decent approximation of the man, but suggestion counts for much in the spiritualism business. And this time, Doc reacted, drawing in a sharp breath before replying.

'I miss you. I miss you both. Where are you? In heaven?'

'More colors than there are on earth, unimaginable beauty, more vivid . . . angelic forces . . . Here there is no old . . . no young . . . no sick . . . the Lord is on his throne and angels like stars gather round . . . God wipes away every tear . . . no death, no sorrow, no crying . . . No more pain, for all former things have passed away.' I sprinkled red carnation petals around the table to remind Doc of his father's boutonniere when the lights came up.

'I wanted to tell you, the evil one is dead. Dead at last and surely in Hell.'

'No need for revenge . . . the Lord will judge.'

'I wanted revenge for what he did to you, to me. I planned it. I wanted to do it. I bought arsenic to put in his drink at the nightclub where I work. He was a regular patron. But when I saw how the waitresses sometimes mixed up the drinks on their trays, I couldn't do it that way. I couldn't risk the wrong person getting the drink.'

'You did right, my son.'

'But then, I heard about a house party and I got my boss to include me. I brought the poison to my bar station and tried

to make a drink that I could hand directly to him. To be sure
he drank it. I had his drink, a Sidecar. I knew he wouldn't
taste anything unusual in it. I handed it to him. Then his wife
came up and told him to go upstairs and check on a girl, the
performer who had gotten sick, and he set the drink down and
left. Next thing I knew, he was dead. Somebody – not me –
whacked him over the head. I wanted you to know, he's dead,
and I'm glad, but I didn't do it. I wanted to. I wish I had, but
it's done now.'

'Praise be, dear son, the sin is not yours. You must put aside
your anger now and look to the future. Your future. Find a
woman, a good woman like your mother. Have a family. Be
content. Covet not thy neighbor's house, nor any thing that is
thy neighbor's.'

'I understand. I just wanted you to know. I didn't want you
to think I'd done it.'

'We will not be parted for long . . . You will come home
to the glory of God . . . where sin and violence do not exist.
I wait to welcome you . . . into the house of the Lord.'

Carlotta's voice trailed off. The séance was over. And Sophie
was no closer to being released.

TWENTY-FIVE

'**W**e need to talk,' I said as I pushed my empty dessert plate back a couple of inches and leaned my elbows on the table. The séance was over; all clients had departed. Little Tommy was asleep. I couldn't put this off any longer. 'I should have come to you sooner with this problem. I'm sorry, but I was hoping it would disappear and I wouldn't need to ever mention it.'

Carlotta and Freddy were looking worried now, so I pressed on quickly. 'We've been caught up in one of Hymie Weiss's plans to kill Capone. He's forced me to invite Capone here for a séance with his dead brother Frank on the thirtieth. That's Wednesday. Weiss's men will be hiding somewhere and kill him while he's at the séance table.'

'Capone will never come here again,' protested Freddy. 'Remember what happened last time.'

'Tell that awful Hymie Weiss there's no place here for his men to hide,' said Carlotta.

'Remember Dan Raymond and his fireman brother?' I asked. Carlotta frowned. Freddy nodded. Of course he did. He remembered everything, no matter how trivial. 'Turns out Dan Raymond was here on Weiss's orders, to scope the layout. He told Weiss where they could hide.'

The parlor clock ticked off the silent seconds as Carlotta and Freddy digested this information. Freddy reached the conclusion first. 'We'll get killed in the shoot-out. On purpose probably. No witnesses.'

'The baby . . .' Carlotta breathed weakly. 'You can tell Capone, can't you? Warn him off. He cares about the baby, doesn't he?'

Well, no, he didn't; not really, but I didn't say that. Freddy provided the answer. 'If she warns Capone off, Weiss kills her. Us too. If she doesn't and Weiss succeeds, Capone's men shoot her in revenge. Us too.'

Carlotta's hand flew to her mouth. Her worried expression changed to fear.

'I've gone over every possibility a hundred times and the only sensible plan I can come up with is for us to leave town. Not too soon, not until Wednesday morning. The way I figure it, we each pack a box or valise with the essentials and take it – separately – to the train station sometime during the next two days. Leave it in a locker. Then on Wednesday morning, we disguise ourselves and slip away to the train station – separately, so we don't look like three people traveling together. Carlotta can bring Tommy. We'll take the train to Aurora, sitting in separate cars or even taking different trains. In Aurora, I've got rooms at a small hotel where we can stay while we look for a place to rent.'

'Will anyone follow us, do you think?' Carlotta's voice trembled. She took a handkerchief from her sleeve and blotted her eyes.

'Not if we're careful.'

'Maybe we should go further. Like California.'

I know what Carlotta was thinking. Her daughter, my school chum from twenty years ago, lived in southern California. 'Lots of people around here know that your Alice and her family live in California. That would be the first place a gangster would look, and we'd be placing Alice's family in danger. No, I think Aurora would be good because none of us has any ties there. And we'll change our names, of course.' That part went down hard with me. I was proud of my husband's name, Pastore, and would regret tossing it aside, especially for little Tommy.

We talked of other details, how Carlotta could start up her new business, how we could hire a lawyer to sell this house, and what we might take with us and what we would have to leave behind. In his mind, Freddy was already sorting through his special enhancements, dividing those he would take from those that could be replaced easily later. Carlotta was looking longingly at her curio cabinet where her collection of spiritual knickknacks was stashed. I could almost see her wondering whether they could be packed up and shipped to Aurora.

'I've never been to Aurora,' she said timidly. 'In fact, I've never been outside of Chicago, even for a day.'

'Me neither,' said Freddy.

'Me neither. But it's supposed to be a nice town, and we'll have each other. It'll be an adventure!' I tried to inject some enthusiasm into my voice, but it fell flat. What the hell – we had no choice. They knew it and I knew it. I just hoped Weiss and Capone didn't know it.

TWENTY-SIX

'The Perry case is closed, Maddie,' crowed Detective Alice Clement when she telephoned me Monday morning. 'I've solved it.'

'I am delighted to hear that, Detective.'

'With your help, of course.'

'A few suggestions are all I contributed,' I protested. I couldn't afford to have my name associated with anything like this. 'All credit goes to you.'

'Everything will come out in the papers soon, here and in San Francisco as well. I made sure to mention Officer Eisenhart's help.'

'That was most generous of you. Have you arrested Mrs Brent?'

'On my way to the Public Health Service building now. I've got an officer with me, but there's room in the motorcar for you if you care to come along.'

'I wouldn't miss it for the world!'

'We'll stop at your house in an hour. What's your address?'

'Please don't go to the trouble. I'll meet you out front of the Public Health Service building in an hour.'

I was standing in front of the stern-looking façade of the Public Health center when the police car pulled up to the curb. Detective Clement introduced me to her uniformed driver, Officer Robert Ryan, a reedy young man with curly red hair sticking out from under his cap. He was armed, as was Detective Clement, but he looked like a good gust of wind might blow him out to sea. No doubt the authorities figured arresting a lone woman wouldn't require much in the way of brute strength. I followed the pair into the building where they showed their badges to the receptionist, a watery-eyed man with sniffles and a cough who was plainly awed by the presence of Chicago's famous female detective.

'Yes, ma'am. Right away . . . Mrs Jane Brent . . . let's

see . . . she works in the lab on the sixth floor. Room 635.'
When he reached for the telephone, Detective Clement laid a
hand on his arm.

'We don't want to warn her that we're coming, if you please.'

'Oh. Yeah. Sure. I understand. Of course. Go right on up
then. Elevator's over there. And, if I might be so bold, good
luck to you, Mrs Clement. You're an inspiration.'

The strong smell of rubbing alcohol greeted us as we stepped
off the elevator and onto the sixth-floor corridor. With its
linoleum floor scrubbed so clean you could eat off it and
its windows polished so clear the glass practically vanished,
the place had the sterile feel of a hospital ward. Men and
women in white lab coats bustled about importantly, sending
us many a curious glance but no direct challenges as we
made our way down the hall toward room number 635.
Detective Clement did not knock, but entered boldly. Six or
seven people looked up with surprise at the interruption.

The large room was crowded with desks piled high with
files and impressive-looking books. Black laboratory counters
were topped with microscopes, burning equipment, mysterious
vials, sinks and measuring devices, none of it recognizable to
a girl like me who never finished high school. Electric wires
ran helter-skelter, tangling with rubber tubes. Shelves crammed
with hundreds of glass bottles of all shapes and sizes, neatly
marked with paper labels, lined the walls. Doors marked
STORAGE and SUPPLIES hung open to smaller rooms
packed with boxes and jumbles of scientific paraphernalia.

Work ceased at our entrance. Workers froze.

'I'm Detective Alice Clement,' came her commanding
voice. 'I am looking for Mrs Jane Brent.'

All heads turned as one toward a middle-aged woman seated
on a stool beside a sink, washing glass vials. One vial fell
from her hands and smashed to bits against the porcelain basin.
Her face turned white as paper. Her lips moved, but no sound
emerged. Her eyes told us she knew why we had come.

Jane Brent stood and staggered a few steps toward us, one
hand reaching out as if in supplication. Then her eyes rolled
back in her head and she crumpled to the floor in a dead faint.

Several men sprang to her assistance. Someone stuck a bottle of smelling salts under her nose, jerking her back to bewildered consciousness. When she caught sight of the detective and the uniformed cop at her side, she burst into tears.

'Mrs Jane Perry Brent,' intoned Detective Clement, 'you are under arrest for the murder of Eileen Perry.' Her colleagues reacted with gasps and soft cries.

Crying, then sobbing wildly, she broke down completely. 'Yes, yes. I'm so sorry. Yes, I did it. I'm sorry. It was wicked, wicked, yes, but I was driven mad by greed.'

'You wanted title to her father's land?'

'Yes, yes. In Colorado. They found gold on the property. Lots of gold. I knew I was my brother's next of kin, should anything happen to Eileen. She knew nothing about her father's land. I'm so sorry. I shouldn't have done it. So wicked . . .'

'Where did you get the typhoid fever germs?'

'Here,' she hiccupped. 'Here in the lab. I took a petri dish with some of the bacteria. So small, no one noticed it missing. Just a tiny bit.' The others in the lab gasped at the confession.

'You took it to her home intending to infect her, didn't you?'

'I was going to leave a trace on her toothbrush or drinking glass,' she gulped. 'But when she played her dulcimer, I saw her lick her fingers to turn the pages of her music, and I knew that was a safer method. A drinking glass might be used by someone else, and I wouldn't get a second chance. No one else would touch the dulcimer.'

'We tested it. The strings were crusty with poisoned residue.'

'I'm so sorry, so sorry . . . greed made me do it. I'm so ashamed, so sorry. What will happen to me?'

'That's for the jury to decide, Mrs Brent. Come now. We're going down to the police station.' She signaled to Officer Ryan to help the woman up.

Still sobbing, Mrs Brent blotted her face on a handkerchief. 'Wait, just a minute, please. Let me retrieve my handbag.' She motioned to a door that opened into an adjacent office with a small window.

Detective Clement nodded her permission and the distraught woman limped into the room. Seconds later, there came a wild scream. Officer Ryan rushed into the room with the detective on his heels, but it was too late. Mrs Brent lay on the ground, blood gushing from a wound in her throat. A penknife lay on the floor beside her. Officer Ryan tried to staunch the flow of blood with his handkerchief but she bled to death in seconds, moaning, 'I'm so sorry, I'm so sorry,' over and over until she gurgled her last breath.

No one in the laboratory moved. No one even breathed. The silence grew louder, until finally Detective Clement took charge. 'All right, everyone here is a witness,' she said, her voice booming throughout the laboratory. 'Maddie, write down the names of every person in this room. Only then can they leave.' She looked down on the lifeless form of Mrs Brent and continued in the dispassionate tone of someone who has seen way too much violence. 'A pity, yes, but I can only believe she preferred this to the hangman's noose, which was a certainty in her case. Where is the nearest telephone, if you please?'

Speechless, I pictured tomorrow's grisly headlines and the accolades that would follow. Detective Clement had solved another important case, a death that had been ruled from natural causes but turned out to be murder most foul. The incident would reverberate across the country and her star, already high in the sky, would shine even brighter. Yet I had to admit she was right – the poor woman would have endured a grisly trial or, if she pled guilty, a quick death sentence, and I understand hanging is not a pleasant way to go. I could not mourn Mrs Brent. My sympathies lay with young Eileen Perry, whose life was over before it had started. A girl unlucky enough to have had an evil aunt who would kill her own niece for title to a goldmine. Little Miss Eileen Perry, seventeen years old forever.

TWENTY-SEVEN

My head was so full of the death of Mrs Brent that Sophie and her troubles got pushed to the back of my mind. So later that night I telephoned Detective Clement to bring her up to date with my news about Doc.

'What was the reaction at the police station about Mrs Brent's death?' I asked.

Her voice sounded slurred. I guessed she'd been celebrating her triumph. 'An unfortunate occurrence, but a satisfactory outcome all in all, since there was a clear confession, heard by a dozen people, and it saved the city the cost of a trial and execution.'

'What do you think?'

'About what?'

'About the way the case ended.'

'Frankly, I wish she hadn't cheated the hangman,' she said, sniffing. 'That poor girl . . . her whole life ahead of her. I care about Chicago's girls, Maddie. I really do.'

'Then I'm afraid I have discouraging news about the Bardo murder. Remember I was sure the bartender had done it?'

'Yes, you told me about him. Doc Makepeace, the son of the disgraced former owner of the Adler.'

'I was right in part – he did plan to kill Bardo. Went so far as to put arsenic in his drink. But before Bardo could drink the poisoned cocktail, someone else bludgeoned him to death. It wasn't Doc.'

She could hear the defeat in my voice. Doc was my best – and last – suspect, and with him out of the picture, I didn't know what else to do. Detective Clement was Sophie's only chance. I was about to flee Chicago and leave Sophie's fate in the detective's hands. I had failed my sister.

'You must have some other ideas,' I pleaded. 'Some other avenues to investigate. You're so very clever at solving crimes and protecting young women from danger. You couldn't save poor little Eileen Perry, but you could still save Sophie Dale.'

'Look here, Maddie. I'll be honest with you. I wanted to help your sister, I really did. I believed you when you said she was innocent. And I even believe that *she* believes it. But the evidence is simply overwhelming. Ellie Bardo and Sebastian Dale escorted a drunk or sick woman upstairs. Ellie returns downstairs and never goes back up. Shortly thereafter she asks her husband to check on your sister. We can trace Nick Bardo's movements right up to the point when he put his hand on the doorknob to the room where your sister was resting. There were people in the hall who could testify that no one else entered the room after Bardo. He pushed himself on your sister. She pushed back; not very hard because the fight left no marks. She grabbed the nearest thing and hit him. Several times. She collapsed back on the bed. There just isn't anything more to investigate.'

'There must be something else . . .'

'You can do something. You can help her by offering to testify to her character. Her lawyer will want to use you and perhaps some others for that. It's highly unlikely that she'll get a death sentence. More like a few years in prison. You have to accept the facts.'

My throat had closed up too tight for a reply. Finally I squeezed out a feeble, 'Yes, thank you,' and hung up. A few years in prison. How many? Ten? Twenty? Would Sebastian be waiting for her when she got out? Would she get out? Plenty of people died in prison from the bad conditions, terrible food and rampant disease.

To add insult to misery, I realized I hadn't heard from Hymie Weiss like I thought I would. The séance date was approaching and I hadn't cleared it with him. I thought I'd better try to contact him, so I called the number he'd given me earlier. However, this time, there was no old lady on the other end of the line. There was no one at all; the harsh bell just rang and rang until the operator cut it off. I understood. People like Hymie Weiss and Al Capone did not like to use the telephone because they suspected the cops were listening in or that the operators were in cahoots with the cops, eavesdropping on selected conversations and reporting back to the police. Those new direct-dial telephones that bypassed the operator were much in demand but converting the entire city would take years. Meanwhile, Weiss would not risk ruin by exchanging any pertinent information over the telephone. We would have to meet in person. I would have to wait until he was ready. Until he contacted me.

I thought he might come for me in a big motorcar like Capone did, but no. He sent his thugs to fetch me the next morning in an ordinary yellow-and-black taxicab. That's why no one on my block thought anything of it when I climbed into the cab in front of my house. The only unusual thing was the extra man who rode shotgun – literally – alongside the driver.

'Where are we going?' I asked without much hope of an answer. The men in front didn't even turn around. After a few blocks, I guessed we were heading toward Schofield's florist shop, located on North State Street comfortably inside North Side Gang territory.

But no. To my surprise, the cab pulled over to the curb in front of Holy Name Cathedral opposite the florist. Both men escorted me up the steps, through the main entrance, and inside the most beautiful church in Chicago.

My lungs filled with the calming scent of frankincense. Sunlight pierced the jewel-like colors of the stained-glass windows, bathing the cold white marble pillars in a warm glow – beauty that went unappreciated in my current state of anxiety. One of Weiss's bodyguards jerked his thumb toward the altar but the cathedral was empty. Where was I to go? They planted themselves beside the racks of flickering prayer candles where they could turn away anyone who tried to enter. I stood, uncertain of how to proceed, when the door to a confessional opened and Hymie Weiss stepped out. With a glance in my direction to acknowledge my presence, he moved to the center of the nearest pew and sat. Waiting for me.

A priest exited the other side of the confessional and made his way to the altar where he began rearranging altar linens. Must have been his last confession of the day. There was no one else in sight. I wondered if he had emptied the church of parishioners for this meeting with the notorious gang leader.

My footsteps tapped weirdly on the cold stone floor, but Weiss didn't turn until I reached his pew. Then he twisted his lips in what I supposed was meant to be a smile.

'Welcome, Mrs Pastore,' he said. 'Come. Sit. We have much to discuss, and I have no time to waste. Cut to the chase.'

'I did as you ordered. I met with Mr Capone and told him his brother had been prayed out of purgatory with all the masses they bought and was in heaven now, wanting to speak with him. We settled on tomorrow, Wednesday, at seven o'clock. He'll be there.'

'Nicely done, Mrs Pastore. You have great potential for a woman. I knew you would come through for us.'

'So now what do I do?'

'Very little. I will organize my men and meet at your house. They will position themselves as they see fit. You will open the door to Capone when he arrives. You should then go directly to the basement and not come up until the police arrive when everything is accomplished.'

'What about Madame Carlotta?'

'She will wait in the séance room.'

'She'll be in great danger there.'

'Not at all, Mrs Pastore. My men are professionals. They know their business. She won't be harmed.'

'I hope not.'

'Listen good. No one knows about this plan, Mrs Pastore. No one but you and me. And those two lugs there. I find it's best to keep such things to myself, which means, if I might be so bold as to say, if anyone else learns of our little episode, I will know exactly where it came from. And I don't take kindly to snitches. You understand, don't you, Mrs Pastore?'

'Yes.'

I didn't believe a word of it. No way would he share his real plan with me. Most likely he was feeding me some bogus scheme while he prepared something completely different, like an ambush on the street right as Capone's McFarlan pulled up, or a man inside the front door who would take out Capone as he crossed the threshold. I had warned Capone of the existence of the plot but I had no clue how either man would really act.

In any case, who showed up when was none of my affair. I trusted no one. Carlotta, Freddy and I would be long gone, having decamped that morning before the shooting started, before the losers in this deadly game could mount reprisals. Rooms at a small hotel in Aurora were waiting for us under aliases. I had bought train tickets two days ago so we could bypass ticket sellers when it was time to board. If anyone questioned them, no one would remember me from two days prior. We would wear wigs and fake spectacles and travel separately. I would put ribbons in Tommy's hair to make him look like a girl. Anyone on the lookout for a young mother and her baby boy would not notice an old woman carrying her granddaughter. I had only to get past this meeting and we would all be safe to start our new lives outside gangsterland.

The priest at the altar was packing folded linens in a box. He paid no attention when Weiss stood to leave. I stayed behind for an earnest prayer, then followed him at a distance, wondering if the taxicab would return me to my home or if I should catch the streetcar. Weiss left the cathedral flanked by his two bodyguards.

Seconds later, just as I reached the open doors, a staccato drumbeat crackled through the air. I had never heard that noise before but I knew instantly what it was – the terrible Thompson machine gun, developed too late for the European war, but just in time for the Chicago war. Tommy guns. I hated that nickname. There was a second of stunned silence from the street, then a chorus of screams and shouts. This was Chicago – everyone knew exactly what was happening.

It's no good saying I wasn't scared out of my wits, because I was. Instinctively I ducked back inside the protection of the church to a spot where I could peer around the edge of a stone arch and figure out what was happening. A barrage of bullets spattered across the ground in front of the cathedral, kicking up sharp bits of pavement and biting into softer flesh, mowing down anyone unfortunate enough to be within ten yards of Weiss and his gangsters.

Pedestrians scattered, screaming as they ducked into shops or dropped to the pavement, covering their heads in terror. Pigeons took flight with a frantic beating of wings. One man threw himself on top of a little boy to protect him; a young woman stumbled out of her high-heeled shoes and ran for cover. Others bent double and sprinted for the intersection to get away from the melée. Two wounded men cried out in pain; one called, 'Medic! Medic!' like he was in a trench on the Western Front. A wounded Hymie Weiss dragged himself to the motionless form of a bodyguard and tried to use it as a thin shield, but the deadly stream of bullets came from higher up and found him anyway. I could just make out the tip of the submachinegun barrel protruding from a second-story window above the shop next to Schofield's.

The gun went silent, but the screams of the wounded didn't stop. The three bullet-riddled bodies lying on the pavement in pools of blood were silent too. The king of the North Side Gang was dead.

Hearing the gunfire even from the far-off altar, the priest ran up the long aisle and paused beside the doorway, panting hard. He was in his middle years with a heavy stomach and a balding head, and the sprint had turned his chubby cheeks crimson. 'What . . . What's going on out there?'

A police siren blared in the distance. Two uniformed officers came running from opposite directions, guns in hand. Pedestrians pointed up at the window where the shots came from, and the cops crashed through the shop door to storm the second story. They'd find nothing. The torpedo would be long gone by now, having ducked out the back. Two police cars screeched to a halt at the corner. I retreated further into the church. No good could come of me being visible to the cops or anyone else.

I knew what had happened. I should have expected it. I should have figured it out. Weiss should have figured it out too. Capone had double-crossed me just as Weiss intended to. No doubt Capone's torpedo had been stalking me ever since our meeting in the McFarlan, knowing Weiss would need to talk with me again, and waiting for us to meet in person. Waiting for me to lead him to Weiss. And it had worked.

'Al Capone's men have ambushed Hymie Weiss,' I said to the priest who had just absolved Weiss of all his sins. Oh good, I thought cynically, now he could go to heaven, pure in spirit. 'There looks to be three dead men on the cathedral steps. Can't tell how many others.'

'Holy Mary Mother of God,' he said, crossing himself. I could see him weighing his duties against his apprehension.

'The police are here. I think it's safe for you now.' With a curt nod, he hurried down the steps, his robes flapping like the wings of a great blackbird, and began administering last rites to Weiss.

Anger flared hot inside my breast as I railed against the injustice of it all. The needless killings. The affront to God. The Capone brothers, Weiss, O'Banion, Moran, the Genna boys, all of them masquerading as pious, church-going Catholics with their silver Saint Jude medals, their gold crucifix necklaces, their gemstone rosaries in their pockets, working every angle, playing religion like it was another gambling scam with marked cards and loaded dice. Make a donation to the church, confess to the priest, chant a few Hail Marys and presto! Sins forgiven. Clean slate. Heaven awaits. God was just another politician with a palm to be greased. Spread around enough dough and the bishop himself would preside over a murderer's funeral and bury him in consecrated ground; a little more would buy enough Masses to boost his degenerate soul from where it belonged all the way to the angels. Fixing God was no different from fixing City Hall. It just took more money and a little lip-service to seal the deal.

Meanwhile, I needed to get out of there without seeing the cops or anyone else. According to what Weiss had told me, everyone who knew of his plan to murder Capone had just been eliminated. Except me. If I could extricate myself from this scene, no one in the North Side Gang would ever know I had been involved and maybe, just maybe, no one would come looking for revenge.

I tore down the aisle and turned into the right transept which, if the door wasn't locked, would open onto Superior Street around the corner from the carnage. There was no 'back door' behind the altar that would lead to Wabash, so this was my best chance to escape the scene while everyone's attention was on the dead and dying. The transept was dark and the massive door must have weighed a ton. It was indeed locked, but I threw the thick iron bolt and pulled with all my might. The hinges protested as the door creaked open wide enough for me to squeeze through, and I was gone.

TWENTY-EIGHT

September thirtieth came and went like any other day. There was no Al Capone séance. No fleeing Chicago for Aurora. No more living in fear of Hymie Weiss. Nonetheless, I was jumpy as a cat all day long.

Of course, someone stepped into Weiss's shoes before they could be buried with him. Bugs Moran was every bit as nasty as Weiss and maniacally focused on revenge. Moran made no effort to disguise his loathing for Capone, saying often and loud that low-life filth like Capone who profited from prostitution did not deserve to live. (That was a good one – Bugs Moran, protector of female virtue.) Unable to get at Capone directly, he launched a reign of terror on everything in reach, burning down his nightclubs, hijacking his liquor supplies and slaughtering his gang members. Capone hit back even harder. The press called it the Beer Wars. The public called it madness. I tried to take comfort in the fact that at least Carlotta and I were not targets. Evidently Weiss had been right about one thing – Bugs Moran knew nothing about my part in the séance plan that had led to Weiss's murder. No one knew. I just had to stay out of his sights. Moran wanted revenge on Capone, not me. I could almost wish him luck, except that whenever one gang leader was knocked off, the man who took his place was even worse.

Life goes on, however, and Sophie's trial was fast approaching. I decided I was done waiting for her lazy lawyer to get in touch with me. I telephoned him that morning only to learn he was with her at the jail that very moment. His secretary arranged for me to come to his office that afternoon. Meanwhile, Carlotta ambushed me with the names of two new clients who needed investigating.

'William Durand,' she told me, 'passed into the Great Beyond last August. He was a postman and he died while walking his route. So sad. His two grown sons want to contact him. And the wife of Dr Theodore Young would like to contact him. The good doctor was a professor at Northwestern University, so the title may not refer to a medical doctor. I couldn't learn when he died. I'm sorry.'

'That's no problem,' I reassured her. 'I'm sure I'll have no difficulty getting that information from someone at the university switchboard.'

I retreated to a quiet corner of the public library with a stack of newspapers and my baby boy and spread out on a large table. Here, Tommy's soft babble and wobbly steps wouldn't bother anyone. He was content to stick close and play under the table with the toys I'd brought in my bag, while I plowed through the obituaries of Chicago's most-read newspapers. As was my practice, I started with the *Tribune* and began with August first, intending to work my way through the month until I came across Durand. Obituaries are arranged alphabetically, so it took no time at all to skim along the tops of the columns for the right letter, in this case, the Ds for Durand. That's the only reason I saw it. D for Duval.

There was my father. Duval, Henry.

For a second, I thought it was a coincidence. Someone else with the same name as my father. After all, my father spelled his name the French way, Henri not Henry. And in a city of more than two million people, most of them immigrants or children of immigrants, a common French name like Henry Duval would not have been unique. But of course, it was not someone else. It was my own father.

> **Duval, Henry**. Born June 1, 1870, Quebec, Canada; died August 10 of heart failure. Son of Jean Baptiste Duval of Quebec and Marie Jeanne Duval of Brittany, France. Immigrated to the U.S. in 1880. Worked as a pressman for the Chicago Daily News. Preceded in death by his parents. Survivors include his wife of thirty years, Pauline Limon Duval; five sons: Jacques, Andrew, Allen, Claude, and Marcel; four daughters: Madeleine, Renée, Sophia, and Pauline; brother: Jules Duval. Services at St James Catholic Church on Friday, August 13th at 10:00.

I felt nothing. I read and re-read the short piece without quite believing it was real. Gradually the numbness changed to sorrow, not because my father was dead, but because his death had made me numb rather than sad. The last time I saw him, I'd been eight months pregnant and begging for a place to stay until my baby came. I should have known better than to go home, but I was desperate. Mean as ever, he cursed me for marrying a wop, called me a whore when he learned my husband had been married before, said he would have nothing to do with me or my bastard, and wrenched my arm badly when he threw me out. And now he was dead. Heart failure? Somehow I doubted that. He'd been a heavy drinker and a violent man all his life – or at least all the years I'd known him. His death was far more likely to have been the result of a drunken brawl with someone he tried to bully. Someone who fought back.

Tommy toddled over, said 'Ah,' and handed me his little tin car. I scooped him up in my arms and squeezed him until he wriggled to get back down. Had my father ever felt any love for me? For any of his children? How could a parent *not* love his child? There must have been something dreadfully wrong with him, and I could only feel pity that he missed one of life's greatest joys.

Well, I thought, he was gone for good. He couldn't hurt anyone anymore, and that was a blessing. I picked up the next newspaper and continued my search for William Durand.

My appointment with Lawyer Farnsworth was at two o'clock that afternoon. I tracked him down in his office in the South Loop, not far from the Maxwell Street Market. Putting on a brave face – my previous experiences with lawyers had not been happy ones – I trudged up three flights of narrow stairs and through the door stenciled Farnsworth and Beatty.

'I'm Madeleine Pastore, here for my appointment with Mr Farnsworth,' I said to the bespeckled clerk in the outer office. He stood when I entered, then indicated a wooden chair where I could wait and offered me a cup of coffee. The frosted glass door to the lawyer's office prevented me from seeing inside, but I could hear him talking loudly to someone in an angry tone. Another unhappy client, no doubt. Weren't all clients unhappy for one reason or another? Why would a happy person go to a lawyer? A copy of *Time* with Frank Kellogg on the cover lay on the table before me. Too nervous to read, I picked up the magazine and pretended.

I didn't have to wait long. In ten minutes, the unhappy man burst out of Farnsworth's office and without a glance at me or the clerk, careened toward the stairs. On his heels came the lawyer, wearing a white shirt and a black scowl, which he quickly rearranged when he caught sight of me. 'Mrs Pastore? Please come in.'

If his lawyering career didn't go well, I'm pretty sure Mr Farnsworth could get an acting job in the pictures playing the part of a lawyer. He looked like what a lawyer should look like: tall and handsome, with silver hair combed neatly back from a high forehead and eyes that could flash from sky blue to ice gray in a second. His desk was a mess with papers and files helter-skelter and a half-empty bottle labeled Seagram's Fine Old Canadian Rye Whisky beside a smudged glass. Just as I was wondering how he could find anything in all that chaos, he dipped through the clutter and pulled out a thin file.

'Let's get right to the point, Mrs Pastore. I'm glad you've come. I saw your sister at the jail a few hours ago, and I'm sure I don't need to tell you that she is in poor spirits. Your offer to speak at the trial on her behalf will be helpful.'

'Just tell me what to say and I'll say it.'

'I appreciate that, but I'm just asking you to tell the truth. The first thing the prosecutor will do is ask whether you were coached by me. You will say no. I will now proceed to advise – not coach – you.'

'I understand.'

'At the trial, I'll begin by asking you the usual questions. Your name, your address, your occupation— What's wrong?'

This man missed nothing. 'I . . . my occupation . . . I'm not sure it's a good one to mention.'

'What are you, a bargirl? A hooker?'

'Heavens no!'

'Well then, it can't be all that bad.'

'I think it's best if I just say I'm a mother. I have a baby boy. I take care of him and do the usual household chores.'

His eyes narrowed as he considered his options. 'OK, Mrs Pastore. You're a mother. Good enough. But you'd best tell me the truth now, so I'm not blind-sided if it comes out.'

I could feel my face turn red. This was the first time I'd ever told anyone outright what I did. I took a deep breath. 'I help a mystic stage her séances.' His eyebrows shot up in surprise, but he made no comment. He was waiting for details. 'I, uh, investigate the backgrounds of her clients and the deceased persons they want to contact, and I, uh, assist with her séances.'

'Assist how?'

'A little help with some spooky gimmicks to make the séance more real. I can't have that come out at the trial.'

'I can see that. Just say you're a mother.'

I thought I'd better come clean about the rest of my background, just in case. 'And I'm a widow. Should I say that?'

'Not unless the other side asks.'

'My husband was murdered last year. He worked for the Outfit. Should I say that?'

'What did he do for them?'

'Deliveries.' I didn't need to tell him what he delivered.

'It's unlikely they'll ask about your late husband, but if they do, you can say he drove a truck. It's the truth. All answers to all questions should be as short as possible. Never elaborate.'

'I understand.'

'I'll establish that you're Sophia's sister. I'll ask you to tell me about her. Now, I know you haven't seen her for the past ten years – she told me that today. When did you become reacquainted?'

'Just two days before the Bardo party.'

'So you really don't know her from Eve.'

'I knew her when she was a little girl. A kinder, sweeter, gentler little thing you cannot imagine.'

'That won't fly. Your character reference won't mean a damn if the jury learns you haven't seen her since she was ten. So you gloss over that if you can without actually lying. For instance, you could say she was on the vaudeville circuit for a few years and you didn't see her then. Be sure to look at the jurors when you answer questions, not the lawyers or the judge. And not your sister. Try to look each juror in the eye at some point. A good witness is likeable. I can tell you'll do well there.'

'Thank you. I'll do my best.'

'I'll ask you to describe your sister's character. What will you say?'

'That she's honest, kind, truthful, caring—'

'Yeah, yeah, that's nice, but after that string of adjectives, try giving an example or two. Tell the jury a story. Something that shows what a swell gal she is.'

That would be tough since I had shared no experiences with her as an adult. 'I could tell about the time our father was beating our little brother and she threw herself into the fray to protect him, knowing she'd get beat up even worse.'

'Hmm.'

Clearly that wasn't what he had in mind. 'Let me think about it. I'll remember something better.' Even if I had to make it up.

'After I finish my questions, the judge will give the prosecutor a chance at you. This will be harder. He's not your friend, even though he'll smile and act friendly to try to throw you off. Just remember to keep all answers as short as possible.'

'Will I be allowed to stay in the courtroom during the trial?'

'Afraid not. But trust me, I'm the best there is.'

'I've tried and tried to find out who really killed Nick Bardo. Were you aware that Detective Alice Clement was helping with the investigation? She's convinced Sophie is innocent.'

'I talked with the detective, yes. She said she'd hit a brick wall.'

'Temporarily.'

'Well, I'm afraid we're up against the clock now, and if she couldn't find anything by now, she isn't going to.'

'What do you think will happen?'

'I'll tell you what I told Detective Clement. The odds are just so-so that I can get her off completely, but I'll try. She's facing a charge of first-degree murder, which was overkill on the prosecutor's part, but he's new on the job and got carried away by all the publicity. No way is a jury going to convict a pretty young miss like your sister for cold-hearted, premeditated murder, even if she did it.'

'She didn't.'

'My original idea was to say it was self-defense, but the absence of any signs of a struggle on Bardo or on your sister makes that untenable. Their clothes were not in disarray, there were no scratch marks on Bardo's face or hands, no bruises on Sophie, not a hair on her head out of place. Bardo's reputation with women was clean – he was no masher. He'd never come on to Sophie before, and here she was in his house with his wife and a hundred guests by his side. If he was going to make a play for her, that would be the last place he'd choose. Talking with Detective Clement convinced me to go for complete exoneration. I'm arguing that she was set up.'

'I think so, too. But then, who did it?'

'I'm going to hint at the mob. Bardo had relations with the Outfit, supposedly giving them fifty percent of the profits of his bars and clubs. But one of Bardo's bookkeepers says he was shorting Capone, cooking the books to make it look like profits were lower than they were. If Old Scarface knew about it, that would sure make a good motive. Anyway, it's not my job to produce the killer. All I have to do is show that there is too much doubt to convict your sister. My best evidence is her dress. How does a girl commit a messy murder like that and come away without a speck of blood on her dress? And why was she so unconscious that she can't remember anything and couldn't even walk out of the house without help? The cops practically carried her out. No one noticed her drinking and she wasn't sick the next morning at the jail. My supposition is that she was drugged, but there's no way to prove that.'

'I'd thought about that – drugs. I wondered if maybe someone dropped a powder or something into her drink. But who?'

'These days, coroners can find traces of arsenic in lungs, livers and kidneys, but that's after death. No one can find poisons in living persons. So I'm just going to hint at that, too. The jury will draw the right conclusion.'

My spirits soared. 'So you really think she'll get off scot-free?'

'Don't get your hopes up too high. The jury might find her guilty of a lesser crime, like voluntary or involuntary manslaughter. She may well face some prison time.'

'Have you explained all this to Sophie?'

'Just today.'

'How did she react?'

'She's afraid to hope. But it won't be much longer. This can't drag out in court for more than a day. You could help with her clothes. Bring her a dress to wear in the courtroom so she doesn't show up in that god-awful prison garb. Nothing flapper. The jury will probably be all men, and we want them to see a pretty, modest, very young girl who could be their daughter, not some painted-face performer.'

TWENTY-NINE

After leaving Mr Farnsworth's office, I went directly to Early's. Sebastian was out, but I applied to Frank Ricardo, the owner, and he gave me the key to their apartment on the third floor.

As I turned the key in the lock, I felt a twinge of unease. I wasn't exactly breaking and entering – Mr Ricardo had given me the key and Lawyer Farnsworth had directed me to fetch Sophie's clothes – but I couldn't ignore the fact that neither my sister nor her husband had invited me to enter their home and rummage around in their privacy. Tamping down my doubts, I persuaded myself that the virtue in helping Sophie overcame any lapse in propriety, but it only brought home how little I knew my sister. What would she think?

She would have been mortified if she could have seen me in her home at that moment. The place was a wreck. It looked as if Sebastian had invited in a band of monkeys to tear the place apart. Not that I blamed Sophie – she'd been in jail for more than four weeks – and I could hardly blame Sebastian, who like most men was all thumbs when it came to caring for clothes or home or food, even when they weren't paralyzed by despair as he was.

A bit dazed, I stepped into the living room and without thinking picked a woolen shawl off the floor, folded it, and draped it on the back of a sofa. I reached for a vase of dead flowers intending to dump it into the trash until I noticed the trash can had overflowed onto the floor. It was too late to water the plants; they'd expired days ago. Old newspapers, Chicklet wrappers, and ashtrays full of Lucky Strike butts covered the end tables. The walls were hung with colorful vaudeville posters printed two or three years ago that advertised *The Dales, A Delightful Duo of Song and Dance*, and a few smaller black-and-white programs that someone – Sophie, no doubt – had lacquered onto wood to preserve them.

I smelled the kitchen before I got there. It was small but furnished with a modern gas stove and an ice box I dared not open. The drip pan had overflowed but most of the water had evaporated, no new ice having been brought in. The porcelain sink was stacked with dirty dishes crusted with dried scraps of food eaten days ago. A tiny herb garden in the window had given up the ghost. The soles of my shoes made sticky sounds on the linoleum floor.

In the bedroom, rumpled bedclothes looked as if they hadn't been changed in weeks. Trying not to step on the cast-off clothing, I picked my way toward an immense wardrobe and flung wide the doors to reveal five feet of hanging dresses, skirts and blouses, all clean and neatly pressed, ready to welcome their owner home. I sighed with relief and got to work.

Flipping through Sophie's collection, I rejected one-by-one the fancy silk party frocks she wore for performances and the summery cotton dresses meant for everyday, until at last I came to a smart gray worsted dress, pleated below the waist, with a white baby-doll collar that looked like something a girl in her teens would wear. Perfect for playing up Sophie's youth. I folded that one over my arm and added a pair of demure Mary Janes from her shoe rack. Rummaging around in her dresser drawers, I found stockings, handkerchiefs and clean undergarments.

I picked up a fingernail file from her vanity, then set it down. No way would those steely-eyed matrons let me bring in a pointed metal weapon like that, but I had an emery board in my purse I could give her. I left her make-up untouched, thinking that Farnsworth knew what he was talking about when he said it would detract from her youthful persona. Some men, particularly the older sort who were apt to be sitting in the jury box, equated made-up women with actresses and prostitutes. It occurred to me that braiding Sophie's hair in two plaits would also enhance her girlish look. Luckily she was small and thin and not heavy in the chest.

Avoiding the WC in the hall, I foraged next in the bathing room. A quick survey of the Dale medicine cabinet revealed nothing you wouldn't find in anyone's home: Bayer aspirin for fever and headaches, Lydia Pinkham's for female complaints, cocaine throat lozenges for sore throats (especially recommended for singers and teachers), opium drops for toothache, Noah's Liniment for aches and pains, Veronal for a good night's sleep, and mercurochrome for small cuts. There was a little bottle of Watkins shampoo that I added to my finds.

I bundled everything into a grip Sophie had stashed above her wardrobe and, giving the place a final survey, locked the door behind me and set out for the jail where Mr Farnsworth had arranged for me to see my sister one last time before her trial.

To my great surprise, Sophie had perked up since my previous visit. She sat up straighter in that dirty oak chair and her blue eyes shone brighter, more alert. She'd lost that resigned-to-her-fate, pathetic manner. Farnsworth had given her hope. I didn't want to do anything to burst that bubble.

'You're looking much better, Sophie,' I told her brightly. 'I've talked with your lawyer and he told me to bring you some clothes to wear at the trial so the jury wouldn't see you in that dreadful prison dress. So I stopped by your apartment – Sebastian wasn't in his office so I borrowed the key from Mr Ricardo – I hope you don't mind – and did my best to follow Farnsworth's instructions. He wants you to look demure, young, sympathetic, like someone's sweet daughter.'

'I can do that.' She examined the items I'd brought. The matron had already gone through them.

'I thought you could wash your hair and braid it in two plaits, like in that Heidi book. Look younger.'

'Good idea.'

'He's got a lot of good ideas, your Farnsworth fella. He's optimistic. Things are looking up.'

'I know.'

'And I have some news. Family news.' She looked up from the parcel, her eyes wide. Neither of us had any contact with any family members. 'Our father died.'

She paused for the time of three heartbeats. 'He did? When?'

'Last August. I didn't know about it at the time. I still wouldn't know if I hadn't happened across his obituary in the newspaper by accident.'

She turned this idea over in her head for a moment, then asked, 'What do you think?'

'Me? Well, I'm glad he's gone. He can't hurt any of us anymore.'

She nodded her agreement. 'Me too. You tell any of the others?'

She meant us kids. 'No. I've no idea where any of them are.'

'Maybe that's for the best. I wouldn't want any of them knowing about this. About me.'

THIRTY

An errand for Carlotta sent me to a client's house one street over from Clark Street, which put me near the building where Eileen Perry had lived and died. My thoughts inevitably turned to Daisy King. How was the girl making out? Had the trauma of a murdered roommate cowed her spirit? It was evening; she should be home from the soap factory by now. On an impulse, I turned down her block and into her apartment building.

It was a veritable Tower of Babel with a different foreign language coming from each apartment, some I could identify even from behind closed doors. The building fairly shook with the slamming of doors, pounding of footsteps on the stairs, and shouts from children playing on the landings. The smells of cooking food made my stomach rumble. I fancied I could tell what was for supper as I passed each door – tomato sauce for pasta, boiled cabbage and corned beef, fried fish caught that day. Daisy's apartment was an oasis of calm by comparison.

And Daisy was home. Her face brightened when she saw who had knocked.

'Oh, Mrs Pastore! What a nice surprise! Do come in.'

'Thank you, Daisy, and do call me Maddie. I won't stay long, I promise. I was passing by and thought I'd stop for a moment and see how you were doing. I'm sure you read about Eileen's aunt in the newspapers.'

She motioned me to the sofa and took one of the chairs to sit opposite me. The table was set for one with knife, fork, spoon and napkin placed just so, and a glass of water, but no sign of any food yet, only a small white box. She saw me looking at the table and said, 'You haven't interrupted my supper; I've not started yet. And I have plenty tonight. Would you be so kind as to join me?'

'Thank you very much, but I'm expected home shortly. Perhaps another time?'

'Of course. A drink maybe? I can make tea.'

'That would be lovely.' And she set about putting a saucepan of water on the hotplate and reaching in the cupboard for two cups and saucers and a tin of black tea.

'I thought you'd like to know what happened with Eileen's aunt. Apart from what you read in the papers. All in all, the stories were pretty accurate. Especially that *Tribune* reporter, Lloyd Prescott. He's a friend of mine, and I know he tries to get the facts straight.'

'You were there, weren't you? When the detective tried to arrest Mrs Brent?'

'I was. So was a police officer, in case of trouble. Which there was, just not the sort of trouble anyone was expecting.'

'I read she jumped out of a window.'

'No, worse than that. She indicated she would come with us peaceably and went to collect her handbag. She had a penknife in the bag, or it could have been in a drawer or on a table, we couldn't really see where it came from. The next thing we knew, she screamed and cut her own throat. She died almost instantly.'

'Poor woman!'

'She confessed to everything. She would have hanged in a matter of weeks.'

'No doubt. Still, it's an awful fate, either way. If only she hadn't been so blinded by greed! How do people get like that? Eileen was a dear girl, quite generous with her things. I can't help but think that if the aunt had befriended her, she would have been happy to share any windfall from the gold found on her land. She was that sort of girl.' The water boiled. Daisy poured it into a pot and dropped the tea ball in to steep. 'I remember when I got home that evening, after the aunt's visit, Eileen was quite excited. I believe she knew that her father had a sister, but they had never met and she was happy to have a relative. One who seemed kind. And all the while, that woman was planning her death.' She shuddered.

'You're lucky you didn't touch the dulcimer strings yourself. And that Mrs Brent didn't stick with her original plan, which was to wipe the edge of a drinking glass or toothbrush with her typhoid fever bacteria. She might have gotten the wrong toothbrush or you might have used the glass . . .' Now it was my turn to shudder. 'Have you disposed of Eileen's things yet? The police have found no other relatives, so I think you can safely sell the jewelry and clothing, unless Eileen's things fit you.'

'I was planning to do that.'

'And the dulcimer should fetch a decent sum.'

'The police still have it as evidence, but Detective Clement said they would return it to me as soon as it was no longer needed. I'll clean it carefully, of course.'

I glanced about the tiny apartment with its cheerful paintings on the walls. I was no judge of art or artists, but Daisy's lifelike flowers and sentimental pastoral scenes would brighten any home. The bedroom door was open. There were still two narrow beds in there, so I presumed the girl was in the market for a replacement roommate. She noticed me looking.

'I take it you're looking for another roommate. Any luck?'

She sighed. 'I'm afraid I won't be able to attract anyone respectable, now that the apartment has a reputation for typhoid fever. Not to mention murder.'

'People have short memories. Maybe after a couple of months, the story will be forgotten.'

'I wish I was that optimistic. Anyway, I can't wait that long. I'm going to have to move. I can't afford to live alone, even with two jobs.'

'Two? I remember you said you worked at a nearby soap factory.'

'Just four days a week. That's all they have for me. My catering job pays better, but it's only three days. They tell me they'll take me on fulltime when business allows.'

'Catering?'

'The business is owned by a really nice couple, Mr and Mrs Rose, who cook dinners and party food for rich people all over the city. Most of the work is weekends, so I can help with the cooking and the serving and still keep my weekday factory job. Plus I learn things and even get tips occasionally.' She reached for the white box in the table and opened it. 'And I get fed during the day and can take home leftovers. Look at these.' The box was neatly packed with dainty hors d'oeuvres so pretty they looked almost too good to eat. 'Try one.'

I put one morsel in my mouth and moaned with appreciation. 'Delicious! What is it – cheese and pastry and . . .?'

'A bit of ground ham. Have another if you like. Sometimes there's enough food left over from a party to last me a couple of days. Eileen was wild about the shrimp croquettes.'

I looked more closely at the box and saw some printing on it I hadn't noticed earlier. Rose Catering it said in black letters with a small red rose to accent the name. Rose Catering. Something clicked in my head. Sebastian had mentioned them when he talked about the Bardo party. How they shared the kitchen as a staging area. How good their food was. And Sophie had remarked on the excellent food too.

'Daisy, this Rose Catering . . . I think they served the Bardo party on August thirtieth. Did you happen to work that party?'

'I sure did! And that was another murder! Chicago must be the murder capital of the world.'

My pulse quickened. 'Tell me about that night, please. What you did. What you saw.'

'I can tell you what I told the police, which is not much. A detective – not Mrs Clement, some rude man – questioned some of us, but with me, he only asked if I'd seen anyone go upstairs after one o'clock, and I said "No". I was in the kitchen most of the evening.'

'Doing what?'

'We brought hors d'oeuvres that night, no meals, but they were elaborate hors d'oeuvres. No expense spared! Some were supposed to be served warm so I set them on tin sheets and heated them in the oven. I arranged some on platters for the dining room and others on plates for Mrs Rose to carry around. I had my white apron so I could help serve, but I stayed mostly in the kitchen. That's why the detective didn't bother to question me.'

'You didn't see any of the arguments that went on during the party? Or see the singer, Sophie Dale?' This wasn't the time to explain my relationship to Sophie or my interest in the murder.

'I did see her briefly, when she came in and sampled a few

of the hors d'oeuvres. Such a pretty green frock that was! I wish I'd heard her sing. I'm sorry she killed Mr Bardo. He was nice to us and so complimentary about the food. So was Mr Dale, although he was too fidgety to eat.'

'He was?'

'Yes, he was in and out of the kitchen several times, always nervous that things would go wrong. So shaky he spilled tomato juice on his apron and was in a panic about how that looked. I lent him one of our clean white ones. We always take extras for just that reason. Anyway, he never returned it, but I can't quibble about that. The poor man had more on his mind than a stained apron.'

'You gave him a clean apron? When was that? I mean, was it early on in the evening?'

She squinched up her face in thought. 'Not early. Just before the police arrived. I'm not sure of the time. I don't have a wristwatch.'

Was it possible? Could Sebastian have stayed upstairs in the room with Sophie after Ellie Bardo returned to the party downstairs? Could he have waited there until Nick Bardo was sent up to check on Sophie? Could he have hidden behind a door and bashed Nick over the head, spattering his apron with blood? Young Stanley Jones said he saw Mrs Bardo come back downstairs, but he never said he saw Sebastian come down. And Stanley went to Sebastian's bar to replenish his tray and waited a good while before giving up and going to Doc's bar for refills. The questions swirled around in my head until I nearly forgot to breathe.

'And what did you do with his stained apron?'

'Nothing. I mean, I tossed it in the laundry basket with the rest of ours. It's still at Rose Catering. I could tell which one it is because ours all have a red rose on the bib.'

My heart sank. 'But it's clean now?'

'Oh, certainly. We wash up linens every day.'

'Daisy, this is a strange question, I know, but think back. Could the red stains on the apron have been blood and not tomato juice?'

THIRTY-ONE

Chicago's streets are reasonably safe during daylight hours, but when darkness falls, it's best not to stroll about alone. No one is likely to bother dog walkers, especially if the dog is large, and men are generally left alone, but women, either singly or in pairs, run the risk of being accosted by mashers, purse-snatchers, or worse. I was alone and absorbed in my thoughts on the dark walk home that night from Daisy's place on Clark Street, and not as alert as I should have been.

Could Sebastian have exchanged a bloody apron for a clean one of Rose's? Could he, with Ellie Bardo, have escorted Sophie upstairs and then remained in the room while Ellie returned to the party, and waited for her to send Nick up to 'check on' Sophie? Was he lying in wait, the deadly instrument in hand, ready to beat Nick to death? Did he murder his good customer and Sophie's patron? And why on earth would he have done that? The only possible reason I could fathom was jealousy. He believed Nick and Sophie were having an affair. Was it possible? Surely not. Sophie would never be unfaithful to the man she loved. But honestly, how well did I know my sister? Could she have been stepping out on her husband? Could he have discovered her infidelity and plotted revenge? Nick Bardo was dead and Sophie was in jail – is that what Sebastian wanted all along? If so, he was a damn good actor.

Sebastian admitted to having served Sophie at least one drink. Could he have put something in it to knock her out? I'd seen Veronal in the medicine cabinet. Veronal was a common sleeping powder that, if she'd swallowed a heavy dose, would explain her unconsciousness better than illness or drunkenness. But how could he have deliberately implicated his wife in the murder, leaving her to take the blame? Clearly they were devoted to each other. Or was it a charade? Could he be counting on an acquittal based on the self-defense argument?

The Roosevelt Road bridge was brilliantly lit with gas lamps and busy with pedestrians, but when I turned on a side street nearer our house, I found myself listening to my own footsteps on the pavement. Shops were shuttered, buildings dark and gaslights glowed only at the corners. Ahead of me, three sailors, recognizable in the dark by their snow-white uniforms and round white caps, stumbled noisily out of a speakeasy – there seemed to be one on every block – and headed in my direction. Prudently, I started to cross to the sidewalk on the opposite side of the street when a man stepped out of the shadows not six feet in front of me. Without a word, he grabbed my handbag from under my arm and took off running.

I shouted out, more in surprise than fear, 'Wha-at! Hey! Stop, thief!'

Unfortunately for the crook, he ran toward the sailors. Evidently not as drunk as they seemed, two of them blocked him on the sidewalk while the third crouched and tackled him as he tried to veer into the street. With their three-to-one advantage, they soon nabbed him.

'Here's your bag, lady,' said a sailor.

'What do you want us to do with him?' said another, shaking the villain by his collar.

The sailors looked very young. So did the thief. I knew of no police station within several blocks. 'Oh, hell, I've got my purse. You may as well let him go.'

After a punch to the gut, the sailor boys did just that. The wounded thief loped off, and the sailors insisted on walking me the rest of the way home.

Carlotta was waiting with a message. 'Sebastian Dale telephoned. He has some new information for you. Said to come by his office tomorrow morning. Nine o'clock.'

'Good,' I said. 'I have some new information for him, too.'

I'm Chicago born and bred, meaning I'm not some naïve country hick who would waltz off to a meeting with a murder suspect by herself. I telephoned Detective Clement's home to arrange for her to meet me at Early's. No answer, so I tried the police station telephone which is always manned. The cop who picked up promised to get her the message first thing tomorrow morning. 'She comes in at eight,' he said. Just to make sure, I telephoned again the next morning at eight, hoping to catch her before I left, but she hadn't come in yet. 'There's already one message on her desk from you, Mrs Pastore,' said the cop who answered. 'Would you like me to leave another?'

'Yes, please.' If nothing else, it demonstrated urgency.

The morning sun shone bright on Early's coarse pink brick façade when I walked up to the place. It's open twenty-four hours a day, but at nine in the morning, customers are few and far between. The all-nighters have staggered home and the lunch crowd hasn't shown up. The place wasn't quiet, though, not with the clatter from the canning factory across the street and the screech of the trains rattling through the city on railroad tracks that ran behind the factory.

I made my way inside past the bar and checked to see if Doc was on duty, but he'd gone home. To my surprise, there was young Dan Ward wiping martini glasses. At a nearby table, two customers huddled over their drinks, talking in low tones even though there was no one close enough to hear a word. In the opposite corner, a drunk lay slouched across his table, passed out with his drink still in hand, dead to the world.

'My, my, Dan, aren't you the early bird! Manning the bar by yourself, are you?'

'Sure thing, Mrs Pastore,' he said with pride. 'Doc gives me the morning shift 'cause it's slow they only need one. I'm on duty now from seven in the morning to six at night. 'Course, Doc and another fella or two are here during the busier hours, but I'm in charge of the place myself in the mornings.'

'I'm sure your mother's proud of you, Dan. Have you seen Mr Dale this morning?'

'Nope, he's usually asleep in the mornings, since he's awake down here most of the night.'

'I'm meeting him at nine. So's another woman, Detective Alice Clement. She should be here any minute. You know her, don't you?'

'Everyone knows her.'

'Please send her right up when she arrives.'

'Sure thing, Mrs Pastore.'

I knew exactly what I was going to say to my brother-in-law. I'd been thinking about this moment all night long. I would wait for him to go first, for him to tell me what his 'important news' was. Then I'd say, 'Tell me about your apron, Sebastian. Was that tomato juice you'd spilled or was it Nick Bardo's blood?' When he paled, I'd tell him I had the apron – still dirty with so-called juice stains – and was turning it over to the police. A lie, of course, but it should elicit a confession, if indeed, he was guilty of murder. Detective Clement could arrest him.

I was going to wait in the hallway for her, but I noticed Sebastian's office door was ajar. Through the crack, I could see the corner of his desk and one arm. The sight of that man working calmly while my poor sister languished in jail enraged me so much I forgot all about Mrs Clement. I barged right in.

My brother-in-law was sprawled across his desk. In my mind's eye, I saw the drunk downstairs, similarly slumped across his table, both of them unconscious, and I turned hot with anger. How dare he pass out at a time like this! It only took the blink of an eye to realize Sebastian wasn't like the drunk downstairs – his body had collapsed in a puddle of blood that soaked the papers underneath him and was dripping over the edge of the desk. No one could lose that much blood and still be alive.

Sebastian Dale was dead.

One hand had flopped on his mail basket at the corner of the desk as if he had reached for it in his last moment. In the basket, peeking out from under another letter, was a pink envelope.

All at once – and way too late – I understood the connection. I knew who had killed Nick Bardo and I knew why. It wasn't one person. It was two working together.

Behind me came the creak of the door hinge as it swung closed.

'I was gonna push him off a cliff in the Swiss Alps,' she said, 'then I thought of a better way.'

I turned to face Ellie Bardo, standing six feet from me, pistol in hand. Her eyes widened when she saw my face. 'Well, well. So it's our own little girl reporter, is it, with all those questions about the hotel? I should of known you weren't the real deal.'

'You killed him,' I said stupidly, pointing at Sebastian's lifeless form.

'No, hon,' she said in the patient sort of voice best used on a dimwitted four-year-old. '*You* killed him. With this gun. Then you killed yourself in a fit of remorse.'

'No one will believe that. And Detective Clement is downstairs, so you won't get away with this.'

'Nice try. If she were coming, she'd be here now. And that bitch is the reason everything started going wrong. Her and you. Without your meddling, she wouldn't have pushed her nose in where it didn't belong and Nick's death wouldn't have been more than a one-day wonder, but no! You had to bring in the famous lady detective and it's all over every goddamn newspaper in the country, day after day after day. And then Seb starts getting nervous and demanding, and I knew I couldn't take him with me. Not now.'

'You can't seriously think you'll get away with this.'

'No? No one knows I'm here. I came through the delivery entrance.'

'They'll hear the gunshots downstairs.'

'Not when the train goes by.'

So she was waiting for the next train to screech and rumble by on the tracks across the street. I had a few minutes, maybe. Detective Clement would arrive any second. I gave a quick glance around the room, looking for any sort of weapon I could wield against a gun. The telephone would take too long. The letter opener sticking out of the pencil case was a poor match for a bullet, but it was something. The wooden chair was light, so was the coat rack, but both were out of reach. I started inching my way toward the coat rack while keeping her talking.

'How did you persuade Sebastian to kill your husband?'

'Tell a man you've never had sex so good and he believes it. And he'll do anything. Works every time. The chance to get his hands on some of Nick's lovely money didn't hurt either. I wanted rid of the old fool and Seb was the way to do it.'

'You said you already had Nick's money.'

'Yeah, and you believed it. Everyone did. Truth is, Nick was a tightwad. But I got him to write that new will where I got all the money. And everything else too, but I didn't really want the real estate – the girls coulda had that and welcome to it if they hadn't been such bitches. Nightclubs and hotels don't travel in the suitcase like cash. I sold all that to the Outfit last week. For cash.'

'You sold the Adler to Capone?'

'And Nick's nightclubs. Didn't get near what they're worth, but I was lucky to get anything after Capone found out Nick was shorting him on his cut. I kept waiting for him to do in Nick for me, but he didn't seem to be getting around to it fast enough, and I got tired of waiting.'

She glanced toward the window, impatient for the next train. I was stalling, too, for Detective Clement and the handgun in her purse.

'So you're going to leave town?'

'Leave Chicago? Hell, I'm leaving the damn country. Always had a hankering to see the crowned heads of Europe. I mean to change my name and marry me a title. Shouldn't be hard, not with all the money I got now. Imagine me, Lady Bountiful or Countess So-and-So. Ha! Or maybe I'll buy me a king and be queen. Queen Eleanor the Great.'

She was insane. I shifted my weight, easing another two inches closer to the coat rack. 'How'd you get Sebastian to do the dirty work?'

'Sex.'

'And get him to frame Sophie for it?'

'Told him she'd never do more than a little jail time if he got her a good lawyer. That'd be reason enough to divorce her, then he could leave town, meet up with me, and we'd get married. Which he believed, the poor sap.'

'So the plan was all yours?'

'Seb's not smart enough to plan his way out of a cardboard box. Of course it was mine! Seb stayed upstairs with drugged-out Sophie, I sent Nicky-boy up to check on her, and Seb surprised him from behind the door, like I did you just now. Only Nicky never saw him coming.'

'Couldn't do it yourself, huh?' Another inch closer to the coat rack. Still, it was beyond my reach. If the train came by, I'd have to lunge for it. I tried to think of a distraction that would pull her eyes away from me for just a second.

'Lil' ol' me?' she simpered girlishly, then returned to her normal voice. 'I'm not big and strong enough, but yeah, I admit, I don't like blood. This . . .' She waved the gun toward Sebastian's limp form. 'This is sickening but it had to be done. And at least it's quick. There are a lot worse ways to go, believe you me.'

Very faint, so faint I might have been imagining it, I thought I heard a train in the distance. There was no more time.

I looked toward the half-opened door and shouted, 'She's got a gun!' Instinctively Ellie turned her eyes toward the door, expecting Detective Clement. Her arm followed, and she was pointing the gun toward the door when I grabbed for the coat rack with both hands. For a brief second, her attention left me. I didn't have time to swing the coat rack back like a baseball bat for a good hit, so I just shoved it toward her, as hard as I could.

Ellie twisted back around to face me and fired in my direction, but she hadn't time to aim and the bullet went wide. The coat rack struck her full force and with my weight behind it, knocked her on her back and jostled the gun from her hand before she could get off another shot.

Scrambling for the gun, I snatched it up and pointed it at her. She had shoved the coat rack aside and was coming for me. I'd never fired a gun in my life, but needed no instructions on how to pull the trigger. What I needed was Detective Clement to come *now.*

Click, click. There were no more bullets.

Disgusted, I threw the gun down just as Ellie tackled me head-on. I was bigger than she was, but Ellie Bardo had far more experience in dirty fighting than I ever had. I'd been my father's punching bag in my youth, yes, but I'd never been able to effectively fight back, so small was I in relation to him.

Ellie and I grappled and rolled on the floor, grunting and kicking. I pulled her hair so hard some of it came out in my fist. I hit her in the stomach and pulled away from her grasp, stumbling toward the open door to escape but she managed to grab my ankle and drop me to the floor. She tried to gouge out my eyes but I rolled over on her, pinning one hand beneath her, and struck her repeatedly in the face. With a twist of her hips, she somehow flipped herself over until she was on top of me, straddling me. Gripping my shoulders with both hands, she pounded my head on the floor until the world went dark.

THIRTY-TWO

Fire and water. Water and fire. My thoughts wandered through Carlotta's recent séance, the one with the hero fireman who charged into a burning building to save a child. Images of burning buildings and crackling flames were so real I could feel their heat. Fire and water. It was getting hot. I managed to open one swollen eye and saw fire – real fire – burning vigorously a few feet away from where I was lying on the floor, stiff as a wooden doll.

Ellie's pistol was in my hand. Ellie was nowhere to be seen.

I dropped the empty gun and pulled myself to a sitting position. My head pounded as my brain struggled to reassemble the events of the past few minutes. How long I'd been unconscious, I couldn't say, but judging by the fire creeping closer by the second, it couldn't have been very long. The pungent smell of gasoline reached my nose. I realized with horror that Ellie had started the fire herself. And that my clothes were damp with greasy gasoline.

At that very instant, my skirt erupted in flames. I grabbed the burning fabric with bare hands and, with strength I didn't know I possessed, ripped it off before the fire could spread up to my blouse. Heedless of the burns on my hands, I leaped to my feet, only to fall back onto hands and knees when the move triggered a dizzy spell. My head throbbed. I began crawling toward the one door that was not engulfed in flames – the door to Sophie's dressing room. Suddenly a man burst through the flames in the hallway and into Sebastian's office. Frank Ricardo, Early's owner.

'Jesus!' he shouted, taking in my appearance and the body on the desk at the same moment. 'He dead?'

'Yes,' I gulped.

'Anyone else here?'

'Not upstairs.'

'The boy called the fire department. Come on, we gotta get outa here.'

He glanced back at the way he'd come. The flames now blocked all passage and were roaring down the hall. 'We can't go that way. Not now.'

The one large window in the room was closed. Mr Ricardo thrust the sash upwards only to find it stuck tight. He was not a large man, but he threw body and soul into the effort. Still, the sash didn't budge. Snatching up the wooden chair, he smashed through the glass and ran the chair legs along the jagged bits that stuck to the edges.

'Two stories. We'll probably break a leg but we shouldn't die.'

Cold comfort, that.

By this time, I'd managed to stand on shaky limbs. A sudden impulse made me snatch up the pink envelope from Sebastian's wire basket and stuff it inside my blouse. I had no idea what it was, but if it related to Sebastian's and Ellie's affair, I wanted to save it from the fire. I scurried to the window, away from the flames dancing across the office floor toward my feet, following the streams of gasoline that had soaked into the wood, making me think of a line of dominoes falling fast. In seconds the fire would overtake us and we would be pinned against the exterior wall. I reached up and grabbed a fistful of one of the ugly brown draperies, yanked it off the rod, and threw it out the window in a ball. Mr Ricardo didn't need to ask what I was doing – he pulled the other one down and sent it out as well, forming a little bit of padding for our jump. The cushions on the sofa would have been nice too, but they were already burning.

'Every little bit helps,' he yelled. 'Go, go, go!'

The alley pavement looked a lot farther away than two stories, but there was no point in debating the wisdom of this way out. It was that or burn to death. As I gripped the edge of the window frame, I saw a bunch of black wires – or more precisely, four wires, each enclosed in black rubber sheathing – running up the side of the building. Thin wires that entered the second-floor offices through their window frames, three that ran to the telephones on the desks of each office and one that continued up to the Dale's third-floor apartment. Thin, yes, but they were something to grab that might, if they held my weight for even a moment, slow my fall.

'Wires!' I shouted to Mr Ricardo.

'Go!'

I gripped the strands and heaved myself out of the window, pushing my feet against the rough bricks of the building in a futile attempt to get a toehold. The uneven brickwork had left slim crevasses between the rows of bricks where stingy masons had applied less mortar than they might have, giving me the littlest bit of a toehold, not enough to rest on but enough to turn my fall into a downward slide against the brick wall. And so I went, until I hit bottom. Hard. There I sat, shivering in my bloomers, the breath knocked out of my chest, but alive.

The thin wires had held until I reached the ground. They could not, however, support the weight of a man who had fifty pounds on me. Mr Ricardo's attempt to follow my lead ripped the wires away from the building and left him dangling. He dropped to the drapery pile, landing on his feet rather hard. His knees gave out and he collapsed in a daze.

Fire is serious business in Chicago. There are probably more fire stations per city block here than in any other city in America, thanks to memories of the Great Fire of 1871 that destroyed most of the city. From the back of the building, I could hear more than one wailing fire engine pull up in front of Early's and lots of shouting as men stormed into the night-club. Another group circled around to our side of the building where they found me and Mr Ricardo breathing hard from our brush with death. A police car pulled up, then another and another. Onlookers from the factory across the street rushed over to gawp. In no time, the drama attracted spectators like wasps to a picnic, surging forward against the police who were trying to wave them back. One woman darted over and took off the shawl she was wearing to wrap around my waist, shielding my white bloomers with the pink eyelet ruffles from prying eyes. I couldn't have cared less, but I thanked her for her kindness.

I heard her voice before I saw her – Detective Alice Clement bustled on the scene, trying to take charge of everyone and everything. 'Thank the lord you're safe, Maddie,' she said. 'I'm so sorry I was late. It's the usual maddening excuse – an accident on one of the bridges delayed me. Oh my, look at your hands. Officer Kelly!' she called, turning to one of the idle cops. 'Get the first aid kit out of the patrol car. This woman needs medical attention.' I was glad she'd noticed. My hands stung like the devil. The burns happened, I think, when I ripped off my skirt, but I couldn't be sure. The sequence of events was already hazy in my mind.

Meanwhile, a small army of firemen was charging through Early's back entrance, each man hauling a section of a fat black hose that resembled nothing more than a long anaconda. 'It's gasoline,' I shouted a warning.

Moments later, another patrol car brought another policeman, this one in a suit. A detective. How did the police know about Sebastian's murder already?

The new man looked surprised to see Detective Clement on the scene, but he wasted no time introducing himself to me. 'I'm Detective Samuel Wilson. And you are?' he asked, looking me straight in the eye.

'Mrs Pastore. Madeleine Pastore. I . . . we've just escaped from the second floor. There's a body in that office,' I said, pointing up with my bandaged hand. 'It's Sebastian Dale.'

'Yes, I know,' he said, pulling a pair of cufflinks out of his pocket. 'And you're under arrest for his murder.'

THIRTY-THREE

'Hands behind your back,' ordered Detective Wilson. Detective Clement, who had stepped around the corner of the building to talk with one of the cops, returned to the drapery pile where I was sitting just in time to hear his command. 'What's going on here?' she demanded haughtily.

The detective bristled at her imperious tone. 'I'm arresting this woman for the murder of Sebastian Dale.'

'This is Madeleine Pastore,' she said, as if he was mixed up as to my identity.

'That's right.'

'Maddie? She couldn't have done such a thing. Where did you get that idea?'

'We had an anonymous tip.'

'Was it a woman?' I asked.

'I don't know. I didn't take the call.'

'It was Ellie Bardo,' I told the two detectives. 'She was the one who shot Sebastian Dale, not me.'

'Did you see her do it?' asked Wilson.

'Well, no, but she told me she did. She was holding the gun that killed him. And she tried to kill me.'

'Where's the gun now?'

'On the floor upstairs.' With my fingerprints on it, damnit. I thought I might as well come clean about that – they'd find out soon enough. 'You won't find her fingerprints on it, though. She wiped them off and put the gun in my hand so it would look like I killed him.'

Detective Wilson's expression said he'd suffered through nonsense like this far too many times in his career.

'Wait a minute, Wilson,' said Detective Clement. 'I'm familiar with this case.'

'Sorry to step on your toes, Mrs Clement,' he said, without a sorry note in his voice, 'but the chief sent me.'

'He didn't know it was the same case I've been working on. I'll straighten him out.'

Frank Ricardo limped closer. 'Is the fire out? Can I go inside now and check on my office? I wanna see what's left.'

'A few questions first, if you don't mind,' said Detective Clement. 'Then you can go.'

'Sure thing, ma'am. Shoot.'

'What time did you arrive this morning?'

'About nine, my usual time.'

'And you knew Mrs Pastore was upstairs?'

'My bartender said she'd just gone upstairs to see Dale.'

'No one else?'

'She told him to send you up right away, but no, no one else had come in but a few customers.'

'Were you the first to find the fire?'

'I smelled something burning when I came inside the building but thought it was just something blown over from the factory across the street. When I opened to door to the stairs and saw the flames, I shouted to the barboy to call the fire department and get everyone the hell out.'

'And you ran upstairs into the fire?'

'I thought maybe I could put it out. Didn't know it was gasoline. Didn't know how far it had spread. And I knew there were at least two people upstairs who maybe didn't know the place was burning.'

'It's a gasoline fire. How did it get started?'

'Can't say for sure, but I keep a can of gasoline in the kitchen. I'll see if it's still there. Someone coulda used that or brought their own, I guess.'

'How far had the fire spread when you found it?'

'A lot farther than I realized. Someone had spilled gasoline inside Dale's office and down the stairs. Those parts were burning fast and hot. I managed to get to my office but the fire traveled so fast I couldn't go back the way I came.'

'And that's when you found Mr Dale and Mrs Pastore?'

'It was pretty clear he was dead. She was on the floor. Her skirt had caught fire just as I came into the room and she pulled it off.'

'And there was a gun?'

'Beside her on the floor.'

'And what did you do then?'

'Got the hell out. Through the window, like you can see.'

'You had to break it?'

'It was stuck. Is the fire out now? I really need to go in and check the offices.'

Detective Clement called to a fireman and Ricardo repeated his question.

'Yes, sir. It's still smoldering in places and there's always the danger that some dry space with gasoline'll flare up again, but I think it's safe enough right now if you take care.'

Nodding his thanks, Ricardo ducked into the building through the back entrance. One of the cops followed him, whether for safety or surveillance, I didn't know.

The two detectives stood over me discussing my fate like I was a little girl and they were the parents. I didn't have the strength to stand up with them, so I just listened to their conversation from my place on the ground.

'As I've already said, this is my case,' insisted Detective Clement. 'I'll take the heat if the boss is mad about it.'

'But what about . . .?' Meaning me.

'She isn't going anywhere. Dale was her brother-in-law. She and I were supposed to meet him here this morning. If I hadn't been late, none of this would have happened.' A few more sentences, spoken in an undertone, were exchanged and an unhappy Detective Wilson slouched off.

Detective Clement sat down on the brown draperies beside me. 'Now then, Maddie, let's get to the bottom of this.'

Before she could say another word, I reached inside my blouse and pulled out the pink envelope. It was bent and damp, but in reasonable condition. 'I found this on Sebastian's desk. In his mail basket. It's from Ellie Bardo.'

'How do you know that?' She took the envelope from me and tore open the flap.

'When I was at her house, in her all-pink drawing room, I saw her at her writing desk using this pink stationery. I don't know what it says, but when I saw this letter on Sebastian's desk, I realized how stupid I'd been not to have suspected that they were working together. They planned

Nick Bardo's murder and framed Sophie so they could run off with his money.'

Detective Clement read the letter to herself. Then she gave me a speculative look as if wondering how much to trust me. She must've decided I was worth the risk, for she read it aloud.

> Darling Seb,
> It won't be long now! It's been agony not seeing you these weeks but I know it will make our reunion all that much sweeter when we are together forever and I can . . . Never mind, that's filth – I bought passage. Your ticket is in the usual place. I am counting the days.
> Your own precious, E (Burn this)

'Well, well. Sebastian wasn't very good at following instructions, was he? I don't know that this is enough to convict her of murder but it sure does help your sister's case.'

Just about then, Frank Ricardo came back outside. The crowd that had gathered to watch the excitement had gotten bored and drifted off. The firemen were winding their hoses onto the wheels and loading their equipment back on the trucks. Except for one patrol car, the police had gone. Detective Clement remained with me. Ricardo set a cardboard box on the ground and snarled, 'The place is a goddamn mess. Those guys wrecked everything the fire didn't.'

'I'm sorry, Mr Ricardo,' said Mrs Clement. 'But at least your building was saved.'

'Yeah, be glad for small miracles, huh? The first floor's soaked but it didn't burn. They put out the fire before it could spread past the second.'

'Was your office destroyed?' I asked.

'My desk didn't burn, so I got these files, but Seb's desk and all his papers were burnt to a crisp. The fire didn't get to the cash,' he said, patting his coat pocket, 'and the other important stuff in my safe, and I got the stuff out of Seb's safe too. That detective fella still think you killed Seb?'

'Probably.'

'Well, that's pretty stupid. Who do they think set the fire? Couldn't of been you – what idiot would set a fire to burn themselves into a corner and spill gasoline on their own clothes? And I sure didn't do it. OK, I'm gonna check on the third floor now. I'm starting to think we could be back in business in a week.'

He bent down and dug through the box of papers. 'Oh yeah, I found these in Seb's safe,' he said, handing Detective Clement three pink envelopes. 'Only took a quick look but it seems like good ol' Seb had a dame on the side. Can't say I'm shocked. Thought you might be interested.'

THIRTY-FOUR

Sophie's trial was canceled. Instead of spending that day in court testifying to her sterling character (about which I knew nothing), I finished the laundry, diced vegetables for Carlotta's goulash, and took my favorite boy to Lincoln Park Zoo. It was a fine fall afternoon, blustery and cold but the sun thought it was still summer, and I had long wanted to show him the real animals to match the pictures in his baby book. He took in the elephants with round eyes and the monkeys with giggles; he clapped his hands at the giraffe. The zoo was full of families strolling together along the pavement. The absence of the head of our family hurt my heart.

It was nearly dark by the time we got off the streetcar at the stop nearest home, and I was chilled. Carlotta had no séance tonight, so I was in no rush to get home. A hot drink sounded like the cure. I ducked into the Greengrocer's for some of Mrs Ward's soon-to-be-famous mulled cider with rum. The place was quiet, with only a few others relaxing after a busy day. Mrs Ward was tending the bar herself. I settled into a comfortable chair and set Tommy on the floor to wander.

'Here, Maddie. And here's something for the baby.' She handed me a steaming mug and a slice of apple for Tommy. 'That's wonderful news about your sister being released. I read about it in this morning's paper.'

'Yes, it's a relief for me and a godsend for her. Thank you.'

'How's the poor girl doing?'

'After a month in jail, she's looking pretty haggard, but she'll recover.'

'Bring her over. She's staying with you, right?'

'We don't really have room. And she couldn't stay at her apartment – the fire didn't ruin the place but the smoke did. She took a room at a hotel. She'll be more comfortable there, and I'll see her nearly every day.'

Just then, Detective Kevin O'Rourke came down the stairs.

'Madame Carlotta said you'd probably be here if you weren't home by now. How was the zoo?'

'A big success. We made all the right noises for the animals and played with bits of gravel along the walk.'

Tommy held up his chewed apple slice as if to share it with O'Rourke. 'No thanks, buddy,' he said, patting him on the head. 'I'll have what you're having, Maddie.'

'Mulled cider. You're not on duty?'

'It's my day off.'

I was sorry I hadn't known that. I might have invited him to come with us to the zoo. Might have. Probably not.

'I was hoping to see your sister here.'

'I stopped by her room at the Adler Hotel this morning.' Sophie and I had something else in common now – a murdered husband. I might not have known her during the past ten years, but I knew how she was feeling right now, losing a husband who turned out to have some very serious hidden flaws. Bitter, angry, betrayed, yet still in love with the man she had believed him to be. We'd stay close after this, I was sure, no matter where she moved or how far she traveled.

'How is she?'

'About as you'd expect. At first she refused to believe what we told her about Sebastian, so we had to show her the letters. Copies, anyway. Mrs Clement gave the originals to the state's attorney along with the other information she had. Sophie was devastated at the betrayal. They were more than just love letters, you know. They had some pretty incriminating details about the plan to murder Nick Bardo. Sophie believes us now, yet she still defends Sebastian. Says he was tricked by that viper, and was trying to free himself from her when she killed him.'

'Unlikely, but possible.'

'I think at some level he still cared for Sophie, in spite of his blind passion for Ellie. He thought she would suffer only a short prison sentence. I can see that now.'

'You've talked with the state's attorney?'

'He wants me to testify at Ellie's trial about what happened that morning at Early's.'

'How are your hands?' he asked, with a glance at my bandages.

'Better. Hurting, but healing. I'm lucky that's the only part of me that got burned.'

'Did you hear about Ellie's capture?'

'Just that she was picked up at home later that day. I was hoping you could tell me more.'

'I was there with Detective Clement and others. It was about eleven o'clock. Ellie was still in her dressing gown, all set to talk her way out of everything. And she damn near did it, too.'

'Tell me.'

'She said she'd just woken up at ten and hadn't left the house at all that morning. There were plenty of servants to corroborate her claim.'

'Well, of course. They're her servants. She pays them handsomely, I'm sure.'

'Naturally that's what we thought, but they seemed quite sincere. I believed them.'

'I'll bet she sneaked out. There would have been time for her to drive herself to Early's at nine, shoot Sebastian, set the fire, and slip back into her house by ten thirty without being seen. It's not that far. Did you check her motorcar?'

'Sure did. It was warm. But that's circumstantial evidence. A lawyer could say it was the chauffeur warming it up.'

I was starting to feel nervous. 'Does she still claim she wasn't at Early's that morning?'

'You are the only witness who can refute that. But don't worry, she won't be able to dodge what's in those pink letters. Boy oh boy, you should have seen her purple rage when we told her Sebastian had saved them in his safe! She figured the fire would have burned up any evidence he hadn't already destroyed, which it pretty much did: the papers and files in Sebastian's desk were burnt to cinders. She hadn't counted on him keeping the letters with the cash in his safe – not to mention his passport with his first-class ticket on one of the White Star Line ships sailing from New York next week.'

'Next week, huh? He couldn't leave until after Sophie's trial. I expect they were planning to meet up on board the ship.'

'Looks that way.'

'So is your evidence solid? I mean, solid enough for a conviction?'

'There's enough to prove she planned her husband's murder and persuaded Sebastian Dale to do it, so we'll get her as an accessory to murder. You're the only link we have to her killing Sebastian and setting the fire.'

'You never found the gasoline can? I'd hoped her fingerprints would be on it.'

'We searched her house, with no success. But there are a lot of vacant lots near Early's. Maybe it will turn up. I am confident that your testimony will persuade the jury.'

'I can't believe she almost escaped.'

'Not really. Even if she'd made it on board some ocean liner, we could have wired ahead to the ship's first port of call and had the local cops pick her up. Still, she's one slippery dame.'

'I wonder . . .'

'What?'

'I just wonder if Sebastian was saving the letters for sentimental reasons – which would be stupid – or because he thought of them as insurance in case Ellie planned a double cross – which would be shrewd.'

'We'll never know.'

'One good thing – when Frank Ricardo found those letters in Sebastian's safe, he also found a wad of banknotes that Sophie knew nothing about. Evidently Sebastian had been putting money aside for months. Or maybe it was Ellie's money, who knows? Whatever the case, Sophie has plenty to pay for a nice room at the Adler for as long as she wants. I think she'll get her bearings soon. Probably be back on the stage in no time.' No one could say we Duval girls weren't tough as granite. 'What's the lowdown on Alice Clement? I see her face splashed over all the newspapers again. No sooner does the frenzy over her solving the dulcimer murder die down than it flares up again for the Bardo/Dale murders.'

O'Rourke gave me a long look, like he was evaluating how much to tell me. 'Yes, indeed, accolades are raining down on our Mrs Clement, Chicago's famous "copette", they're calling her, for yet another spectacular success story. Unfortunately, Chief McWeeny's well of patience has run dry. Mind you, there are other female officers in the department – no other detectives, but a few female cops – and none of them manages to generate as much antagonism as Mrs Clement.'

'What can he do? He can't fire her. She's a celebrity. Practically a national one.' I understood the chief's prickly reaction to her flamboyant manner and her craving for publicity, but her support for women's rights and her work saving Chicago's young women from lives of shame and degradation balanced that out in my eyes. She hogged credit and strutted like a peacock, but she did a lot of good, too.

'He could cut her off from the most interesting cases. Or he could transfer her. Which is what he's done.'

'What? Where?'

'West Chicago.'

'Jeez Louise, that's like the Gobi Desert.' Nearly as far as Aurora. Conflicting emotions battled within me. I was relieved that Detective Clement wouldn't be around to continue her crusade to sweep Chicago clean of phony mystics and fortune tellers, yet she was good at her job and had taught me some useful lessons. A woman in a man's world . . . not an easy balancing act anywhere.

'Knowing Alice, she'll soon have that town's criminals locked up tight and get herself transferred somewhere else. I wouldn't worry about her.'

'What'll happen to Ellie, do you think?'

'It's all but certain she'll be found guilty of masterminding the scheme to murder her husband. If the trial goes well, she will also be found guilty of Sebastian's murder. Not to mention charges of arson and attempted murder – you. I'm betting she hangs.'

'And Nick Bardo's money?'

'Goes to his good-for-nothing, thoroughly undeserving pair of daughters.'

I heaved a great sigh and hauled Tommy onto my lap. 'Proving what we've all known since childhood: life isn't fair. You have to take the thorns with the rose petals.'

'Another cider, Maddie?' called Mrs Ward from her stool next to the bar. 'And you, detective?'

'No, thank you. This young man needs his supper and his bed. I should be getting home.'

'Wait a moment, Maddie,' said O'Rourke. 'I have something for you.' He reached inside his jacket pocket and drew out a folded piece of paper, which he unfolded slowly and passed to me. 'I picked it up at the station this morning.'

It was a notice. There was a sketch of a police badge on the top of the page and a few words in large print below. Short and to the point.

> Job opportunities . . . Recruiting police officers . . .
> $2,000 per annum . . . apply at . . .

'What's this about?' I smiled. 'I think Tommy's too young for a job.'

'I'm thinking of you. You'd make a darn good detective.'

'Me?' I was flabbergasted.

'Of course, you have to start as a private, but you're smart and a hard worker and in no time, you could move up to detective, where you'd earn an extra five hundred dollars.'

'But that's such dangerous work!'

The moment the words were out of my mouth, I burst out laughing. So did O'Rourke.

When the hysteria subsided, he managed to say, 'More dangerous than what you're doing now? Getting shot at, nearly burning to death, tangling with gangsters, and almost drowning in the Chicago River last winter? In fact, I believe it would be far *less* dangerous, because you'd not be working alone. Police detectives have training and support and backup and they can call on help from many quarters. And you're an ace investigator.'

He knew! He knew about my investigations. Or was he fishing? At a loss for words, I ducked my head and made a show of retying Tommy's shoelaces while I gathered my thoughts. But it was useless.

'When did you know?'

'I always knew. From the time you first came to me with your suspicions about the death of that boy in the North Chicago River. I always knew it was you and not Madame Carlotta. I tried to discourage you, because I know how dangerous this sort of work can be, but you've proven hard to discourage.' He gave a rueful smile. 'I strongly suspect it was more your work than Alice Clement's that led to the capture of Ellie Bardo and the woman who killed little Eileen Perry. You have the instincts to make a really good detective.'

'But Chief McWeeny doesn't like women detectives on his force.'

'McWeeny won't be chief forever.'

'But I . . . but I . . . I have a baby. I can't have a job like yours, all day, every day.' Tommy must have sensed my distress, for he started whining and squirming until I put him down.

'I didn't mean tomorrow, Maddie. I thought this was just something you might consider in the future. Right now, you seem to be managing well enough as Madame Carlotta's assistant.'

So he knew about that too. About the séances. I was grateful for the semi-darkness in the basement speakeasy. It made it harder to see my red face. All this time, I thought he wasn't aware of what Freddy and I were doing. But he had known all along and never let on.

'Well,' he said rising from the chair, 'your young man seems like he's hungry. I am, too. I'd better be going. I'm glad your sister is free, although I'm sure you had all hoped for a different end to her story.'

'Carlotta has made a pot of goulash,' I blurted out before I could consider whether it was wise or not. 'It's a recipe she says was handed down from her royal gypsy ancestors. There's plenty, if you'd care to join us.'

'I'd be honored.' And slinging a giggly Tommy over one shoulder, he followed me home.

AUTHOR'S NOTE

Readers of the first two novels in the Mystic's Accomplice series, *The Mystic's Accomplice* and *Spirits and Smoke*, will recall my enthusiasm for the Roaring Twenties, the decade I consider America's most intriguing. While my main characters – Madeleine Duval Pastore, Madame Carlotta Romany, Freddy, Sophie and Sebastian Dale, Daisy King, Nick Bardo and his daughters, Ellie Bardo, Doc Makepeace and Detective O'Rourke – are all products of my imagination, Detective Alice Clement and Officer Kathyrine Eisenhart were historical figures, pioneering policewomen during a time when jobs outside the home were just starting to open up to women. Eileen Perry and her aunt were real too, as were the gangsters – Al Capone, Bugs Moran and Hymie Weiss – who were, if anything, more deadly than this story makes out. Few gangsters managed to 'retire' from the mob and die of old age. Most were gunned down in the proverbial barrage of bullets while in their twenties or early thirties, save for Capone who died in Florida of syphilis after serving a long prison sentence for income tax evasion. (It was the only crime the feds could make stick.) It's not hard to understand the motivation for such violence when you understand that Capone's Outfit *alone* grossed about seventy million dollars annually – the equivalent of around one billion in today's money. Each year.

The Roaring Twenties also brought interest in the occult to the highest level it has ever seen. Mystics, fortune tellers, mind readers, hypnotists, Tarot readers, astrologers, ESP practitioners, Ouija board players and spiritualists flourished. Spiritualism, a quasi-religious movement that began in the 1840s and peaked in the 1920s, had millions of followers. Many (all?) of its practitioners were frauds, and the great magician Harry Houdini set out to prove as much by offering ten thousand dollars (about $158,000 today) to any genuine spiritualist who could contact the dead. As a magician, he was always able to expose their fakery, so no one was ever able to claim the reward. His book, *A Magician Among the Spirits*, published in 1924, reveals many of their tricks. As you can imagine, this was a great help to me in describing Madam Carlotta's séances. Houdini's book is still available if you want to read about his success in exposing the frauds. Detective Alice Clement was also serious about pursuing fraudulent mystics in Chicago. (And by the way, much of her dialogue is authentic, taken from the quotes I found in the newspaper articles.) Sadly, she died a year after this story takes place. No one knew she was diabetic, and after her transfer to West Chicago, her health declined rapidly. Chief McWeeny, another real-life character, really did dislike her enough to have her transferred out of his jurisdiction.

The story of Eileen Perry and her death-by-dulcimer may seem absurdly far-fetched, but it is an example of truth being stranger than fiction. Detective Clement figured out that Eileen had been murdered when others thought it was just another case of typhoid fever, then a deadly, scary disease. I invented the roommate, Daisy King, so as to give more information to Maddie and Detective Clement and put the girls in a boarding house instead of the 'rickety tenement' where Eileen purportedly lived alone. Kathyrine Eisenhart was one of the first three policewomen in San Francisco, and while I know of no contact between the two female cops, I thought it highly likely that they were aware of each other since both were featured in national publications. Readers of the day were fascinated with the idea of a woman succeeding at such a masculine job.

Hymie Weiss is all too real and his death happened just as I wrote it, although I confess to moving the event up a year. He was murdered on the steps of the Holy Name Cathedral directly across from the florist shop where his friend and former leader of the North Side Gang, Dean O'Banion, had been gunned down two years earlier. Both deaths are well documented in newspapers of the era and you can find gruesome photos of their bullet-ridden bodies online. Although several civilians were wounded in the attack at the cathedral, thankfully only gangsters were killed. Don't believe anything you read about the bullet holes in the cathedral stone being visible today – they were patched up shortly after the assassination and can no longer be seen.

I am always grateful for the expertise of librarians and others who help me get the facts right. Thanks go to Jon Handlery of Handlery Hotels in San Francisco for the story idea about the fictional Adler Hotel; to Dr Carol B. Pugh, PharmD MS, and Dr Mark C. Pugh, PharmD, for their superb advice on poisons and medications; and to my sister Margaret H. Miley, who read my early manuscript and made it better with her suggestions.

Do let me hear from you; I can always use suggestions for the next book! I'm on Facebook and my website www.mary-mileytheobald.com and can be reached most easily by email at mmtheobald@gmail.com. To see pictures of the real people and places mentioned in the book, have a look at my Pinterest page: www.pinterest.com/mmtheobald/the-mystics-accomplice.